GREED'S SIREN

STEPHANIE HUDSON

Greed's Siren
Lost Siren Series #5
Copyright © 2024 Stephanie Hudson
Published by Hudson Indie Ink
www.hudsonindieink.com

This book is licensed for your personal enjoyment only.
This book may not be re-sold or given away to other people. If you would like to share this book with another person, please purchase an additional copy for each recipient. If you're reading this book and did not purchase it, or it wasn't purchased for your use only, then please return to your favourite book retailer and purchase your own copy. Thank you for respecting the hard work of this author.
All rights reserved.
This is a work of fiction. Names, characters, places, brands, media, and incidents are either the product of the authors imagination or are used fictitiously. The author acknowledges the trademark status and trademark owners of various products referred to in this work of fiction, which have been used without permission. The publication/use of these trademarks is not authorised, associated with, or sponsored by the trademark owners.

Greed's Siren/Stephanie Hudson – 1st ed.
ISBN-13 - 978-1-916562-67-7

Whilst this book is being released during the holiday season, I wanted to dedicate this book to all of those who will feel the loss of a loved one on Christmas Day.

A season known for spending time with loved ones and family members, I think it is only right to remember those that are no longer with us. To dedicate these words to the memory and hearts to those that loved us and would wish for nothing but our happiness in life.

And even though we may shed our tears at the sight of the absent space they used to occupy on Christmas day, please remember that they are still with us, in our hearts and in the great spirit of their memories.

So, remember on this day the gift of good times shared. The laughs and funny Christmas mishaps. The smiles and excitement. The stories told around the dinner table over food cooked with love. And even though there is now a space left empty, tell those stories once more and invite those wonderful memories back to the family feast.

Tell the stories that mean the most. The stories that are passed down through generations so as they may live on, and forever be...

A seat at your dinner table.

CHAPTER 1
SON OF GREED
RYKER

"My Lord?"

I sighed the moment I heard the knocking at my office door, already regretting my choice to leave the lower levels where I kept my training room. But seeing as I was one of the King's Enforcers, charged with finding where the next illegal black-market auction was to be held, I knew I would get nothing done with my fists. No, I would get more done by utilizing the skills of my men rather than sparring with them and testing their talents on the mats.

Although, one was definitely more fun than the other, for it had to be said that sitting behind a desk was by far the most tedious part of my existence. But then the way of the world had certainly changed.

These days, most wars were fought with a keyboard and a computer screen rather than with a sword and shield. Long ago were the days of glory from beating your enemy on the battlefield as you emerged victorious from the smoke and dust barely settling on the blood staining your amour.

No, these days you were forced to simply exchange chainmail and breastplates for a designer suit, and your weapon of choice was, of course... *money.* A threat that spoke to most, for there were those out there more terrified by the thought of stripping them bare of it than soldiers of old facing the tip of my sword.

Speaking of money, the Lega Nera, also known as the Black League, dealt not only in cash but mainly in blood. For these bastards had been trading not only stolen mortal treasures, but they had also been dealing with black market goods from a world hidden to humans. Everything from Heavenly relics to Demonic artifacts had been sold.

With only a few rules to follow, anyone, including supernatural creatures, were allowed to bid. First, you needed enough money to pay for whatever you bought and second, you didn't speak of the auction... *ever.*

Which meant that even to this day, and thousands of years after the first had been held, we still didn't know who was the master of it all. Of course, we had caught many of those involved in the past, but each had been hexed with a spell that prevented them from ever uttering a single name. Meaning the head of the snake was one we had still yet to sever.

That was the only way it would fall, once and for all.

Of course, what made it more difficult was that it was never held in the same place twice. And with barely any notice given to the listed elite as to where the next one was to be held, it was often hard to prevent it from happening before it could take place. So many times, had my men and I arrived, only to find the place empty and all evidence of it ever happening long gone. A frustrating end to a lot of hard work that felt nothing but wasted.

Which is why I knew that more information was discovered by sitting at my desk rather than putting my men through their paces on the mats. After all, those on my council were the best of the best, just like most of those that were chosen by the King of Kings. His own elite group of powerful rulers, chosen to become one of the King's Enforcers.

But then the King of Kings was only one man and couldn't control the mortal world's supernatural alone. He may have reigned supreme but with millions of supernatural's living upon this Earth's plane, then it was an impossible job to keep the peace without granting power and rule to those he trusted not to abuse it.

Which meant that the world had been divided into sectors. My job was to rule over most of Canada, where there were more portals close to the veil of Hell than I would have liked. In other words, it kept me fucking busy. And now, after finally discovering the possible place that Lega Nera was planning on holding their next auction was in my sector, well, it gave me the perfect excuse to get in undercover.

For I had many aliases in business, some of which not even the rest of the Enforcers knew of. Which meant that if they didn't know, then neither did those in the Lega Nera. But then this was also what I had been waiting for. For this auction was illegal, and crimes committed in my sector gave me the right to do whatever I saw fit to do.

Like bid, pay, and keep whatever I wanted, and there was something I very much wanted. Something I had been searching for ever since it was stolen from me, and I had my money on it being sold in the next auction. It was something I very much wanted back in my possession as I knew, more than most, of the dangers it presented if such a weapon were to fall into the wrong hands. Meaning it was up to me to find the rest of the pieces of the scepter before it was too late.

"Come in, Faron," I replied in what I knew, even to my own ears, was an exasperated tone. But then, being thousands of years old, even with all the riches the many worlds had to offer, life often lacked luster. Especially for a being that was born and bred for the battlefield. I had spent far longer in Hell by my father's side leading his armies than I had here on Earth's plane. But then shit was far simpler down in my realm of Greed than it was here. Fucking Demonic politics solved with a sword rather than with a pen and cheque book. But like I said, money was the weapon of choice here and although far less bloody, it was often far more effective than most things. Like placing the end of my weapon at the enemy's throat and forcing them to yield with threat of relieving them of their head and of their soul.

But then the greatest of honors came when Asmodeus paid a visit to the realm of Greed and charged me with becoming an Enforcer for his son, Dominic Draven, the King of Kings. My father could not have been more fucking proud and told me it was a chance to carve out my own rule, one the Greed running through my veins compelled me to do. Because, like him, I wanted it all and after conquering most riches in all of Hell, I was now to do the same in the Mortal Realm.

Yet there was one thing I still wanted to possess. As if a vital piece of me was still missing, and naturally, I had searched the globe trying to find it. There was a part of my dark and possessive soul that didn't even know exactly what it was I was looking for.

Extreme wealth I had ten times over. An army of men under my command was at my fingertips, a whispered order away from jumping when I fucking told them to. I had everything I could ever want and, yet, my Demon still pushed at me to keep searching for more. Half of me wondered if I would ever stop. If this dark, twisted Greed would ever let me. Would ever find the one thing that would finally make its journey to the very end of our quest.

It was a blind need searching in the darkness for what felt like an eternity. Would I ever know what it was like to feel satisfied? Time, after all, was the slow death for the minds of an immortal life.

Perhaps I would get T-shirts made.

"What is it now?" I all but snapped at the tech genius who still looked like a fucking teenager that had grown up in the eighties and never left it. Of course, he was an old soul locked to a young vessel that had been gifted to him when crossing over to this realm. One who found a lust for life in all the strangeness that came from popular culture. The ripped jeans and a cartoon truck robot on his T-shirt was only further proof of this. But then he had never been one for a suit like I forced my large vessel into after having it custom made to fit my muscular build. One more fit for amour and wielding my favorite sword, known here in Earth's plane as the Zweihänder.

Of course, it was better known in my own realm as a Colossus Killer and was far bigger than the German t͡svaɪhɛndɐ, which literally translated into two-hander. A sword on Earth that was a large two-handed sword that was used primarily during the 16th century. Zweihänder swords were developed from the longswords of the late Middle Ages and I, of course, had many in my collection. In the right hands, the Zweihänder could kill with such skill, strength, and efficiency that you could behead several people with it in a single blow.

Oh, but what I wouldn't give to have one in my hand now and not the fucking paperwork I was trying to engage my brain with enough interest to read.

"We have finally tracked the shipment." Now this did finally grab my attention, and the paperwork ended up crumbled in my fist.

"Tell me," I all but snarled.

"It's in San Francisco." I released a quick breath hearing this, as it had been the first mention of it in so long, despite our best efforts. However, a few weeks ago, a man came to me after he had heard I was offering money for any information about it.

The Scepter of Dagobert.

Or better known to my people as the Scepter of Psychopompós, literally meaning the 'guide of souls' in Greek. It was a scepter created for one purpose and one purpose only. For it was capable of opening gateways big enough to deliver large amounts of souls, ones either lost to war or great natural disasters. However, over time this method was eradicated, as gateways didn't only offer passage from one side. No, both sides were open during this time, and even if for only a short period, it proved to be too much of a temptation for those in Hell not to take advantage of it.

In fact, it was because of this mighty Scepter that most knowledge of Demons had been discovered by the mortal race. Thankfully, the power of time had aided in this, as what were once considered facts to our kind at one time, soon turned to myth in the more modern mortal world. Becoming nothing but stories passed down from generation to generation, with details often lost along the way. Myths that began to lose their strength like Chinese whispers making their way down the line of thousands.

And as for the many races of Demons that had managed to break through the portal, well, not all of them were so quick to want to abide to the rules set before them by the King of Kings. Not like today, where most knew how to fall in line and live what was essentially a peaceful existence in the mortal realm.

These days, an Enforcer dealt with a few rogue Demons here and there but back then, there had been so many of them, it had been like a Demonic plague sweeping across the land. Hence why this time-period was known among my people as the Great Cleansing.

As for the Scepter, it was broken into three pieces and given to the house of Greed to protect. Once there, it remained hidden for a time in the three mountains our castle was built against. Each piece lay buried in the mass of my father's treasured horde. But then, many centuries later, it was stolen by someone my father was still hunting, even to this day.

Someone only known as...

The Master Luzuh.

A word that meant 'person who steals' in Sumerian, a

Demonic language that was still used to this day throughout many of my kind.

And well, master they would have to be in order for them to steal from the mighty Mammon, my father, ruler and King of the 4th realm of Hell. And this theft is why, naturally, I had taken on this personal mission to retrieve the three pieces that had made their way to Earth's realm.

A sceptre I knew for a fact had last been seen complete back in the 7th century and had been a part of the French crown jewels. Of course, they had no idea what they had in their possession at the time. Hence why, on Earth, it was now known as the Scepter of Dagobert and had been stored for many years in the treasure of the Basilica of Saint-Denis. Stored there all the way until 1795, when it disappeared, stolen in the basilica and never seen again.

Unfortunately, by the time word had travelled far enough to reach me, I had already been too late. For the trail went cold quickly and the only information I was left with after reading the minds of the few witnesses left was that it was no longer whole. That three thieves from Paris who had been working together to accomplish the heist, had spilt the Scepter, each taking a piece for themselves before fleeing the city.

And now, it finally looked like one of them had been found.

"Gather the team," I demanded, standing with a fist to my desk.

"Did someone mention team?" This was said after my cocky ass second-in-command and piss-taking best friend walked through the door like life was one big fucking game.

Vander was a Drude, just like his brother Dante, and could do far more than just control the dreams of others. For starters, he and his brother had the ability to trap a soul within their own mind, believing whatever it was that they wanted them to believe. This mental cage could last a millennia if they so wished, which became a powerful threat to use when in an interrogation. Of course, Vander was also an extremely skilled fighter, and one I respected. Especially, considering he had come the closest to beating me on the mats above all else.

Yet despite being royalty in his own right, the two brothers chose to ignore their Hellish lineage and came to Earth before going their separate ways. A path for Vander that brought him directly to me and, admittedly, he had stayed by my side ever since.

Vander, also known as Van, was the first to join my council and most of the shit he got away with was because he'd had my back more times than I could count. He was as loyal as they came, and that scar across his lips and down his neck was a testament to it, after being on the receiving end of a battle axe that had been aimed at my head at the time. One that had been made from the Phlegethon steel of my home world, A weapon that once forged, was dipped into the flaming river of Phlegethon.

As for the rest of his appearance, he was nearly as big as I was, but where he stood at six-foot-four, I was six-five. He, like I, was also more than equipped to hold a Zweihänder, which weighed in at twenty-five pounds.

With a vessel homed for destruction, I was a beast of a man and undeniably made an intimidating businessman, even in the board room wearing a suit. Now had I been in my battle gear then most people would shit themselves and run screaming from whatever building I was occupying.

But then my name, Ryker Wyeth, literally meant rich war lord, or war strength but either one, they both described my nature precisely. I was a warrior beyond all else and my mortal vessel only mirrored that of my Demon when on the battlefield, for I was capable of such brutality in either world. Although it also had to be said that due to my own lineage, many of my kind also knew me as simply Greed. Or if you were kneeling at my feet, begging for mercy I was unlikely to grant, Lord Greed also worked. To those closest to me, however, much of the time I went by Ryk.

Now as for my mortal features, these were described as dark and foreboding, with a hard, sinister black-blue gaze that took no shit and could stare even the hardest of souls down to submission. Eyes so dark blue, they pierced through the bullshit of men and forced the truth with merely a look. A hard gaze that did nothing to the happy as pigs in shit look of my second-in-command, Van.

Light olive-green eyes with a burst of hazel flecks of honey at the centers seemed to smile back at me, the fine lines at the sides deepening with his amusement. Eyes he shared with his brother Dante. But unlike the smooth shaved head of his brother, his hair was dark blonde and took him Hell only knows how long to style.

As for my own, this was cut short at the sides and slightly longer on top, styled with ease in mind as I only needed to run my fingers through it when wet and it was done.

"Listening as always," I grumbled, making Van shrug his massive shoulders in an easy-going and unapologetic way.

"But of course, plus, it's boring as shit around here and I need something to kill."

At this Faron chuckled, something that ended the second Van grabbed him in a head lock and started to rub his knuckles into his tight curly hair, making them both turn static as was something that tended to happen when either one came into contact with the other. Of course, Van loved Faron like a brother and teased the shit out of him like one, which made the poor, tormented tech whine like a bitch. Poor bastard.

"Get off me, you Gorgon shit bag!" Faron snapped, making Van boom with laughter, before Faron used his slight weight as a way to slip from his hold in a cloud of smoke and move around his bulk before he knew what happened. His vaping shifter abilities made it near impossible for him to ever get caught. He was also one hell of a hacker.

"Slippery as always, buddy boy."

At this Faron gave him the finger that ignited with fire before he extinguished it so as he could pull the paperwork from his back pocket and hand it to me.

"Yes, well if you kids are quite finished," I questioned, just like I always did when dealing with these two. Meaning I was thankful when the more serious member of my team entered and took his stance opposite me, bowing his head first and granting me respect.

"Oh goodie, fucking kiss ass is here," Van complained, making Hadrian growl in his direction. Someone who we also nicknamed Hades due to his mistrust and obvious Hellish temper. But then he was one of the Devourers and therefore a testy motherfucker at best. A race of Demon that weren't not known for their patience but made for the perfect candidate to be granted the title head of my security.

He was another of my men I could count on as being loyal as they came, which was why he was on my council and lead his own team. He also looked like some tattooed biker that shaved his head with a bowie knife before picking his perfectly white teeth with the tip. His piercing grey eyes were almost as dangerous as my own and his skills at fighting were on a par with most high-ranking Demons in Hell.

"Your orders, my Lord?" he asked, making Van mimic him from behind. I jerked my head to silently tell him to knock it off. I valued my brotherhood and friendship with Van but, fuck me, he could be hard fucking work sometimes.

Dressed like some GI Joe, he looked more like a solider boy- Captain America wannabe. Floppy blonde hair styled as always, he fucked anything with an ass, tits, and pussy that was more than a little willing.

As for Faron, he was content with the mortal men at his disposal, but I had one rule. Don't fuck the same mortal twice. I didn't care too much for certain rules, despite never being tempted to dip my wick in mortal pussy before.

No, I liked to play it rough and therefore stuck to my own kind, for the type of screaming I required was one of pleasure and pain combined, not one of solely pain. I needed submission in the sweetest form it came and, thankfully, being at the top of the supernatural food chain helped in this department. Even if most sexual encounters with my own kind I found to be a little lacking these days. Fucking hated it when they topped from the bottom as most Demons tended to do.

There was only one master in the bedroom and if you didn't like my rules, then you got the fuck out of my bed and stayed out of it! Just like that bitch, Madison, emphasis on the 'Mad'. A Demon that still thought she could play me, and one I had scraped off the second I cottoned on to her game of manipulation.

Crazy bitch.

"Where are Kenzo and Katra?" I asked after the brother and sister duo that completed my council.

"Still away on a recon mission, but they should be back next month," Feron informed me, now leaning his slighter frame against the large carved oak table I had in my office for whenever we had council meetings.

"Gather a few of your best men, Hades. It looks like we have a warehouse to break into," I said, now looking down at a picture of my next target. But then even as I said this, I had a strange feeling there was going to be more in this warehouse than just my missing treasure.

Perhaps something new.

Perhaps something exciting.

Perhaps something…

Fated.

CHAPTER 2
ETERNALLY FORBIDDEN
EVIE

"This job is bullshit!" I complained for what felt like the millionth time, once again staring at myself in the bathroom mirror and talking to myself. Somewhere which seemed to be my only place of solace when finding myself in yet another crap job.

Now, how I kept finding myself working for assholes, I just didn't know. I only knew when it all started. My dreams of making something of my life after collage hadn't quite worked out the way I had hoped.

But then again, it felt as if my dreams had died the moment after I graduated. I wanted to be so much more than this. I wanted to be more than some puppet with strings tied up in knots and tugged by another's hand. With each job I took, I just ended up adding an extra string that wound me up tighter, and all I wanted was to be free.

All I wanted, was to paint the world.

But in reality, all the color from my work had been drained away to nothing but a lifeless gray shade that was far too sombre to be considered for an art gallery. It was too macabre, too gothic, too dark to see the light of day. But that was what happened when art intimated life, and what I saw in the mirror was nothing but what felt like a cursed soul. Because nothing exciting ever happened to my boring-ass life.

There was no epic love story to tell.

There was no shining career to be proud of.

There was no adventure waiting for me around the corner.

There was nothing but a turbulent past I had long ago ran away from.

But as for now, it was simply wake, eat, loath my day, sleep, and repeat. The only time I felt free of this lonely existence was when I was in my crappy little apartment painting, despite how depressing the subject matter was. But then it didn't take a genius to know I was depressed and had been for a long while now.

I kept putting it down to each dead-end job and dickhead I worked for. Perhaps it was down to having no blood family to speak of. With only a deaf old man who raised me after he had found me on the streets, there was no one else.

Essentially, I was a runaway.

And well, if I were truly honest with myself, I hadn't really stopped running since. Because my childhood died at only ten years old, right along with my mother after one terrifying experience had ended both our lives that night. So, I fled the only home I had ever known before things could get worse. After navigating myself in a brutal world for six months, the kindest soul I had ever known, since my mother, found me and took me in.

Arthur Parker.

He became my entire world, and still was in many ways. He taught me how to paint away my nightmares. He taught me how to sign away my anger, and how to keep fighting for what I believed in. He taught me never to give up and every time I locked myself in a bathroom, I would look at my reflection and see his face in the background telling me to be strong.

So, I nodded to no one and fixed my long, dark-brown hair into a neater braid that I always kept to one side. Then I told myself,

"You can do this, Evie Parker."

I took out my concealer and reapplied the matching skin-tone cream across my freckled nose and cheeks. Doing this so I didn't look like someone who was fresh out of high school and more like the twenty-seven-year-old I was. Then I smoothed out the crease of dusty pink eyeshadow over my lid, unsure if the color went with my light brown eyes or not. Thankfully, my eyeliner wasn't smudged and still flicked out to the side. Which meant a swipe of tinted-red cherry-flavored lip balm and, voila, I looked more human.

To be honest, it felt like a pretty shitty version of armor, but it was all I had. That, and my secret sign language that meant I would always be able to get away with saying exactly what I wanted behind the next asshole's back. And speaking of assholes…

"Where the fuck have you been?" This was snapped at me the second I walked back into the office.

I resisted the urge to throw a stiletto heel at him… I always dressed professional, despite looking completely different at home, and losing one of my shoes would ruin the look. I was currently wearing a pair of navy wide-leg trousers that were pleated at the front. To this I had added a light-blue striped shirt, fitted to my slim and petite body with a navy cable-knit sweater-vest that had thin, light-blue lines at the V-neck collar.

The outfit was killer and despite finding elements of it from eBay, like the pointed-toe stiletto shoes in electric-blue that, granted, didn't exactly match the rest, I didn't care. It was all part of my amor. The one labeled "office professional". Now all I needed to do was find a boss that had the same ethos.

Something Bill Samson didn't have a single cell of. But then, maybe he had lost all of it with his hair, as wasn't that what happened to Samson when they cut all his hair? That he lost his strength? Well, maybe Bill had lost all his will to be a decent human being when he became as bald as the ass-end of a baboon.

Case in point, as he barked his question at me, one I was unfortunately used to. Just like my response, because the moment he turned his back to me, I would tell him to "go fuck himself, the bald twat," in sign language.

"I was in the bathroom," I told him, barely able to keep the exasperation from my tone.

"Yes, well the next shipment doesn't give a shit about your slutty make up!" he snapped, making my mouth drop.

"What!?" I scowled, making him grin. The sadistic asshole.

"A joke. Jeez, lighten up. The new crate is in the warehouse. I want it all cataloged but when you find lot seventy-seven, I want it brought back up here right away," he ordered, making me refrain from telling him exactly where he could stick lot seventy-seven, hoping it was something sharp, pointy, and the size of a prized zucchini!

"You know that will take me hours," I told him, making him scoff,

"So?"

I wanted to roll my eyes, already knowing it was pointless but said it anyway.

"So, my working day ends in ten minutes," I reminded him, wondering if my left-over Chinese food would last another day before going bad.

Yep, that was what my life had come to. Perhaps I would make that my next painting, a grayscale half-empty Chinese carton with rotting Kung Pao inside.

"Then I suggest getting your ass down there," he said, walking toward me and smacking my ass after saying this.

I swear I nearly broke his nose this time, fisting my hands as if I could feel the satisfying crunch of bone as my knuckles broke it. Arthur had also taught me how to punch but, then again, Arthur had taught me a lot.

However, I thought of the many things I usually did in these moments, which was my rent, electric bill, water, internet, phone, and one credit card bill I had to rack up when my car needed four new tires, brake pads, a new fan belt, oil change… and, well, the list goes on.

Which meant I walked out of the office praying that by the time I eventually got home, there would be emails waiting in my inbox offering me an interview. I had seriously lost count of the number of jobs I had applied for now. At this rate, I would be back to waiting tables. At least most customers weren't assholes and the job usually fed well. But like Arthur always signed,

'Keep looking to the path in front of you. There will always be something new just waiting for you around the corner.'

But that was Arthur, he was always saying something wise like that. Like a calm cloud in the storm that was my mind. He directed all that bitterness and pain into something I could use. He taught me how to punch a bag instead of some kid at a playground who was bullying someone smaller. Like directing pain and upset into a painting, therefore letting it go like the colors that faded from the brush when dipped in water. He taught me never to give up when things got hard. Which was why I didn't hit the sexist pig, but instead I made my way down into the lifeless warehouse.

It seemed all the other staff got to do normal hours. But then I guess that was why they chose to work away from their asshole boss, and I was the fool who was still his assistant or, in other words, the dog's-body slave. How I had lasted six months in this job was beyond me but, in my defense, he hadn't been that bad in the beginning.

That had all changed when I refused to sleep with the little creep. The charm had dropped from him like a slop of hot shit off a shovel and beneath was revealed to be something far worse.

A sexist little pervert.

"Fuck my life," I muttered, yanking back the elevator cage doors that rattled and groaned with desperate need of some lubrication. They weren't the only ones because, damn, I needed a drink. Hopefully the little prick would leave as soon as I found this lot seventy-seven and, that way, I could steal a swig of the whiskey I knew he kept in his bottom

draw. I, of course, wasn't usually in the habit of stealing or drinking at work, but after six months of dealing with this little shit and not managing to get another job, then it had driven me to doing both.

As for my job, Bill Samson's set up was cagey at best, but the most I could gather was that he was an antiquities dealer and often tasked with acquiring these rare finds for the filthy rich. I had seen letterheads with strange symbols on them and the letters LN under them. I tried to google what it might mean but it left me even more baffled because I could find no company name by those letters that could be linked to Bill's business.

I had tried to ask him about it once but after getting snapped at to do my damn job and keep my nose out, I knew that I would learn no more. But I did have to wonder if what he was doing was legit and not against the law. Going so far as dreaming of becoming an inside snitch for the FBI. Well, that would certainly help my boring life get more interesting. And who knows, maybe in doing so I would fall madly in love with some handsome agent.

Okay, so it was unlikely, but a girl was free to dream at least.

Speaking of dreaming, I walked into the warehouse office where I knew Noah's delivery notes would be. He was in charge of the warehouse, one that had a lot of security, no doubt due to the value of most of the antiques we kept here ready to be shipped out. It reminded me of something out of an Indiana Jones movie. There were walls of crates that created a wooden maze I could easily get lost in. Thankfully, the crates were spray painted with numbers and were kept in good order, thanks to Noah, who actually took the time out of his day to show me around when I first started.

As for now, other than the security guard doing his rounds and nodding his acknowledgement to me, there was no one else here. He was only one of ten men hired to keep this place secure and the guns on his belt always made me nervous. Noah had explained that there was also a separate security team at the ready, one privately paid for that could be here far quicker than the police force could.

Meaning that if any of the alarms were tripped, they would have this place surrounded in minutes should anything happen. Hence why I had codes, keys, and security cards up to my eyeballs. If you asked me, I thought it was a bit overkill but then again, I didn't know half of what this warehouse held, so what did I know? All I did know was that my boss was an asshole, and my job was everything from making coffee and picking up dry cleaning, to filing receipts and invoices that I couldn't understand because they were mostly in different languages.

Oh, and not forgetting, cataloguing some items by ticking them off the delivery note and taking pictures with my phone. This was so they could be uploaded to a site, ready to be sold at different auctions or straight to private collectors. Admittedly, this had been a new and recent addition to my job. This was only the second crate I had documented.

But hey, if it got me out of the office of that sleazeball, then it was time well spent. So I swiped my card in the reader, punched in the code, and grabbed the clipboard from Noah's desk. Then I made my way toward another room where the crates were opened, having to swipe the same card and enter a different code. I swear, how my brain retained all this information was beyond me. I had been tempted when I first started to get this shit tattooed on my arm. But that wouldn't have exactly gone with my other tattoos that were a collection of the same thing.

See, some people bought the same book because they loved it so much. Some people went to the same holiday destination every year. Watched the same movie over and over. But as for me, whenever life was hitting me hard, I would get another variation of the same tattoo. The first being on the back of my neck, mostly hidden by my hair if I ever wore it down, unlike today.

It was the rune Ingwaz.

It was known as the symbol for knowledge but also for divine energy. According to God Ing, known as a divine hero, people cannot change the past, but you can influence the present. Inguz teaches us that we are driven by the hope of changing something and from this we draw strength to carry on in life.

So basically, it meant that where there was a will there was a way. It was also Arthur's moto in life and why I got the same tattoo he had on his arm. Well, now I have five of them, one at my neck, one at the base of my spine, one at my hip, and on my ankle, but it was the one on the inside of my wrist that I always found myself rubbing, as if it had the power to give me strength and courage.

It was simple in its design, with two over lapping arrows, or two X's connected with one sitting above the other and creating a diamond shape in the center. The one at my neck had been the first and was therefore the most bold in its design, despite it being no bigger than my thumb. It was thick black lines with no flourishing features, not like the elegant brush strokes at my wrist.

The very same one I played with now, stroking the permanent lines etched into my skin as I stepped up to the crate that had, at the very least, been left open for me.

I didn't know why I was feeling uneasy this time, but it was as if what I was doing now was wrong.

Or more like it was…

Eternally Forbidden.

CHAPTER 3
DANGEROUS JOBS

"Holy shit balls," I uttered the second I came across lot seventy-seven. It was a statue of sorts and was the size of both my hands. Oh, and it looked to be made of solid gold. Its design was of a weird bird, with large talons that looked as if they should have been holding something. But then it was also bizarre because the moment I picked it up, a strange feeling washed over me. Like a sudden warmth I couldn't explain. As if something deep within its core was humming to me, trying to reach out and speak with me.

I tried to shake it off, this feeling I got sometimes when touching something old and doing what most people do in my case, which was to put it all down to an overactive imagination. I carried it over toward an area with better lighting so I could get a good look at it, when something crazy began to happen. It started to change! As if it was hiding something more. However, the second I saw the Demonic shadow on the floor reaching out as if to grab me, I nearly dropped the bloody thing, screaming out in fright,

"Ah! Jesus, mother of God!"

It had looked like some type of Demon stretching out a hand and trying to take me within its grasp. Admittedly, it freaked me the fuck out! Like Freddy Krueger had just showed up in my dreams and his hands were ready to play a game of slice and dice. A thought that quickly made me clutch the thing to my chest and turn away from the light just to make it stop. I knew it was just a trick of the light but, damn it, I swear something Demonic was trying to make a grab for me.

My heart pounded in my chest and, once again, I found myself shrieking out when I heard my cell phone start ringing.

"Fuck!" I swore this time and the thing bounced around in my hands like it was wet soap in the shower.

"Let's just put you down, should we?" I said to no one, now placing it back in its smaller create before answering my phone, groaning before I did when I saw the name 'little bald prick' come up on my screen.

"Sir I was just…"

"Where the fuck are you? I don't have all night to wait!" he snapped, making me scowl down at the phone and childishly stick my tongue out at it, before answering with a roll of my eyes,

"I just unboxed it to check it off the list and I am now…"

"You unboxed it!" I frowned at this new outrage.

"Yes, just like I do with all items I have to check off… you know… how *you* told me to." I emphasized the 'you' in this sentence.

"Right, yes, fine, just bring it to me," he bumbled, making me roll my eyes.

"But the rest…"

"Leave it until tomorrow, I have shit for you to do up here!"

I would have sighed at this had he not been on the phone, meaning in the end I just said,

"I'm coming now… *dickhead.*" I ended this with my favorite name for him when he hung up on me mid-sentence. Then I walked back to the gold bird and looked down at it with a sadness I couldn't explain. As if knowing the likes of my boss getting his greasy hands on it wasn't right. As if it was going against the wishes of what it wanted, which was totally ridiculous and absurd, I know. Hence why I closed the lid and scorned myself,

"You're going crazy again, Evie."

But then this was something that unfortunately happened often. I seemed to have a kind of affinity with old objects. As if they spoke to me or something. It was as if their history was trying to connect with me, using me as a conduit to speak with those who needed to hear their past. Either way, it was a weird gift I had spent years trying to ignore, like muting the whispers of ancient history.

Something not easy to do after accepting this job. Damn it, why did I have to accept this job…?

"Because it was this or Papa Party Pizzeria's new delivery girl, that's why," I complained after trying to juggle the heavy box and locking the door. Of course, I had been cataloging the crate for so long that security was making its next round, making me nod hello to Derek… or was his name Darren?

Well, lucky for me he was far enough away that just a

nameless nod was fine. I then struggled with the elevator, trapping my finger in the cage doors.

"Oww!" I complained, shaking out the painful sting of grazing off the skin from both knuckles and getting blood smeared on the box.

"Great, just peachy, Evie, the boss is gonna love that," I said before crying out when the lift jerked, and the lights flickered.

"Oh shit… come on, come on, *come on!*" I said when it stopped suddenly, making me start pressing all the buttons like my life depended on a fucking blue button!

"You piece of shit! COME ON… eureka! Ha!" I shouted in happiness when the last button I touched made it spring back into life, because clearly, I was desperate to get out of this rickety old thing.

I grabbed the box from the floor and stepped out into the office part of the building. However, I didn't know what was going on with the power but even the lights in here started flickering, making me walk faster down the hallway, getting more freaked out by the second.

"I told you, I will have confirmation soon and send you all the pictures you want but I want that money in my account before it leaves my hands!" I paused when I heard this angry statement being barked down the phone from Bill. A conversation that had me soon frowning down at the box in my hands, feeling it near screaming at me not to give it to him. But then the door was wrenched open, and the second Bill saw it was me, he snatched it right out of my hands, making me yelp in shock.

"Good, it was about damn time!" he snapped, turning his podgy little body and placed it down on his desk.

Then his beady eyes widened, and he actually sighed in pleasure the second he opened it. As for myself, I couldn't help but narrow my own gaze as his was suddenly filled with the gold bird reflecting menacingly in his eyes, as if all he saw was a briefcase of money.

Fucking Greed, it was the downfall of all men with power and the cause of so many innocent lives lost.

But wait, where had that thought come from? Had it been my own or that of the bird? I shook my head to rid myself of the feeling once more and stepped inside as he started taking photos of it, no doubt ready to send it straight the buyer. I therefore decided it was better to just pretend that I hadn't overheard his conversation, now asking,

"Did you want me to put it on the website?"

"No, no, this little beauty already has a buyer, but he won't be in 'til tomorrow. No, he just needed proof I have acquired the artifact," he said as if forgetting that he was speaking to me, being agreeable for once.

"No, for now I will put it in my safe," he said, jerking his hand at me and prompting me to turn around to face the window to find night had fallen on this September day.

Of course, I knew the drill by now, but the clueless asshole thought I was oblivious to most things when it came to his business. Just like knowing the combination to the safe in his floor and that the key was kept in the wall safe, which I also knew the combination to. But then I also wanted to roll my eyes and resisted the urge to mutter, *windows reflect asshole.*

But this wasn't the only combination I knew, or the fact that he had a panic room with a hidden latch to open it. Like I said, he thought I was stupid, and I freely let him because being underestimated was sometimes a person's greatest weapon. Thank you, Arthur, for that. So I let him continue to keep his low opinion of me, having no idea that I was good at remembering things, having a photographic memory for shit like this.

Which meant that when a bunch of maintenance men came in to do work on the panic room, I took notice. What good it would do me, I didn't know. Although, admittedly, I kind of just had a sixth sense for this shit. Which was, no doubt, why I seemed to file everything away in my mind, believing there was a chance I would need it someday. Just like I knew that it not only needed a code to get inside it but a thumbprint as well.

"Right, I am leaving, but I need that shit filed before you go," he said, making me turn around and gape at the pile of papers on his desk, wincing in disbelief. It would take me fucking hours!

The sound of him slamming his now empty glass of whiskey on the desk managed to draw me out of my dread after he had finished his drink in one.

"And clean up this mess," he said waving a dismissive hand over the rest of the shit tip that was his desk before grabbing his jacket and leaving me to my misery.

I shook my fists while doing an angry dance, stomping my feet like a child having a tantrum! Then once I got it all out, I brought my hands down in front of myself and took a deep, calming breath. After which, I got to work, slipping off my shoes to move around the office quicker.

At this rate, I would be bringing sneakers into work with me because I stopped at one point to lean against his desk so I could rub my feet, sighing in pleasure when I did. Then because I was always creeped out being here so late by myself, I fished out my MP3 player, plugged in my headphones, and started singing and dancing to 'Somebody to Love' by the legends that are Queen.

Soon I was getting so into it so much that I ended up using a stapler as my mic as I danced my ass across the office, then stepping onto the dickhead's chair and up to the desk, playing my air guitar at the solo and bending my knees as I really got into it. But then just as the chanting started in the song, the lights suddenly died, and I was left with the fast beat competing with that of my pounding heart. Then before the last of Freddie's voice was asking for someone to love, I screamed when flashes of light erupted, as if someone just blew open the doors at the end of the hallway because I could see sparks through the frosted glass.

I quickly ripped out my headphones, hit the stop button over and over again until it switched off, and ran around to hide under the desk, yanking the chair in to keep me from view.

Hopefully, they would just see an empty office and move on to where they kept the expensive shit in the warehouse. Something that would set off an alarm for who was, in all likelihood, nothing but a bunch of thieves. Jesus, but why oh why didn't I pick free pizza over this?!

I swallowed hard when I heard footsteps getting closer, making their way down the hall, and the temptation to poke my head up was one I fought against and labeled as suicidal. However, my hands ended up flying to my lips to hide my gasp of fright the second I heard the door opening. Please oh please, just take one look around and move on, I prayed silently.

A prayer that went by unheard as I heard more than one pair of footsteps enter.

"You're sure it's here?" a voice asked, but it was the strength of the one that replied that caused my heart to start hammering a beat named fear. It was a voice so deep it sounded made for commanding armies and leading the way into battle. Shit, but where had that thought come from?

"It's here... *I can feel it.*"

I swallowed hard, flinching when I thought it was heavy enough to hear. Which was when my fear doubled as that same sinister voice informed the room,

"And that's not the only thing I can feel."

I winced at this, hoping like holy fuck he didn't mean me! I also closed my eyes tight and waited, half expecting to be dragged out of here any second. However, when that didn't happen and no movement was heard, I released a relieved breath, realizing now that they must have moved on.

But my sigh of relief was quickly chased by a cry of fright as the chair was moved and a large hand shackled my ankle. Then I was dragged out of my hiding place and soon looking up into the most startling eyes of darkness I had ever seen. A foreboding figure of a man now stood over me, making me think of only one thing...

The Death I had once escaped...

It had finally found me.

CHAPTER 4
FACES OF DEATH

Naturally, I screamed when faced with Death.
Literally!
Because the towering figure had the body of a God but also the face of Death himself!

Or, at the very least, what I imagined death to look like. It was a face that looked like a Demon had been stripped of its flesh and skin, right down to the bone, before it was then dipped in matt-black paint. There were high cheek bones, so angular, and sharp enough they could have cut you. A jawline that aided the triangular shape, drawing down into a pointed chin that you would have imagined on the devil himself. The nose followed in the same style, being thin and pointed like that of an arrowhead, and not like you would find on a skull at all.

But it was the high-barbed brows that made me want to quiver back in fear as it regarded me with a permanent expression of harsh displeasure.

A startling darkness lay beyond the eyeholes, with the

slightest whites of his eyes being the only part that told me there was anything there at all. That, and the way he now regarded me as he tilted his head to the side slightly, as if questioning what he had just found.

The high forehead was covered in a series of spikes running in three lines. The middle row started above his nose, whereas the two either side framed the lines of his eyebrows. All of which, molded over the top of his head between a pair of black horns that were directed behind him and ended with sharp tips. His thin lips were completely unmoving as they continued to regard me silently.

Strangely, the terrifying Demon seemed so surprised at finding me, he even took a step back away from me, as if *I* was the one with a Hellish face. Which was why I reacted, quickly scrambling to my feet and running from him, stopping short the second I found myself faced with not one, but six of them all in the dark office. Demons that were only illuminated by the screen on the laptop and the full moon beyond the large window. One that cast a soft yellow glow over the office, along with the clueless city below that had no idea the horrors that walked among them.

I frowned as I took notice of what they each wore, seeing tactical vests, black military style uniforms, and thick black boots. Five out of six of them were also huge, with the biggest one easily being the one who had dragged me out from hiding under the desk. This was also when I let out the slightest of breaths, realizing now that they weren't Demons but men in disguise. I also would have said that my earlier thoughts of the FBI turning up had been right, but since when do they all wear Demonic masks?

I started backing away, holding my hands up in surrender

and before I had chance to say a word of protest, I was grabbed by the only one I could see had a shaved head. Because I soon realized there was only one of them that wore a full-face mask because the others had a variation of the design. One which was cut in half and allowed some of their human features to be seen. Like their lips, jawline, and most of the tops of their heads. They didn't have horns like the first man.

As for my predicament, I cried out in pain when I was suddenly slammed against the wall, making the picture of the Golden Gate Bridge next to me rattle before smashing to the floor. Then I found myself with a large deadly knife held up against my throat, making me close to peeing myself.

"P-p-pl-l-lease," I stammered out, now being forced to look up through my veil of unshed tears of fear into a pair of dead gray eyes. A pair hidden in the depths of the death mask he wore. However, the moment he growled down at me, and I saw fangs growing, I was ready to beg for my life. Even if I had to do this with my eyes closed because it looked like he was about to take a fucking bite out of me!

But then I heard the name of a Greek Devil being growled and, this time, the sound came as a warning. Thankfully, it wasn't a threat meant for me.

"Hades."

I opened my eyes and turned to find that the first man to drag me out from my hiding place was now standing towering next to the monster in front of me. Then I watched as the gray eyes looked down to see a large, gloved hand restraining him, forcing him to lower the knife held to my throat.

"Let her go," he ordered.

It was an order I doubted many would have ignored because there was such strength behind it, I would have dropped to my knees had he asked me to. Not surprising then when the one he called Hades dropped his weapon and stepped away, lowering his head in what looked like submission.

I would have started breathing easier had I been given the space to do so, but the moment I tried to take a step away from the wall, the one in charge was taking my previous captor's place.

"Ah ah, you're going nowhere, little bird," he said, walking me backward against the wall with a large hand spanning my belly, pushing me slowly.

Of course, he did this far gentler than the other brute had done, so I had to hope that meant he didn't intend to hurt me. At least I didn't find myself with another blade held against my throat, so thank the Gods for small mercies.

"Go help the others," he ordered the shaved-headed Hades, who bowed ever so slightly once more and stepped away to join the rest of the team. One that soon started trashing the place as they started looking for something by literally punching holes in the walls. Which was when it hit me…

They were looking for the safe.

But of course they were, they were thieves after all.

"Bill Samson, you work for him?" The scariest one of them all asked me this. It was now obvious he was clearly in charge here. I nodded my head quickly and, I couldn't tell behind the mask, but I swear that he was smiling.

"Good, then you know where the wall safe is."

I swallowed hard and braved to ask,

"And if... if I show you... will... will you let me go?" I asked, and again, he seemed fascinated by my voice, tilting his head slightly just like he had done when towering over me when I'd had my back to the floor. But then he raised a gloved hand to my face, making me flinch back as if he were ready to strike.

However, this didn't happen. He paused his hand, holding his palm out the moment I winced as if telling me silently that he wouldn't hurt me. Then once I was still, he ran the backs of leather clad fingers down my cheek before telling me,

"As tempted as I am to say no and keep you, I will, at the very least, vow that no harm will come to you should you aid us in any way you can."

I didn't know why but I believed him. Although the part about keeping me only ended up confusing me enough to be forced to ignore. But as for his vow, well it could have been his gentle touch or the way he purposely forced his voice to take on a smoother tone. Either way, I trusted in what he just told me, foolish or not. Which was why I nodded and told him,

"The other bridge." At first, I saw him frown before he looked behind him, finding yet another picture and told one of his men,

"Van, the bridge." At this, a tall, muscular blonde man wearing the same mask as the others nodded before walking to one of the many pictures in the room, removing it to find the safe there. As soon as it was revealed, the leader in front of me turned back to face me and praised softly,

"Good girl."

I couldn't help but bite my lip at that, lowering my eyes and just glad he couldn't see the blush I could feel rising. Damn, why was I having this kind of response to him? Wasn't he the bad guy? I mean, sure, I wanted something more exciting in my life to happen and that old saying, *be careful what you wish for* hit me like a fist to the gut. But, in my little fantasy, I had also been daydreaming of falling for the hero agent, not the villain thief.

"You will need the combi… oh." This ended in a gasp of shock as the one he called Van tore the handle clean off, opening the safe as if it had been made from cookie dough. At this the leader, whose name I naturally didn't know yet, looked to be smirking again, if the change in shape to his dark eyes was any indication.

However, this didn't last long, because one of his men soon snarled,

"It's not fucking here!"

At this, a slimmer man I didn't know the name of pushed him out the way and demanded,

"Let me look."

"One of you better give me something and fucking now!" the leader seethed, and I couldn't help but hold my breath in fear. However, the second he felt my reaction to it he turned back to me and commanded,

"Take a breath, little bird."

I did as I was told but it was one quickly stolen as the one called Hades snapped,

"I can't read her mind, but she knows something!"

He was storming his way back over to me when the leader snapped his hand up, stopping him in his tracks.

"Fear is not always the answer."

The one named Hades scoffed at that but backed down anyway.

"What are your duties here exactly?" the leader asked me, and after swallowing down the fear he spoke of, I told him,

"I am just his assistant."

"Ah, but any good businessman worth his weight knows that a good assistant is key for a successful working day."

I wet my lips at that, something he seemed fixated on for the moment before I told him,

"Bill isn't a good businessman, nor does he think much of his assistant."

"Then Bill is a fool," he replied with ease and, again, my cheeks grew hot.

"Thank you," I replied shyly. Even if he only said it so that I would give him what he wanted, shamefully, it still felt good.

"I am looking for something very… precise, should we say," he told me, prompting me to reply with the truth,

"Then it is most likely down in the warehouse. He rarely keeps anything in his office. In fact, tonight was the first time it ever happened," I told him, and I knew behind the mask he raised his brow in question before asking,

"What happened?"

"He wanted me to bring him lot seventy-seven." At this he looked back at the slim man who was listening to us. He nodded to his leader, telling him silently this was what they were looking for.

"And where did he put it, little one?" I swallowed hard before asking,

"You give me your word you won't just kill me after I tell you?" Again, this seemed to amuse him before he told me,

"Do you hold any loyalty to your boss?"

At this I couldn't help but scoff a laugh and tell him honestly,

"Not likely, Bill's an asshole."

He seemed surprised by my answer before a slight chuckle escaped him.

"Then you have nothing to lose by telling me, for trust me, little bird, it certainly won't be your life," he told me, making me sigh before I admitted,

"There is a hidden safe in the floor next to the desk, he thinks I don't know about it." At this he most definitely smirked.

"Foolish Bill indeed," He replied, making me grin and it was something he seemed fixated with once more.

"Van, if you would do the honors."

I watched as the blonde found the hidden panel of carpet and revealed the safe, making me quickly tell him in a panicked tone,

"You can't just rip it open!" Honestly, as soon as I said it, I was questioning myself as to why I did. Why was I helping them? Was it because this was my chance to stick it to Bill? Because, let's be honest, my ass was getting fired after this regardless.

The leader lifted his hand quickly, seemingly trusting me instantly.

"Tell me?" he asked and, again, it was as if he had one tone for his men and a far softer one for me.

"It will trip an alarm without the key and code."

He nodded once as if telling me he understood before enquiring,

"And I am assuming that a smart girl like you knows where I would find both?" he said and, like before, I knew it was a compliment he gave me just to get what he wanted but, again, by this point I didn't care. Clearly, I was already fully invested with the fantasy.

"The key is hidden in the book of War and Peace in his wall safe and the code is 46. 58. 92. 7650," I told him, and this time his eyes crinkled at the corners, something I could barely see because it looked as if they each wore black make up under the mask around the eye holes. Although, this close, I had no clue what they used. It looked more like his skin was dyed as black as night.

"You have a good memory and, clearly, a boss that underestimates you," he commented when I was proved right and the safe opened.

"Lucky for you guys," I replied with a slight smile, one that I could tell was received with one of his own, despite it remaining hidden.

"It's here," the man named Van said, making the leader say,

"Excellent."

And damn, the way he said that, Christ, I could have heard it over and over again in my dreams and sleep happily. However, the second I saw Van about to slam it shut, I shouted,

"No! Don't shut it!" But this warning came too late because the second it closed, an alarm started blaring. I flinched as my panicked eyes shot up to his, when his own narrowed down at me.

"I'm sorry… I tried to…" I was quickly cut off by anger.

"Lies! She did that on purpose!" the one named Hades growled, now storming over to us. I started shaking my head quickly as panic set in once more.

"No… I… I…"

"Think about it, genius, if that were true, she would have not told us about the code and key so as not to trip the first alarm," the slim man said, surprising me by coming to my defense and making me more than a little grateful.

"It matters not. We have what we came for, now it is time to leave," the leader said in a hard tone that meant I was back to being terrified. Then he motioned for his men to leave, making he irrationally grab his arm and stop him. A touch I retracted slowly when he looked down at my hand now clutching his arm, one that felt made of so much pure solid muscle that it was frightening.

"If you go that way they will be waiting," I told him after quickly letting him go.

"A few guards will be nothing to us," Hades scoffed arrogantly.

"But there will be a private security team here in minutes, these guys, they are ex-military… mercenaries most likely," I added just to be sure they took me serious enough.

"How do you know this?" the leader asked in a serious tone.

"I have seen the payments, I googled the name of the firm and put two and two together," I told him with a slight lift of my shoulders.

"Smart girl. Alright, little bird, what do you suggest?" he asked, shocking me that he wanted my opinion.

"Boss, I don't trust her, I don't think…"

"Enough! I do not intend to end this in mortal bloodshed," he snapped back at the one he called Van, someone who just shrugged his shoulders like I had done moments ago.

"There is a way," I said, nodding across the room and hinting for him to move. Something he did by first taking a step back and holding out his arm while saying,

"Then have at it, little one." I nodded before rushing to the bookshelf, running my fingers along the third shelf until I felt the hidden button. I pressed it, causing the whole thing to open up, showing a hidden metal door behind it.

"A safe room?" the slim guy asked.

"I saw some of the blueprints one of the installers dropped, I think it has a secret passageway down to the back of the warehouse," I told him, making the leader nod.

"It's got another code and fingerprint access. So, unless we have Bill's severed finger lying around here, we can't gain access as not even brute strength is getting through this one," Van stated, making the slimmer one take his place at the keypad.

"You can't bypass it?" the leader asked him, making someone I was now naming as slim, reply,

"I'm good, Boss, but not that good," he admitted, making me quickly think before my eyes settled on Bill's desk.

"I think I know a way," I shouted over the blaring alarm, now hurrying to the desk and finding the empty glass before yanking open the draws, looking for what I needed.

"What the fuck is she doing?" Van asked.

"The humans are coming," Hades stated, forcing me to ignore the word humans, because what the hell did he class himself as if not human!? A fucking terminator perhaps?

"How long?" the leader asked, maintaining his calm tone.

"Forty-five seconds," one of the other men said, one who up until now had remained silent.

"And their minds?" This was another strange thing to ask from the leader, a question I purposely ignored as I continued with my search.

"Too many of them all spreading out," was the even weirder reply from one of the others.

"Well, girl scout, if you are going to do something, then now is the time," the one named Van said, just as I found the roll of clear tape I knew was in here.

Then I grabbed my handbag, rummaged through it, and found the blush powder I knew was in there. At this I blew a little onto the glass before tearing a piece of tape from the roll, using it to cover where I knew his thumb print had been. I then carefully pealed it away, mentally counting down the time and wondering why I was still helping these guys try to escape.

Because you're still invested in the fantasy, you idiot!

I quickly ran over to the panel that slim was standing at and stuck the tape with Bill's thumb print over the sensor, praying it turned green. When it did, it allowed me to put in the code I knew, and I finally let out a breath of relief when the door opened.

"Just in time, here they come," Van said as one-by-one they all stepped inside and just when I was about to step out of the way, the leader grabbed the top of my arm and told me,

"Tut tut, little bird, I am not letting you go just yet." Then he did the unthinkable as he pulled me...

Deeper into his world.

CHAPTER 5
LASTING IMPRESSION

The door slammed shut, sealing us in, and the lights illuminated the space as we heard the turning wheel of what sounded like heavy locks sliding back into place. I blinked to adjust to the brighter light, finding a pair of intense eyes looking back at me.

Dark blue, not black like I first thought.

"Will they hear us in here?" the one named Van asked on a whisper, making Slim answer,

"Not fucking likely, not with how thick those doors are."

"Well done, girl scout, that was pretty clever thinking," Van praised, grinning down at me before ruffling my head as he passed me like I was a good little pet.

"Clever indeed," the leader agreed without taking his eyes off me. making me want to squirm under such a penetrating gaze.

"There is a tunnel back here," one of the others said.

Van nudged into Hades. "See, just like she said there would be."

However, the bald man scowled my way and growled at

the blonde before following toward the back of the room where there was indeed a door open. It led to a room that was nothing but dark-gray walls filled with cupboard doors, a bed against one wall, and another door at the far end. I couldn't help but blush when looking at the bed.

"Where did you learn how to do that?" the leader asked after following my gaze to the bed and, no doubt, wishing to get my mind back to what just happened... away from the fantasy that would never happen.

"I watch a lot of cop shows," I said, shrugging my shoulders.

"Well, I hope you don't root for the good guys," Slim said with amusement in his tone before he followed the others, which left only myself and Mr. Intimidating as being the last to leave.

"It was certainty resourceful," he commented, before I couldn't help but ask,

"Why did you pull me through?"

At this he tilted his head to the side a little as if contemplating the answer for himself. But then he raised his gloved hand to my face and rubbed his thumb down the side of my nose and under my eye. However, before I could question this, he looked down at the black leather, making me do the same and seeing for myself the smudge of foundation across the pad of his thumb.

"Why would you hide your true self?"

"Says the guy in the mask," I replied before I could think better of it. I could tell this had made him grin because his eyes danced with mirth. Something that was easier to detect now we were in a well-lit room.

"I think it's obvious why I hide," he said. This time, the

blush he caused was easier for him to see with some of my makeup gone.

"But why you would hide unique aspects of your beauty, I am at a loss."

At this my mouth actually dropped a little and, oh yeah, he was definitely smirking at this. He even raised the backs of his fingers to my cheek and ran them over my freckles, commenting softly,

"Cute."

"Are you... *flirting with me?*" I asked on a shocked whisper.

"Ah but that would be inappropriate now, wouldn't it?" he teased, and again those incredible eyes glistened with amusement. I swear I could barely breathe, holding my breath captive in my surprise. Especially when he stepped closer and used a bent finger to tip my head right back so I could still see him.

Damn, he was so tall!

Something made even worse without my heels. Man, I had loved those shoes. Well at least I had my bag with me, one nestled against my hip. But then fuck my bag because I was close to passing out, especially when he lowered his head and, for the briefest of moments, I thought that he would kiss me.

"Breathe for me," he whispered, and as if he had just slaughtered all other puppeteers and taken their place, I did his bidding by inhaling suddenly. After which he tapped under my chin twice with his finger that had remained there before taking a step back. Then he held out his arm for me, this time telling me without a commanding tone to leave the room and follow the others.

I swallowed hard and tried to get myself back under control, finding the tattoo on my wrist and rubbing it like I always did when feeling vulnerable. But after walking down the hallway, he quickly fell into step beside me and I braved asking once again,

"You never answered me before…"

He looked down at me over his shoulder as we walked side by side, and it felt weird to be so comfortable communicating with someone in a Demonic mask.

"A mistake I am sure to rectify, no doubt," he replied once again in a teasing tone and I had to say, he was the most well-spoken thief I had ever encountered. Well, okay, my experience was all based on living on the streets when I was a kid, but still, he wasn't what you would consider your typical thief. That, I could be sure of.

"Why did you bring me with you?" I asked again, and I swore I heard the slightest sound of a sigh coming from him before he answered me.

"Like I told you, I wasn't done with you yet."

"That doesn't exactly fill me with confidence that I am going to survive this," I replied dryly, despite finding it hard to believe that he would harm me. Now as for Hades, hell yeah, that guy wanted to see me dead, for sure.

"You think I would reward your trust with deceit?" he asked in a slightly affronted tone.

"Well, you are supposed to be the bad guys," I replied, making him scoff.

"Oh, we are most definitely the bad guys, make no mistake in that, little Dove."

"Dove… I thought I was just a bird?" I teased back, and again I wished I could have seen his lips. I would put money on it being a handsome mouth, especially when smirking the way his eyes told me he was.

"Yes, well, Doves can be the symbol for many things, good luck and freedom only being two of them." At this he actually winked at me, admittedly, making my heart flutter. But afterward, I didn't know what to say, so I chose not to say anything as we continued down the hallway until we reached a ladder leading down.

"I will go before you," he said, and my face must have asked why.

"That way, if you fall I can catch you," he told me, and again my mouth opened a little in my surprise.

"Oh... but then what happens if you fall?" At this he stepped into me once more and asked with clear satisfaction coating his words,

"Worried for me, little bird?" I swallowed hard but refused to answer. It was far too dangerous to admit it to myself, let alone admitting it to him.

But when I remained silent, he gripped my chin in between his thumb and his index finger, using this hold on me to tip my head right back as he stepped flush with me once more.

"Then I suggest you do not fall, little Dove." Again, this caused my heart to skip a beat and I would have closed my eyes in preparation for him to kiss me had he held me for much longer.

However, once again it was not meant to be, because he soon stepped back and allowed me some much needed space. This was before he started to lower his body down the shaft that was barely big enough for one large person to fit. Good job that the guy who had this secret escape commissioned was my fat ass boss, or the group of bulky muscular men would have had no chance.

I couldn't help but look down to find the leader looking back up at me. Then he warned,

"Keep your eyes ahead and on the rung of the ladder."

I resisted the urge to gulp at the order and did as I was told.

When did I get so damn submissive? Oh yeah, when those orders came from someone big enough to squeeze me to death, and with a voice that made me want to both run and hide as much as I wanted to roll over and show him my belly. Okay, so being honest with myself, showing him my belly was the very last body part I would have started with.

Although it had to be said that any hopes of cooling these sexual thoughts wasn't helped the moment I felt a pair of large hands grip my sides. This was before he lifted me down from the last rung of the ladder. Something he really hadn't needed to do, but in this fantasy of mine, I liked to think he did it because he wanted the excuse to touch me. Admittedly, the connection was far too fleeting and I wished he had made more of an excuse to keep his hands there for longer.

"There is a doorway up ahead." This was whispered from someone ahead of us as we were both still at the back. It was also a darker tunnel we travelled through, making me wonder if we were walking along a false wall of sorts. Or perhaps it was one made to look like a wall of crates? Either way, it ran along what I assumed to be the full length of the warehouse because it went on for a while.

"It leads straight into the loading bay," another voice said, before we indeed found ourselves out in one of the loading bays. It was one that was rarely used… and now I knew why.

"Go get the van," the leader ordered, and I knew with that, our time was soon at an end.

"But, my Lord, we should…"

"I said go!" he snapped angrily; however, my mind was still lingering on the 'my Lord' part and questioning why? Lord of what exactly? Was it like some weird nickname and if it was, then wow, egotistical much?

"I think this is the part we go our separate ways," I said, looking back at the door we had just come through.

"No, I think this is the part where you tell me your name," he countered, stepping up to me and making me quickly start to take quicker steps backward. Something that didn't exactly go as planned when I found myself against a pair of roller doors.

"Wh-what are you doing?" I questioned fearfully, although admittedly, there was also a great deal of lust in there too. I mean, Christ, I hadn't even seen this guy's face yet! Of course, my treacherous little heart didn't care about this annoying insignificant fact. Not when he placed an arm above my head, something easily accomplished seeing as I still was without my shoes, and he towered above me in height.

"Your name, beautiful?" he asked again, and this time his tone told me I better not refuse him, despite it coming out like a demanding, lustful purr. This, combined with hearing him call me beautiful, well, it was naturally doing strange things to me.

"I don't even know what you look like," I argued weakly, and this time when he smiled, it was one I saw for myself.

As he finally...

Removed his mask.

Something that caused me to gasp and for more than one reason. Not only did my eyes see the impossible, as the darkness I had thought was makeup seeped back into the mask, leaving the face of perfection behind. But he was also...

He was utterly breathtaking!

But despite being astonishingly good-looking, I couldn't help but feel as if he was less intimidating with the mask on, because now I was really starting to squirm! It was those high cut cheekbones that screamed authority and leadership, and that straight nose that made me believe he could easily have been born from royalty. His perfectly proportioned lips with neither the bottom nor the top being bigger than the other. A delicious dusting of stubble casting the lower part of his face in enough shadow that he couldn't have been considered a clean cut and therefore giving him a dangerous, raw edge.

Yet these features all seemed insignificant and a mere afterthought in comparison to his incredible eyes. Eyes so dark blue, they almost didn't seem real. A color I didn't even think existed. I felt as if they could slice through any mental amor I could have erected around myself and pierce right through to my very soul. Eyes made more menacing by the dark, straight slashes of his eyebrows that made him permanently look as though he was studying me. Accessing every move I made, and silently warning me that nothing I did would ever get past him.

And, holy hell, I had never seen someone so handsome in all my life! Hence why I embarrassingly whispered,

"You're not real."

At this he grinned, which turned into a smirk before he tipped my head back with a curled finger under my chin. It was a smile that completely transformed his face into nothing short of spectacular. It managed to soften the harshness to the point I could believe the man was actually capable of laughing. Like some fabled tale you needed to see the proof of before you believed it was real. Oh, and fuck me, but he was very, *very fucking real*, despite my whispered remark.

"Then there is only one sure way for you to find out," he told me, and before I knew what was happening, he leaned down and turned my unbelievable night of adventure into one of pure fantasy.

As he kissed me.

A kiss I could tell was only supposed to start out as a gentle reminder that the two of us existed in the moment. That we were right here and right now. But after I, shamefully and eagerly, opened up to him, something seemed to snap within him. Some unspoken restraint that I didn't know why he had bothered to hold back to begin with.

Because he emitted a rumbled growl before he swept on in and took his first taste of me. An act that caused something darker and more definitive to shift within him. I heard the scraping of what sounded like knifes cutting through metal above me and, at the same time, his other arm banded around my waist and tugged me closer into the wall of muscle that was his chest. As if he had been concerned that the violent sound above me would have had caused me to pull away and, above all, he wanted to prevent my escape.

I gasped and it was one he tasted. He deepened the kiss

into something so sexual I, shockingly, nearly came from it alone. It was something so erotic, I just knew I had never experienced anything like it and never would again.

It was earth shattering.

But then the second I heard a commotion behind me, I knew our time was up and he knew it too. We were both breathing heavy as he placed his forehead to my own, demanding on a growl,

"Now give me your name, girl!" I gulped at this before telling him,

"They are coming, you don't have time for this!" Then I pushed him away, something he refused even after a van appeared at the loading bay.

"Boss!" Hades shouted after opening the side door and hanging half out of it.

"Your name!" he growled louder this time. It was a sound that fought against the sound of men running toward the loading bay behind the roller doors.

"Please, just go!" I pleaded, trying to get him to see the urgency we all could, everything within me screaming for me not to trust him with my name.

"Give. Me. Your. Name!"

I gasped because, this time, the deadly sound that followed it gave more strength to the mask he had worn. It also made me comply and tell him quickly,

"Evelyn Parker." At this he tugged me to him and kissed me one last time before promising me,

"I will be seeing you soon, little Dove." Then he finally turned and ran toward the van held open ready for him.

Meanwhile, I was left panting, wondering what on earth I had done by giving him my name.

After first watching the van speed out of the loading bay, I soon discovered just how dangerous giving him my name really was. Especially, when I turned around to face the roller doors, my breath was stolen at what I saw.

Because my mystery man hadn't just left an everlasting impression on me. Oh no, he had also left his destructive impression on the metal door only inches above where my head had been.

Four long jagged gashes torn straight through the metal as if…

A Demon just clawed through the doors.

CHAPTER 6
EVERYTHING
RYKER

"And how is our Girl Scout doing?" I frowned when Van said this, irrationally wanting to rip out his tongue for claiming her as being anything but mine. Fuck, but what was wrong me, I didn't know. Well, that wasn't strictly true. I knew what was wrong with me...

That fucking kiss.

Why I had kissed her, I still had no clue.

Well, again, that wasn't strictly true. I had fucking wanted to, that was why! Gods, but in that moment, it had felt like I had never wanted anything more. Even the fucking Scepter had been the last thing on my mind. Fuck, but why was I still thinking of her? Why had I demanded her name? Why was I still feeling this way about her?

I had no fucking clue but, either way, the compulsion to kiss her and demand her name had been simply too strong to ignore. Hell's fire, but how I had wanted to steal her away. To not do so had been a test to my will like never before. Just like now, when I had Faron hack the police station so as I may watch the live feed of her interrogation.

Even watching the way she sat there waiting hours for the officer to enter had me on edge for her. But I knew it was a police tactic as we often did the same when conducting our own interrogations. Although granted, ours did include a great deal of torture, whereas theirs usually included bringing coffee.

But then I found myself wondering what that mark on the inside of her wrist was as she seemed to play with it when nervous. I had caught sight of her doing this last night but hadn't had the time to enquire further. It looked like a tattoo of sorts, and I made a mental note to ask Faron to freeze the frame and zoom in so as it could be printed out for me to examine. Again, I questioned why the fuck I cared for all of about two seconds before dismissing the feeling, questioning why the fuck I didn't freely allow myself to care.

Because I knew there was just something about this girl. I could feel it deep within my old bones. And I wasn't just speaking of her obvious beauty, one that had me captivated from the start. The way those light brown eyes with their darker circle framing the ochre and flecks of cinnamon had looked up at me in fright. Those long, thick lashes making her look like some innocent doe in sight of the beast ready to strike. And ready to strike I was, but just not in the way she feared I would.

Fuck me, but that innocence I could have fed from for fucking years, as that alone had been enough to make me fall to the abyss of addiction. But then added to this was a part of herself she had tried to hide, something I quickly found unacceptable. For when I discovered the gentle dusting of freckles across her nose and cheeks, I had nearly been forced to bite my lip from grinning.

She was too fucking cute and to a dangerous degree, for it was my favored type of beauty. The type that naturally occurred and wasn't hidden by makeup, for what was often considered as flaws upon the skin I found to be the most interesting part. I didn't want a perfect canvas glossed over by what convention dictated to gaze upon.

I wanted something real, something pure. Something admittedly hard to find in another Demon. I wanted that dark hair out of place and escaping the confines of the plait she had attempted to keep it contained to. I wanted those breathy sounds whispering my name despite never giving it to her.

I wanted those...

Cherry flavored lips.

I released a frustrated sigh, wishing now I had just acted on impulse and snatched her from that loading bay. That way I would be experiencing that same wide-eyed look she had awarded me so often last night. Although, next time, it wouldn't have been from a floor but from my bed. I needed to possess this woman!

It was a need I only knew one way to sate.

But as for now, I had no choice but to be content with watching her from my computer screen, despite wanting to put my fist into it from anger at how long they were making her wait. Something that thankfully ended moments later, just as my Second was casually taking a seat next to me, making me give him a wry look. One he ignored, as usual.

But then I had to admit the nickname he had gifted my little mortal bird also suited her, as she had certainly been resourceful in that office. Of course, we could have dealt with the human tactical force, but it was doubtful there wouldn't have been casualties in doing so. Besides, I had wanted the excuse to keep her with us that little bit longer and, in truth, I was intrigued. Curious enough to let it play out and wondering when it would be that she double crossed us.

Something that still astounded me to say, hadn't happened. Which was another reason why I wanted to see this integration, wondering now how long it would take her to crack and tell the cops everything that had happened. Not that I would blame her if she did as, well, she did have her own skin to save… *delicious, freckled skin.*

I remember when seeing her for the first time under better light, having the urge to see what she hid under the make-up and promptly giving into it. Again, being utterly delighted to see the freckles there. Gods, but why couldn't I get my damn mind from those freckles?! Because I had never seen anything so fucking cute in all my life, that's why. And it was a long fucking life at that.

But I also knew the dangers of such feelings, for it gave her power over me and that was not something I could ever allow. Despite whatever it was my Demon was trying to tell me as he had seemed just as captivated. The first time I saw her, pulling her from her hiding place, the sight of her looking up at me hit my Demon like a fucking thunderbolt to its chest.

I couldn't fully understand it as, in truth, my Demon had never had that reaction before. Nor could I understand what it was her voice did to me. The moment she spoke was another hit and, after that, they just kept coming. Even so far as to me being forced to resist the urge to beat the shit out of

Hades the second he threatened her. The need to protect her rode me hard and had me intervening, whereas normally I would have let him have his fun and feed from her fear.

Fear that only ended up tasting bitter to me. A soul's acid that filled my senses until I was forced to replace them by easing her fears and granting comfort in what was, no doubt, a traumatic experience for her. And speaking of traumatic experiences.

"Miss Parker," the officer said, making her sit up straighter and pull the hem of her little knitted vest down in a haughty manner that had me suppressing a grin. Brave little thing.

"And you are?" she asked in a tone that surprised the officer as, clearly, his tactic of keeping her waiting hadn't worked in breaking her. Good girl.

"I am Detective Campbell," he replied, taking a seat opposite and placing a thick folder down on the desk that I knew was yet another tactic used. It was most likely two sheets of information and a thick pile of nothing underneath. But then it seemed I wasn't the only one who picked up on it.

"That looks like a whole bunch of nothing you have there... careful, Detective, they might need all that blank paper back at the copier."

At this Van nearly choked on his coffee as he started laughing next to me and, this time, I was unable to suppress my own amusement by grinning at the screen. That was until Van commented,

"Fuck me, but I like this chick!" To which I growled low in the back of my throat, unable to help myself.

"Easy, Ryker, I'm just saying the girl's got spunk."

"Hmm… *indeed,*" I growled before going back to watching as this Detective Campbell flustered.

"And what makes you say that?" he asked, and she simply shrugged her slight shoulders at this and told him,

"Trust me, my life is not that interesting, but I appreciate the effort in making it look more so."

"Well, I would say you just got your wish… now what can you tell me about last night?"

She smirked a little and her fingers rose to run along her lips ever so slightly, and I couldn't help my reaction as I knew exactly what she was doing.

She was remembering our kiss.

Admittedly, the sight made me fucking hard in seconds. I just hoped that my asshole best friend didn't fucking notice the uncomfortable action as I tried to readjust myself to ease the strain against my slacks. Thank fuck I wasn't wearing jeans, that's all I would say.

"Looks like your girl is remembering your farewell," Van said, not missing the action she made either and, because of it, was now nudging me and making me roll my eyes at him. This despite knowing it was all an act. As the same sight meant far more to me than some bored expression I was trying to portray. Although Van knew me better than anyone else, so why I fucking bothered I had no clue.

"Well, I think it's obvious what happened last night," she replied, regardless of our farewell.

"Is it?"

"Surely, you have video surveillance?" she asked, making me grin, but Van got there first by praising her,

"Smart girl."

And that she was, as it was clear she wanted to know what they knew first before she admitted to anything.

"Well, that's the funny thing, Miss Parker. All footage of last night was erased." Her eyes widened at that before she seemed to relax ever so subtly.

"Yeah, that's because we are professional's, dickhead," Van commented with a chuckle, as it was true.

However, before Faron had hacked their systems and erased the footage, I had him send it all to our private servers so as I could watch it back for my private viewing. *Unlike now.* I suppressed the urge to roll my eyes again when wishing I was alone. Something that didn't happen when Faron joined us, along with Hades.

Great, now it was a fucking party.

"Has the canary started singing yet?" Hades commented dryly, and before I could say a word in her defense, Faron butted in,

"Fifty bucks says she doesn't say a word."

"Oh, shit, I am in on that!" Van said, trying to get out his wallet, however, I lost my shit and snapped,

"Shut the fuck up, all of you!" Then I went back to listening, knowing I had missed some parts, when hearing her say,

"What can I say, Detective? It was such a traumatic experience for me that I must have suppressed all memory of it."

"Pay up, douche bag," Van said quietly this time, making Hades growl and Faron chuckle. I shot Van a quick 'I will rip your balls off' look, making him zip across his lips with his fingers.

"That, I find hard to believe," the detective said firmly.

"Am I under arrest?" she boldly asked, making the detective scowl at her before telling her,

"Not yet, no." At this she rose from her seat and told him,

"Then I guess I am free to go."

"You guessed wrong, Miss Parker, now sit your ass down!" he shouted, making me growl at the way he spoke to her, already telling myself that some unfortunate encounter was going to be paying Detective Campbell a visit. Preferably down some dark alleyway at night... something that would award him nightmares for the rest of his pathetic life. After all, it was one of Van's specialties.

"Whoa, Boss, you might want to ease up on the equipment," Faron said, pulling the laptop further away from my hands that had turned Demonic, just as they had last night.

Fuck, but I didn't even have a clue they'd changed, admittedly giving me enough cause to worry. That had never happened before and now twice in less than twenty-four hours, and the only change in me had been...

Her.

I watched as she sat down, now doing so slowly and without keeping her seething gaze from the detective.

"I could have you arrested as an accessory to theft." At this she laughed and told him,

"You and I both know that if you had even a shred of evidence to support that wild theory, I would be locked up already."

"Perhaps I am giving you a chance to work with us and make a deal." At this she scoffed.

"I don't need a deal. I wasn't involved any more than

being taken as a hostage, hence why I ended up in that loading bay where you guys cuffed me and took me in." I gritted my teeth at that, hating the thought of her being treated this way. Knowing that the fault lay with myself didn't exactly sit right in my chest.

"You didn't seem very frightened at the time." At this I couldn't help but smirk, as no, she hadn't.

"And why should I when I thought the good guys had appeared to save the day…? Oh wait, that was until you hauled my ass in here and dumped me in this room for the last two hours. Oh yes, very heroic of you," she drawled sarcastically, making the detective visibly grit his teeth.

"Yes. well, you weren't exactly playing damsel in distress, Miss Parker, so forgive me for not sweeping you off your feet toward my chariot," he replied just as sarcastically.

"No, instead you just treated a victim like the bank robber because you let the real guy's escape, and now you're looking for a scape goat. Well, no offence, Detective Campbell, but why shouldn't I just call my lawyer and say no comment?"

At this I grinned and nodded to Faron,

"Send her in," I ordered, and in return he bowed his head and was on his phone in seconds.

"Because you don't have a lawyer and after looking into your finances, I doubt you could even afford one." At this she scowled at him, and I tensed as something ugly twisted in my gut at the thought of her struggling for money.

"And I am sure that was a gross invasion of my privacy," she retorted and rightfully so.

"Like I said, Miss Parker, we believe you are an accessory to this robbery, so had due cause to look, so did a judge." At this she started to look panicked but, despite this, she folded her arms and stated firmly,

"Then no comment it is."

"Good girl," I said, and if it shocked anyone in the room, they didn't dare fucking say. No, only Van had questioned me about that kiss, but even he knew not to approach the subject of my feelings in front of others. I did, however, feel his questioning gaze on me now.

"You could tell us who they were and what it was they stole." At this she showed a slither of surprise before masking it and replying with,

"No comment."

Of course, I had to wonder why it was that she felt the need to protect us. She could have given them all manner of information and it wouldn't have led the police anywhere near us but then... *she didn't know that.*

"Why is she protecting us?" Van asked, giving voice to my thoughts.

"Did you threaten her?" he asked then, and I tensed my fists, knowing that I couldn't have threatened her, even if I had wanted to. No, for some reason, she meant something to me, and I couldn't yet explain what. Yet, no matter how much easier it would have been for me to say to my men that I had... *I just couldn't do it.*

So, I told them the truth.

"No, I did no such thing."

"Then she must really hate her boss," Van replied, looking at me and no doubt at the ready to gauge my reaction, one that made me grit my teeth and force out,

"Perhaps."

Now he had planted that doubt in my mind, I had to

wonder if this wasn't to protect us at all but like Van had said, was merely a way for her to get back at a boss she hated? I knew which one I preferred, despite it being wrong for me to give heed to hope.

"She's on her way, Boss," Faron said as soon as he was off the phone, no doubt giving our 'backup' an update on all we had heard so far.

"Good. I want this put to an end," I said firmly, for I had my answers. The girl had not said a word and I was assured that she would continue with her silence. She had passed my test and now it was time to reward her loyalty.

"Make no mistake, Miss Parker, I will get to the bottom of this and when it comes to light that you were involved, then I will nail your ass to the… excuse me, what do you think you're…"

At this I had been ready to put my fist through the fucking screen had not in that moment Miss Green, the best lawyer money could pay for, walked into the room and snapped her heels.

"I should be asking you the same thing, Detective Campbell, seeing as you are interrogating my client without her legal representation present, something I am sure she has enquired about."

At this the detective blustered and Evelyn looked surprised at the lawyer. But she just subtly shook her head at her as if to say, play along. Something I was happy to see, she was smart enough to do. Meaning I was, yet again, trying to suppress a satisfied grin as Evelyn turned her now smug gaze back to the detective.

"She didn't inform me that she had council."

"Oh, did she not? Miss Parker, is this true?" At this the

detective was up out of his chair and gathering his stack of fake papers before walking to the door.

"Well now you're here, I will give you time with your client and I strongly suggest you advise she give us the names of all involved as we are ready to make a deal." At this Miss Green bristled.

"Are you trying to tell me how to do my job, Detective? Or should I take this grave misdemeanor on your part up with your superior chain of command? I know the chief quite well. As well as the judge who issued this warrant to look into my client's finances... oh yes, I know about that, along with the video footage he believed you had that could prove my client as being involved."

"I...I..." He stumbled for words, making Miss Green grin and jerk her hand toward the door, telling him,

"I believe you were just leaving." Something he did quickly, making me turn to Faron and say,

"Give Miss Green a bonus for that, as it was most entertaining."

Faron chuckled and started tapping on his phone with a grin. Something that alerted Miss Green to the fact when she looked at her phone as it vibrated, causing her to grin up at the camera and wink before taking the detective's now vacant seat.

"Miss Parker."

"I think I should tell you that as much as I appreciate you being here, I can't afford a lawyer, definitely not one as good as you."

At this she grinned her thanks and, again, hearing how she couldn't afford this form of protection did something to me.

Why was I so determined to see her cared for? Was it because I had admired her loyalty and wanted it rewarded? Yes, that must be it.

"I will stop you there, Miss Parker, by telling you that your fears are unfounded." Evelyn frowned at this.

"In what way? Do you offer some kind of payment plan spanning the next twenty years, because I have to tell you, I can barely afford my shitty car, let alone having an extra bill to pay and, no offence, but your handbag likely cost the same as my rent for a year." Again, hearing this had me clenching my fists in anger.

"I appreciate your candor, Miss Parker…"

"Please, call me Evie, everyone does." I frowned at this, wondering if this were the case, why did she not offer such to me? Another irrational annoyance that told me I needed my head examining.

"Alright, Evie, here it is. The bill has been paid, so you have nothing to worry about." At this her hands hit the table and her mouth dropped open in a delicious way that once again had me readjusting myself.

"I'm sorry, come again?" she asked, clearly in shock.

"Your legal costs have been covered," Miss Green repeated, and the way Evelyn shook her head made me smirk.

"But why…? Is this some kind of pro bono work? Did you pick my name out of a hat at the office?" I scoffed at that while Miss Green chuckled.

"I am afraid that's not how it works. And no, this is not pro bono work. Quite simply, my client is the one that pays the bill and let's just say that he has a… should we say, invested interested in you," she said, pausing to look up at the camara and, no doubt, being careful about saying too much. Van, however, didn't miss it as he nudged me and chuckled.

"Invested interest is right, but tell me, Ryker, do you kiss all your invested interests? 'Cause if you do, I am pissing off right now."

"I wish you would," I grumbled, making Hades comment,

"I second that." At this Van looked to Faron, who shrugged his shoulders.

"Don't look at me, I like you, but I wouldn't fuck you." I suppressed a laugh at that.

"Yeah, only 'cause I would break your cock, fucker." At this Faron blew a kiss his way, making Hades groan in exasperation.

"And if we have all had enough talk of Van's sexual abilities," I said, trying for patience I was surely lacking today.

"That will never happen," Van scoffed, grabbing his package in a proud way and making me close my eyes in irritation, before snapping,

"All of you, get the fuck out!"

Van grumbled about me needing to get laid, whereas Hades simply did as he was ordered to. As for Faron, I told him to wait.

"I want you to find everything there is to know about Miss Parker."

He frowned in question, before pointing out the obvious and mistaking my reasons. "I think we have established she won't say shit about us by now."

"Just do it," I ordered sternly, making him sigh before telling me respectfully,

"It will be done, my Lord." Then he bowed his head and walked to the door, making me stop him once more.

"And, Faron…"

"Yes, Lord Greed?"

"Include her finances and whoever she owes money to." He showed the briefest hint of surprise before replying respectively,

"It will be done."

I nodded, giving him leave to follow the others. Meaning that the second I was alone once more, I ran a single fingertip over the face of my new obsession and told her from afar,

"Oh, my little Dove, soon I will know you. Soon I will know…"

"…Everything."

CHAPTER 7
THE BLOODY STRENGTH OF A KISS
EVIE

The moment the lawyer, *my lawyer*… told me this, I was shocked. I continued to ask myself who on earth could have paid for my legal costs? I knew it wouldn't have been that dickhead Bill. Of course, I had asked Miss Green this but she continued to tell me that she wasn't at liberty to say. Which, if you asked me, was a very lawyer thing to say. This of course meant that I had no other choice but to ask myself could it be…

Him?

My mystery man who now knew my name, but I was yet to learn his own. Christ, ever since that kiss, I had been plagued with the memory of it. Okay, so not exactly plagued because that suggested something I wouldn't want… after the best kiss of my life, then Hell yeah, I would most definitely be game for more. And, well, if that only came in the form of reliving the moment over and over again in my mind, then I would damn right take it!

But if it had been him to pay for my lawyer, then why? Surely the only reason he was so nice to me had been to get me to comply, because well, I wasn't stupid. Although I certainly was tempted to act like it just so I could kid myself long enough to believe he had felt something the way I had.

Felt that kiss the way I had.

Fuck, I was still in a daze by the time the police had shown up and thank Christ they had. It turned out someone else had called the police after seeing something suspicious. Meaning I was facing them instead of the private security team Bill had hired, who no doubt would have questioned me a lot differently than Detective Campbell had. They were a bunch of mercenaries for a reason, and I doubted they carried with them an ethical handbook on how to interrogate civilians. My head being dunked in a bucket of water and the removal of my fingernails eerily came to mind.

But no matter how much I had kept my cool in the face of being up shit creek without a paddle, I had been silently crapping myself. But not for reasons you would have thought, like helping the bad guys. No, it was more about my past that I was afraid for.

Of course, I had watched enough cop shows to know he had nothing on me after about two minutes, especially when finding out the footage had been tampered with. Thank God, otherwise I really would have been in trouble. Although even as I thought back on that, then what would they have seen? A frightened woman who could have been forced to help them for fear of death? Because I doubted it would have had audio.

Although, despite this lack of evidence, I also felt better knowing that I was being covered legally and, even more so, when I was quickly released without charge. It felt like a veil of protection when Miss Green handed me the card now in my pocket. This after she said,

"Call if you ever need me or the cops come back... oh, and remember, no comment."

Something I knew, once again, from watching too many cop shows. And who knew at the time how handy retaining that information would be? It hadn't been hours wasted after all. Okay, granted, a social life would have been great and all, but it definitely wouldn't have helped me with staying out of the slammer. Cheesy lingo, a must of course.

Either way, I sighed in relief after I finally made it all the way back to the warehouse where I had parked my car. As for my place of work, it was all packed up tight and looked to be most definitely closed for business. Meaning I felt safe enough to make my way back to the loading bay in order to retrieve my bag from behind the X-press pack compactor. Which was basically a big green trash compactor that Bill only bought to save on disposable costs. Of course, there had been only one reason I had felt the need to hide my bag and that was because it contained the only piece of physical evidence that my thief had ever been there.

I had stolen his mask.

I also knew how risky this move was, because doing so meant I could be arrested for tampering with evidence. Something that would give Detective Campbell all the more reason to suspect me of being in league with them. But at the time I hadn't cared about the implications my actions could transpire into. I had just felt this overwhelming need to protect him and, also, to take a piece of him with me.

So, with that in mind, I tucked my bag close to my chest and made my way to where my car was parked, truly believing this would be the last time I saw the warehouse. Because I think it was safe to assume that I no longer had a job there and, in all honesty, I didn't think this was a bad thing. Which essentially meant that if the pizza place wasn't still hiring, then it looked like Arthur was back to having a twenty-seven-year-old roommate.

Well, at least, for now, I had a cereal box with my name on it and a CSI boxset to make my way through. Oh, and let's not forget the job section in this week's paper. *Ah, the joys of being me.* I groaned as I slammed the door on my car and prayed it started up.

Thankfully, it didn't decide to add to my bad day and started up just fine, getting me across town and back to my crummy apartment in Ocean View. Of course, its crime-rate wasn't as bad as, say, the Mission District, Chinatown, or Tenderloin but there was still a one in seventeen chance of becoming a victim of crime in the neighborhood.

Hence why moving at the first chance I got had been high on my list of priorities for a while. Now, however, I was forced to do the math on how much money I had left and how long it was going to last me if I couldn't find another job straight away. Which also translated into, how long I had left in said crummy apartment before I would be turning up at Arthur's.

He didn't have a phone, not even a cell I could text him on. So that usually meant just turning up at his door unannounced because, well, I couldn't exactly send him a homing pigeon. Crazy loon would probably just shoot the thing and make a pie. He was old-school like that. Whereas me, I hated death or, more to the point, being the cause of it.

Arthur, not so much.

The moment my apartment building came into view, or should I say, the graffiti on the side of it, I knew the cops had taken one look at my life, or rather the lack of it, and instantly they made up their minds. Well screw them! Yes, I was broke, but that didn't instantly mean I would steal to change that.

Although, I did have to remind myself that they were just doing their job and as for Detective Campbell, he hadn't been entirely wrong because I had helped the bad guys steal something. Not that I had gotten much out of it...

Okay, not true, there had been that kiss.

Yep, totally worth nearly going to prison over, Evie. I silently reprimanded myself as I put the key into my lock and twisted it. Only, the problem with that was...

It was already open.

I should have run then. I shouldn't have stepped inside. But unfortunately, I did. Because I convinced myself, in those five seconds of hesitation, that I might have forgotten to lock it. Even though, deep down, I knew I hadn't. Of course, I hadn't. I knew that the moment a hand grabbed me from behind and covered my mouth, muffling my scream. Then I gasped into a palm as I felt the cold steel of a blade being held to my throat for the second time in my life, both with not even a day apart from each other.

"Now I am told you are the stupid bitch that helped a bunch of thieves steal a priceless artifact and, well, my boss isn't happy."

I froze in his hold and started trying to talk when my muffled excuses started pissing him off.

"You scream and I will slit your throat!" he warned

before pushing me roughly away from him, making me cry out as I stumbled and hit my knees on the floor.

"I had nothing to do with them!" I shouted, turning to face the thug who had broken into my home.

He was dressed all in black, with a leather jacket cracked and worn around the shoulders and elbows. I didn't know why I focused on that insignificant fact, but my panicked brain did. Just like it focused on the pitted red skin at his cheeks, making me wonder if he had a bad case of pox growing up. His hair was dark gray with streaks of white, giving him this old-school mobster vibe and it was one I knew didn't bode well for me.

"Now we both know that's bullshit and, no surprises, Bill wants you dead."

Well, no, he was right there, that wasn't a surprise, the little podgy prick.

"But I convinced him you were far more useful to us alive, seeing as you are now going to go running off to your little boyfriend and tell him he has just twenty-four hours."

I started to shake my head, before repeating,

"Twenty-four hours to do what?"

At this he sneered at me before snapping,

"To get it back to us, or next time we come for his little bitch, I will do a lot more than beat the crap out of you!" he threatened, and I quickly began crawling backward to get away from him as he came at me.

But then as I kicked out, he grabbed my foot and dragged me back, ready to punch me, which was something he managed, making me see stars as pain exploded across my face. Then after a few more punches, I turned my head, spitting blood to the floor as anger rose to the surface in place of the fear that should have been there.

All my thoughts on Arthur and all the advice he had ever given me. All he had taught me and how I never wanted to let him down. Because he always told me, that no matter what I had to do...

'You do it, kid... you do it to survive.'

A sentence he signed and one I understood more than most.

Which meant as the thug turned his back to me, now picking up the knife he dropped in the scuffle, I silently got to my feet and grabbed the first thing my hands landed on while aiding my recovery. Then as soon as he turned back to face me, I swung the heavy DVD player around and hit him across the face hard enough his whole body spun.

He groaned on the floor, and my rage hit new levels as I calmly walked over to my TV, picked up the flat screen, one Arthur have given me, and walked back toward him.

I also knew my body was working on pure adrenaline at this point, because I remember how I struggled to get this bastard out of my car and up the stairs. As for now, it seemed to weigh nothing at all. Although I doubted the asshole on the floor, who was now missing a tooth, would think so. Especially as I lifted the TV above my head, all the while doing so with his wide-eyed look of panic silently pleading with me not to. But then as he started to lift the knife, I hammered the TV down onto his head, screaming in rage as I did.

"ARHHH!"

The knife fell from his twitching fingers, clattering on my floor, and this was when all adrenaline fled from me. I fell to my knees and cried as I stared at the dead man on my floor, then I looked at my bloody hands, as my busted face dripped the evidence of my attack onto the palms of a killer.

Memories flooded back to me with such strength, I found myself gripping the top of my head, burying my fingers in the strands and welcoming the pain of my new reality. I wanted to cry. I wanted to scream. I wanted to take it all back. Back to a point I had never walked inside this apartment. But I knew more than anything what I wanted to do, and that was… *run.*

Because I knew that, in spite of it being done in self-defense, I feared more about what else they would find when the police started to delve deeper into my past. Something I doubted even Miss Green could get me out of.

No. Now it was time to do what I did best.

It was time to run.

So, I quickly ran to my bathroom and, after wincing when seeing the number that bastard thug had done to my face, I threw water all over the cuts and bruises. Now watching as my blood ran in rivulets down the sink as if this was now a cruel metaphor for my life. I then used a towel to wipe my face before racing around my apartment, trying to ignore the dead guy on my floor as I packed anything and everything that meant something to me, was of value that I could sell, or things I would need.

I also looked around at all my artwork, pained by the fact that I could take none of it. So many hours wasted. So much effort for nothing. The thought made tears well in my eyes, but I fought them back with a grit of my teeth. There was time for my pain later but the time to cry wasn't now.

So, I concentrated on packing. I also made sure it was

shit that I could carry and, just in case anyone else came back here, I removed all trace of Arthur, knowing there was no way anyone could tie him to me. He wasn't even my legal guardian and, despite taking his name, there were hundreds of Parkers. As far as the world knew, Arthur never had kids. No, he just had a cabin in the woods and was known as a reclusive, crazy, deaf old man. Someone who had taught me everything I ever needed to know in life.

Like how to disappear.

Of course, it also had to be said that Arthur had spent a great deal of time after Vietnam being paranoid the government were watching. Hence these lessons and the advice I was now thanking my lucky stars for having. It was also why Arthur's name had never made it to any documents I filled in, like him being my next of kin. As far as the world knew, I had no family to speak of. Which thankfully meant I could walk away guilt-free knowing there was no one to care about that could get caught in the crossfire of all this shit.

Mind blowing kiss or not, I was starting to ask myself even now if it had all been worth it. I would be insane if I said yes. But then again, there was a dead guy in my apartment, so what did I know about sanity?

Well, I knew how the hell to get out of dodge, that was what. So, with everything I could carry in a duffle bag and backpack, I felt like lighting a match and getting rid of all the evidence. However, it was an apartment building, so I knew that was out of the question.

Which was why I picked up my fallen keys and my handbag, then locked my door saying goodbye to this part of my life. Which, unsurprisingly, was why I was shaking like a leaf by the time I got to my car. I had avoided looking at anyone, but when one woman saw me and winced at the mess that was my face, I pulled my hood over my head further, hiding myself away.

"You survived, Evie," I told myself when looking in the mirror and seeing tears in my light-brown eyes, one of which that was bleeding into crimson thanks to the burst blood vessels.

"You're alive and that's all that matters!" I told myself more firmly this time, trying to calm my shaking hand enough to put the key in the ignition. Then I started the engine and drove to the nearest bus station, knowing I was going to have to dump my car. I had no clue where I was going, but I felt like I had at least one phone call to make before I got there.

So as soon as I parked close to the bus station, I got out my phone, one that I also knew I would have to leave behind. I had already stopped at an ATM and drew everything out of my bank account, as well as drawing everything I had paid off my credit cards. Meaning that the math I did in my head now was trying to calculate how long I would last on the run. Because, soon, the cops were going to come knocking and when they did, I would be back on their radar. Oh, and this time, it wouldn't just be for stealing or aiding and abetting criminals but for something far worse.

It would be for murder.

Because dead bodies tended to smell after a while and, well, my neighbors were sure to notice. Plus, the cops weren't stupid. They would put two and two together and get twenty-seven-year-old me. And no matter how good Miss Green was, I doubted whoever had paid her to keep me out of jail would be willing to do so for a murder. Because there was only one man who would have done that for me.

My Mystery thief.

The same one I needed to reach out to now, and there was only one way I was able to do that. Which was why I pulled out Miss Green's card and dialed her number.

However, little did I know that hers wouldn't be the only voice I spoke to, because she wasn't alone.

No.

She was with…

My Demon with claws.

CHAPTER 8
DEADLY PATHS CROSSED
RYKER

"Tell me," I ordered the second Faron walked into my office looking grim. Which had me still wondering why all my attention was focused on the girl and not on the rest of the pieces of the scepter that had been stolen.

"What do you want me to say, Boss? She is barely scraping by."

I gritted my teeth at this but didn't comment. Knowing that my men needed me to focus on the reason we were still in San Francisco, and believe that the reason we hadn't left yet was because of the scepter and not the girl. So, I motioned Faron forward with the box I had asked him to bring. Of course, it had already been confirmed to me that it was the piece we had been searching for, but as of yet I had not even glanced at it. Because, clearly, my attention had been focused elsewhere.

Which was why now was the time to put the girl behind me and get my head back in the game. After all, I had been searching for the three missing pieces for far too long. But the moment I opened the box and grinned down at the golden bird, it lasted only seconds before I was thinking of another bird that seemed to strip me of all my good senses.

It was then a scent started to waft up, penetrating my senses, and it made me tense instantly.

"That scent... can you...?" I couldn't even finish the question.

It seemed as if my mind was spiraling out of control. As if I had suddenly been pushed into the depths of Tartarus and the souls of the Titans locked there were screaming out all around me. I vaguely even heard Faron's voice asking me what I was referring to. A sound muffled and far away as I finally took control of my faculties long enough to take the box in my hands. Its treasured contents were now lost to my thoughts as they were quickly consumed by another. One far more precious, which alone spoke of the strength of it considering how long I had been searching for the scepter. So, I turned the box to the side, seeing the smear of blood along the sides. Then I remembered looking down at Evelyn's hands and suddenly it slammed into me, making me growl.

"My Lord?" Faron said, rightly questioning my strange behavior.

"Evelyn, where did you say she lived?" I forced out, trying to relax my jaw long enough to speak.

"Some shit-hole in Ocean View." Even as he answered me, I was calling Van and telling him to get his ass in here.

"Just escorting Miss Green up here," he replied, making me grit my teeth.

"Be fucking quick, I have your next assignment. And

bring Hades!" I snapped, and thanks to my tone he knew not to question me or joke around. Instead, he replied with a respectful,

"You got it, Boss." Then he hung up and once more I was bringing the box closer. However, this time, I lifted it to my nose so as I could be absolutely fucking certain I was right. But even being a day old, I knew I was. I should have fucking known yesterday.

Gods be damn it, I should have fucking known!

"It's her," I growled, making Faron frown.

"Its who?" he asked, but I never got the chance to answer as Van, Hades, and Miss Green all entered my office together.

"Ryker?" Van said my name the second he saw my face, knowing instantly something was seriously wrong. For the concern was easy to hear in his tone as he tried to search out the impossible. Because that was exactly what it was!

"I want you to... to go to my... to Miss Parker's residence and bring her back here immediately," I told them, trying to control my voice despite hearing it shake for myself. At this, all three of my men looked shocked, however, because they hadn't yet run out of here ready to do my bidding, the second Van question me,

"Come again?"

I roared, "GO GET ME THE GIRL!" Making Miss Green step back in fear as she had never seen me as anything but the cool, calm, collected businessman I usually was. This, despite how ruthless I could be in a boardroom and even more fucking brutal elsewhere. Because the truth was far darker, of course, but the lawyer didn't need to know that.

My men started to back up quickly, but it was Van who

braved calming me down, as I realized I was now standing with my fists curled and the talons emerging from the tips of my fingers. Their deadly tips curled into the wood of my desk as easily as if it had been fresh bread. The spikes already pushing through the flesh and replacing the knuckles at each bend of my fingers. Something Van took notice of before the mortal in the room could, now coming to stand opposite me, hiding them from view.

"Easy, my friend, we will go get your girl."

I nodded, forcing my Demon to submit. Something that was far easier to do now that Van had declared her to be mine, speaking it aloud. So, I took a deep, calming breath, forced my Demon side to withdrawal and nodded once more before he knew it was safe to leave. Van clearly knew now of the seriousness in my order, taking care with his words.

"Come on, lads, we have an important package to pick up and deliverer to our king." Again, like he knew it would, this helped calm me further, despite Miss Green now looking closer to the color of her name, as it had to be said, she looked slightly ill.

"Forgive me for my outburst, Miss Green, and please come, sit, and tell me of my girl's case," I said, now holding my arm out to the seat opposite to my temporary desk, already missing my own office. Conveniently, for me at least, I had property all over the world and in most of the major cities in the Unites States. Just like the one I was in now, utilizing the office I had barely spent any time in, despite my name gracing the business sign in the lobby. A building that also held a number of penthouse suites that both my men and myself could live in while we were conducting business... *of both kinds.*

So many homes and just thinking of Evelyn in even one of them was easing the thought of the shit-hole I wanted her out of... *permanently.* But I should have known the second I saw her who she truly was to me, as my reaction to her had been instant. It all made perfect sense now. The urge to protect her. The urge to touch her. To kiss her.

But mainly the urge to fucking keep her!

Gods, but why hadn't I reacted on impulse? Why hadn't I listened to my gut? Well, regardless of this, I was now, and soon the girl would find herself in my care. Now what came after that, I didn't yet know. But what I did know, was that I would have to take it slow with her. Perhaps under the pretense of a job.

Perhaps she could be my new assistant, that way she would have to remain by my side and the excuse to keep her there would be warranted. It would also give me a chance to ease her into my world in the hopes of her falling in love with me before running from both my true self and that of my brutal, corrupted heart.

I was certainly greedy for more of her.

"Miss Parker's part in the crime can't be backed up as there is no evidence to speak of. It's a clear-cut case and, besides, the judge is an old friend of mine and, let's just say, he wasn't impressed with how he was manipulated into granting that warrant."

I scoffed at this.

"No, I suppose not. Well, I dare say your job is... what is it?" I asked when she started staring down at her vibrating cell phone, now frowning at the number.

"I don't know who is calling but I gave Evelyn my card,

so I guess it could be her." I held my breath before forcing myself to speak,

"Answer it... *if you please.*" This last part came out as forced politeness, seeing as the first part of this had been clearly a sternly spoken order.

"Hello?" a timid voice spoke on the other end, and I didn't need for her to put it on speaker for me to hear who it was. Nor would I have missed the tremor in Evelyn's voice. My superior hearing awarded me both sides of the conversation, however, the moment I heard her distress, I felt my entire body respond to it.

"Miss... Miss Green I... something happened and I..." Evelyn stopped herself after a held sob broke free before she could continue. "I wanted you to tell... to tell your client, whoever he may be, but I think I know... anyway, please tell him I am sorry... I know it's him... my..." She paused at this, as if to stop herself from saying what she really wanted to say before she added,

"He... needs to know that men are after..." She paused again and this time I hit my limit and snapped out my hand, telling her,

"Give me the phone." My tone must have told her this was not a request she could ignore, as she all too quickly handed me her phone. Then I nodded to the door so as she could give me privacy. Thankfully, she got the hint pretty quickly and left just as I was putting the phone to my ear.

"Hello... are you still there?" Evelyn asked, and I took a deep breath, trying to calm my voice enough so as not to frighten her with the Demon that wanted to break out of my skin. Then I told her as gently as I was able,

"I am here, Evelyn." At the first sound of my voice, she gasped as if recognizing it as quickly as I had hers.

"It's... it's you," she stammered, and by the sound of it she was close to breaking, well it Gods be damned near broke my heart. Not that I had one to begin with but if I had, then it would have been hers right in that moment.

"Tell me what happened?" I asked, once again trying to control the temper that wanted to seep through. I heard her sniff as if trying to control her own emotions, ones I was far more concerned for than that of my own.

"I... Something happened," she admitted quietly.

"Are you alright?" I asked, as that was the most important thing to me at the moment.

"I... I don't know," she replied, and I swear my blood turned to ice.

"Are you hurt?" I asked, unable to keep the furious tone from edging my words.

"I have... I mean, I am fine," she said, stopping herself from speaking the truth.

"You're lying to me," I stated firmly, and this time there was no holding back on my anger, making her sniff again. However, it quickly came with a resigned sigh before she told me in a firmer tone than before,

"I don't have much time, but you have to know, men, dangerous men want back what you stole."

I swallowed the urge to snarl, and it was like snorting acid and forcing down rusty nails down my throat but I managed it. Because as soon as she said those words, I was already imagining the worst.

They had gotten to her.

"I am a dangerous man, Evelyn, and therefore I do not fear for my life but, right now, I do fear for yours, so tell me where you are," I told her, making her gasp at the admission.

"I... I can't." At this I growled in anger at being denied and even with the greatest will in the world, I couldn't have helped the sound this time, despite knowing it would most likely only go against me.

"Yes, you can, *and you will.* Now tell me where you are, girl!" I demanded, allowing every ounce of my authority to coat my words in a way that usually got me what I wanted. However, when she sighed again, I knew she would deny me. Because instead of telling me what I wanted to know, she surprised me by asking me a question.

"Why did you kiss me?"

I jerked back a little, not expecting it.

"Why do you think?" I asked softly, not willing to explain the gravity of what we were meant to be over the phone.

"To get me to help you," she replied and, naturally, I frowned at this.

"Oh, my girl, you had already helped me," I reminded her of what I thought was obvious, despising the idea that she believed I had manipulated her this way. That my only interest in her had been for selfish gain and nothing more. I couldn't help but scowl at the box on my desk, despite being thankful for what was inside. And, for once, it wasn't the gold there that I was interested in but more so the means in which lead me to her.

"Is that why then? As a way to thank me?" she asked, making me want to fucking howl in frustration. *To fucking thank her?!* Was she serious?

"No. It. Was. Not," I forced out through gritted teeth.

"Then why?" she pressed after sniffing again and, gods, but ease my soul for how painful this was. Knowing she was out there somewhere in the city, when all I could hope for was that it was in the very place my men were on their way to right now. But even I knew that it was doubtful and a hopeless dream.

"I do as I please, Evelyn," I told her honestly.

"So, you wanted to kiss me?"

I felt my hand fist the phone and had to relax my fingers enough not to crush the fucking thing.

"Yes, Little Dove, *I wanted to kiss you,*" I told her, making her inhale a quick, labored breath, before whispering,

"Then you felt it too."

At this I closed my eyes and told her,

"Yes, and it is a feeling I will get to experience again soon, even sooner when you answer my question and tell me where you are." At this she took another staggered breath before ignoring my demand once again, instead telling me,

"Thank you, that means something to me."

Naturally this reply had me quickly frowning, as I didn't like where this conversation was going. Not one fucking bit! Not when my gut was telling me something that rarely ever happened was about to happen.

I was about to be denied.

"Then you can thank me in person... now tell me, *Where. You. Are. Evelyn?*" I put every ounce of compulsion into those words but, in the end, it was useless, as my power was nothing against her.

"Then it was all worth it... Goodbye, *my Mystery Thief,*"

she said, and just as I was shouting down the phone for her not to hang up, she did the one thing I ordered her not to. Which meant the phone was soon raining down to my desk in crushed pieces before I found my own phone and quickly rang Van.

"Tell me you are nearly fucking there!" I snapped before he even had a chance to say a word.

"Well, we just broke every fucking speed limit there is, but yes, we are just entering her building now."

"Good, call me back when you have her!" I growled before hanging up, knowing I needed to get myself under control. She would be there. She had to fucking be there!

"RAHHH!" I roared, and my hands transformed before I could stop them as I slashed out at the furniture like some wild beast, feeling my human face slip and give way to my monster.

In fact, it was only the sound of my phone ringing did I finally manage to get a handle on my other self, forcing my Demon to submit for the second time today. This so as by the time I reached for my phone I had the hands of a man back.

"Speak to me!" I growled. They might have been my hands holding the phone, but it was *his* voice taking control now. However, what I was to hear next meant that a second after I had finished the call, my office would not survive my rage.

"Shit, Ryker… but you better get down here and see for yourself."

"See what!?" I seethed, but then he said the very last thing I ever expected him to say and, for the first time in my existence, I felt a long, dead heart start to beat rapidly within my chest.

GREED'S SIREN

When he told me...

"The dead body on the floor."

CHAPTER 9
MAKE IT PAINFUL

"*The dead body on the floor.*"

"*What?!*" I hissed, falling to my knees as the first thought was one of deep and agonizing pain, fearing the worst. But then my friend quickly eased my anguish by telling me,

"Oh shit, Ryker, I didn't mean it is her. No, I have no fucking clue who it is."

I closed my eyes at this, as utter relief washed through me, finding I couldn't lift my head from where it hung limp in the grip of my emotions. Emotions I, admittedly, was not fucking used to.

But I knew I needed to act and was back to my feet a heartbeat later, soon snarling down into the phone,

"Get Faron to send the address. I will be there shortly." Then I hung up the phone and, like I knew I would, took my anger out on my office. This whirlwind of rage only lasting mere minutes but it was long enough to achieve two things. First, it managed to calm my fury enough to fucking function and the second, it meant that remodeling this room would soon be someone else's problem.

I ran a hand through my hair just as my Demon side was retreating now it'd had its outburst and, therefore, I didn't end up scalping myself on my claws. I then grabbed my jacket, this time exchanging one that was leather and more fitting, than that of my suit. My choice to change earlier was now one of convivence as my dark gray jeans and a long, navy-blue, sleeved t-shirt was far more practical for what might be in store for me.

After this, I made my way down to the lower levels, speaking to Miss Green as I passed her by, telling her,

"Thank you for your services, a new phone will be delivered to your office shortly."

This comment naturally left her mouth agape at my abrupt departure and, no doubt, left her wondering what the fuck I had done to her phone. Well, it was currently metal dust on my floor and, as for my office, well, it looked like it had been mauled by some rabid beast.

But I didn't give a shit about any of that. Not now I knew that something serious had happened since Evie left that police station. Meaning I was now fucking cursing myself by resisting the urge to have her followed. And why, all because I had been trying to convince myself that the girl was nothing but a mortal distraction. A momentary amusement I had allowed myself to indulge in for a day, forcing myself to let it go before the obsession had truly taken root.

But that was all before I knew for certain what she was to me. And now I just hoped I wasn't too late. And speaking of time, the second I made it down to the underground garage, I ignored my long line of luxury, opting for speed and agility instead. Which meant traveling the only way I knew would get me through the city streets with ease, even if there was traffic to contend with.

"Sorry, my friend, but it's time to see what this Ducati 1198 R Corse can really do," I said, zipping up my jacket, grabbing his helmet and stealing Van's bike without the need for keys as a single thought had it roaring to life.

Needless to say, I fucking wanted one by the time it got me to her apartment building at Ocean View. One that long ago needed to be fucking condemned! I gritted my teeth, in barely concealed fury as I mounted the steps, trying to ignore the trash littering the steps, and finding it harder to do so when among this junk was evidence of the drug users in her building.

Hence why, by the time I finally made it to her door, I nearly ripped the fucking thing off its hinges. However, the shock of what awaited me when I made it inside had me forgetting all about fucking litter or those that were stupid enough to choose to sign up to a slow death of drug use.

"What the fuck?" I asked, stepping inside to find my men giving me a wide birth as, clearly, they hadn't wanted to touch anything until I got here.

"Yeah, not what we expected either," Van stated with a frown as we both took in the sight of the dead man on the floor and the clear evidence of what had killed him. Although the second he suddenly took a breath and groaned, we all took a step back as one.

"What the fuck?!" Faron exclaimed, clearly as shocked as we all were.

"Okay, I swear that heart only just started beating again." I ignored Van and instead ripped the TV off his head before grabbing the bloody thug from the floor. Then I threw him against the wall, making my men give me an even wider birth, despite there being very little room to do so in the fucking glorified shoe box.

"Oh, okay, so we are doing this then," Faron said, shrugging his shoulders.

"Who the fuck are you?!" I snarled, making the dying man cough blood up through his lungs, and I warned, "You don't have long left to live, so I suggest you spend it talking so as you may save your soul from rotting in a place you really don't want it rotting."

When he didn't take my words seriously enough, I allowed my Demon to breathe life into my threat, scaring the ever-living shit out of him. To the point that his body actually functioned enough to piss himself.

"Oh... fuck... no... I... not real..." he stammered.

"Oh, trust me, he is real alright, and if you don't start talking, he will rip you from limb to limb before getting his minions in Hell to do the very same thing to you each day!" Van warned, and it was enough for him to tell me what I couldn't rip from his mind in all the agony he suffered.

"I work for Bill's buyer. He wants the artifact... he... fuck... but he told me to... to rough up the bitch so she would reach out to you... oh fuck, please don't fucking eat me!" he said this last part when I allowed my Demon form to snarl his way, ready to rip out his throat with my multiple rows of teeth as my lips curled back to reveal them.

"I want a name!" my Demon roared.

"Hector Fo..."

"Hector Foley," I finished on another snarl of anger, knowing all too well why the fucker wanted my scepter. He

was one of the 'Marked' and was believed to be a mortal possessed by someone far more dangerous than he. Someone who was thankfully still locked to Hell and would remain there if I had anything to do with it.

But, at the very least, now I had a name, despite knowing what little good it did me. As one of the Marked, it meant he had been hunted for a while now and still had managed to allude us and the other Enforcers. Well, his time was running out, and speaking of things that would soon being finding their end...

"Now it's time for the rest and be warned, fucker, it will determine the fate of your soul," I threatened before slapping my hand over his face and making him scream in agony as I tore the memories right out of him, pain or not, it came to me clearly this time. However, the second I saw it all, there was only one part of it that remained with me.

The one of him punching my girl.

Meaning the second it finished, I ended up dropping him and punching my fist straight through his skull, ending him far too quickly. Then I called forth my minions, causing the floor around his corpse to turn to bubbling black tar then skeletal, Demonic hands dripped from the black river in which they rose, one that flowed right through the city of Kusig. This was the main city in the realm of Greed, and one that translated into the word Gold in Sumerian. Therefore, it was also naturally where my father's castle was situated, towering high above the thousands of golden rooftops below.

Which was why I could easily summon those under my command, watching now with a glowing Demonic gaze as they eagerly reached out through the gateway I created. Then once they found their next eternal victim, I told them in a dark, seething tone,

"And make it fucking hurt!" Then I bit into my palm and let my blood seal the doomed asshole's fate, before the whole thing vanished into a large red plume of smoke. The hands now taking their new play-thing back to the realm of Greed to feast on.

Then, once I was finished with the soul I just cursed to an eternity of being ripped apart, I turned to my men, losing my Demon side that they were right to be afraid of. As most would be foolish not to be. Not seeing as what I was capable of.

"The girl is on the run, I want her tracked down. Nothing is more important this day or the fucking next... do you understand!?" I ordered, making them all bow their heads at their ruthless master.

"Faron, ideas?" Van asked, now in full commander mode and doing what my rage would not allow me to do.

"If she is hurt, she may have gone to a hospital," he suggested.

"Good, check them all. Hades, have your men here and pack up all this shit. I want everything gone through. Any fucking clue as to where she may have run to. Nothing is to be missed or overlooked, even if it's a fucking postcard ten years old, I want every stone turned. Understood?" Van ordered, and Hades, knowing his place, instantly replied,

"It will be done."

Meanwhile, I took a moment to look around her place, minus the carnage left over from the fight, one that never should have fucking happened! However, a surprising sight that managed to calm me slightly was witnessing her artistic talent for the first time. There was at least ten 11x14 inch canvases dotted around the space, adding a haunting kind of beauty to the walls.

Almost all of them were black, white, and gray scenes with only small aspects holding any color. Like the old man sitting on a park bench, his face was pure sadness as he looked down to a shadow of a dog on the sidewalk. However, no dog was painted in the picture, for there was only the memory of him, as a red collar sat next to the old man, no longer a beloved pet to fill the leather band.

Another, less disheartened one, was of a tree that had lost all but one of its leaves, with a pile below the base of its trunk of all of the fallen. The single leaf on the tree was bright orange and there was a child walking off in the distance holding between her fingers the same orange leaf. I knew all her paintings held an inner meaning, some obvious like the man that had lost his dog.

However, one in particular drew me closer, and that was a painting of a cabin. The only one out of them all that held the most color. In fact, the only aspect of the painting that was grey and foreboding were the woods that surrounded the home, as inside, there, through the windows was filled with color. As if it was a metaphor for the safety felt inside those walls. As if none of the darkness and creatures of the night could reach the two people I could barely see inside.

"Faron, tell me of her family?" I finally asked, wondering still about that particular painting. However, when he delayed answering me, I turned around to find sadness in his eyes, a reaction that had me tensing. Then he shook his head slowly and being the most sensitive of my council, he said,

"Sorry, Boss, she is alone."

"What?" I asked in astonishment.

"No family," he repeated, and this time I wasn't the only one to react.

"What? No one?" Van asked.

"No next of kin on her records, it was left blank. Every document I ever found on her suggested that her parents are dead or unknown."

"An orphan then?" I surmised, instantly feeling bad for my little Dove. For it would seem as if she was all alone in the world, and that thought bothered me more than it should. Especially considering what a heartless bastard I was. Well, regardless of this current fact, she would not find herself alone much longer.

"I will check in the system for her name. They might have records of her or if she was ever adopted but I doubt it," Faron offered, and again, my heart ached for her.

"Unless she is a runaway," Van suggested, making me turn his way as he shrugged his shoulders and offered,

"Adoption isn't always a fairy tale solution... plenty of kids on the streets for a reason, Ryk."

I sighed, as it was true and looked to be that if she was a runaway, then this just might be another impulse of hers kicking in. One look at the TV and smashed DVD player she had used as a weapon, and it was certainly evidence enough to speak of her resourcefulness. And, in truth, that was what worried me the most, as clearly she was smart. Street smart at that, which meant finding her was going to be all the harder. I snatched a towel off some rack in her shitty kitchenette, wiping the blood and brain matter off my hand while I told Faron,

"Check all the bus stations, along with trains, as she won't need ID to travel and therefore it's harder to trace. She may still be in one of them waiting to board a train or bus. A girl with a bruised face will be easy to spot in person or on surveillance, so hack whatever systems you have to."

"On it," he replied, already pulling out the laptop he carried with him everywhere in his leather satchel.

"I want all her possessions packed up in case there is anything here that meant something to her. As for the paintings, I want these professionally packed as nothing is to happen to them, understood?" Hades stepped up and bowed his head before telling me,

"I will have that taken care of once a clean-up crew has been in and taken care of all the evidence."

I nodded the once in reply before turning back to Faron, the one I knew I would be relying heavily on for finding her.

"I take it you tracked what car she drives with the DMV?" I asked as an afterthought, and one that luckily Faron had already thought of.

"Of course," he replied, already tapping away on his laptop sitting upon the counter of Evelyn's small kitchenette... *if it could even be classed as such.*

"Then have all of our men on the lookout for her car, I want all her details given to as many of our people we can spare for the search until more arrive from Toronto," I told them, prompting Van to tell me something I already knew.

"You know our window for finding her is getting smaller." At this I released a frustrated breath and made my own point in a hard tone,

"Then we don't have any time to lose, do we?" Then I walked from the apartment, feeling myself tense when Van followed me out into the stairwell and called me by name, stopping me before I rounded a corner on the staircase.

"Ryker... I have to know."

"Just ask, Vander," I replied in a tense tone, already knowing what was coming.

"Just who is this girl to you...? What is it you're not telling us?" I released a pained sigh knowing that this had been all my fault. That I had foolishly let her go. That I'd had her in my fucking arms and yet I stepped away when I could have just taken her there and then.

I lost her.

Which was why I told him the truth, and to finally say the words aloud caused that long-dead heart of mine to beat once more.

"She is my Lost Siren."

CHAPTER 10
LOST SIREN
THREE DAYS LATER

"Not fucking good enough!" I roared down the phone when yet another fucking lead went south, and I ended the call like I did most days by throwing the phone at the fucking wall! It burst into a rain of metal and miniature circuitry just as Van was walking into my office, one that was starting to look more like a fucking war zone.

"Tell me you have fucking good news!" I snapped, making him grin.

"That I do, as it comes with your next lead and one you will be happy to know you can beat the shit out of."

I at least managed to stop scowling at that, but I knew it would take a lot more for me to actually fucking grin. Perhaps when I was finished with the soon-to-be dead man, I would manage to express one.

"Good, I take it you found the little prick?" I replied, making him chuckle.

"Oh yeah, and once he found out who his thief was and

who he was actually fucking with, then he was also on his way to Mexico."

"Ha, like that could have fucking stopped me," I replied, trying for some semblance of calm, wondering who the fuck I had turned into these last five days. I used to be known for my dark, sinister composure, but now all I was known for these days was my destruction and erupting anger. And I knew that even spending time in my vault surrounded by my vast collection of treasures wouldn't have worked in calming my Greed for once.

Because now there was only one thing I truly desired. Meaning I would gladly have set the vault aflame and watched as the whole fucking treasured horde burned to ash had it brought her back to me. A revelation that was shocking to a pure creature of Greed.

But the truth was, that this felt like a punishment for all my sins, as she was still in the fucking wind! My men had found nothing of substance as each lead had run colder than the last, leaving me with nothing! Even Faron was scratching his head wondering how the hell she had managed it. No one ever got anything past him, yet she had turned into a fucking ghost!

The furthest we had been to finding any trace of her, was that of her car, one that had been left dumped. This along with her cell phone still left inside. Her apartment had turned up nothing as everything left there had been bought second hand. The girl never even traveled and kept not a single receipt. Her bank records showed that other than direct bills coming out each month, she must have paid for everything in cash.

I couldn't even account for what fucking grocery store

she used or where she got her coffee from. It was like Faron said, she was either on the run from someone, or the girl was a fucking spy for the CIA. She lived her life as if any moment someone was going to turn up and make her run. Making me question what had happened to her to make her live this way?

What was she truly running from?

There were no records of her other than the jobs she's had and the education she had worked for, which had been no surprise to discover was an art degree. Faron had not even found a shred of evidence that she had ever been in a foster home or that she had ever even been in the system. No record of any couple by the name of Parker dying and leaving behind a child.

Nothing.

Like I said, *she was ghost.*

An enigma I wanted to solve more than I wanted the mountain of gold my father's castle was built upon. But more than anything else, I wanted her to be here by my side so as we could start getting to know more of each other. Or, in my case, everything about her, as for once, I knew nothing about the prey I hunted.

But then I did at least have a slight advantage in this, as she knew me as nothing but her Mystery Thief. I would have chuckled at that, had I not found myself in a perpetual state of anger. No, if anything, the only thing that seemed to calm me now was the footage I had of her the night I first infiltrated her life. All before I had turned it upside down. However, it was not the footage of our encounter I found myself playing over and over again, but instead the time before it.

The cute as fuck dance she did, singing like no one was around and could witness the act. I even found myself with my fist in my mouth to stop myself from laughing aloud, like doing so at her expense was forbidden. Gods she had been funny and sexy all at the same time.

The way she had removed her heels and groaned to herself as she let her head fall back as she massaged her own feet had me hard in seconds. Thoughts of other deliciously sinister things I wanted to do to her made me wonder which would ignite those same sounds from her. Dark and devious things that included tying her up in rope and hanging her body from my bedroom ceiling so as I could do whatever I pleased with her. I would have her spread wide and play with her for hours until she had tears in her beautiful light-brown eyes. Until her voice was hoarse from begging me to stop. However, yet again, I would answer her desperate cries to stop by making her come once more, singing her release so beautifully raw for me.

Then I would take her down, lick away each red mark I made and care for her like no one else ever could. I would bathe her, wash her clean from the mess I made of her, and dry her before wrapping her up in the best sheets money could buy, keeping her tied to me in strips of silk as she slept.

But the one thing I would never let her do ever again...

Was run from me.

"Wait... is that what I think it is?" Van asked, making me frown in question before seeing where his gaze was now centered on. My first thought was to close the screen of my laptop so as he couldn't witness what my own obsession had seen in what felt like a hundred times over by now. But something in his narrowed gaze told me not to.

"What is it?" I asked when he started coming closer.

"Is this the footage of that night?"

"Yes," I said through gritted teeth, as again, I hadn't wanted to share this piece of her with anyone.

"Can you play it?" he asked, and despite it being an irrational response, I gritted out my annoyance, asking him,

"Why?"

"Just trust me on this," he replied and, well, seeing as I trusted my second in command with my life, I forced myself to tap on the mouse pad and brought my girl back to life on screen. This was the part that usually had me seething and the reason we had hunted another type of pray these last few days. It was the part before her boss had left.

"Fuck me, it is."

"What?!" I snapped, having zero fucking patience these days whereas once, I had the fucking aptitude in shapes for my friend!

"See this... what she is doing with her hands behind his back."

I turned so as he could play it again and, I had to admit questioning the funny signals she did, but I didn't think much beyond it being nothing more than learning the quirks of my girl.

"I had wondered," I admitted, looking to him as he turned his blue eyes dancing with mirth.

"It's sign language." I jerked back a little before asking,

"Are you sure?"

Then shocking me further, he signed to me while translating,

"I am sure, as she just called him an asshole." This last sign was made with him stuffing his finger in the circle he made with his other hand, making it obvious now.

"Fuck, so it is," I agreed in shock, now playing it back and seeing for myself once more that he was right. Then before I could even issue the order, Van was on the phone.

"Faron, I have a new search for you, check for any names in the San Francisco area that go by Parker that were either born deaf or have suffered injury, resulting in loss of hearing, as there should be medical records of it."

"On it," he replied but before he could end the call, I quickly added something else that only now came to me.

"Also check if any of them own a cabin or live remotely."

Van raised a brow at me in question, but I shook my head, telling him not now.

"You got it," he said, sounding enthusiastic now he had a new lead to go by.

"A cabin?" my friend asked as soon as Faron hung up.

"It was one of the paintings that stood out in her apartment."

"Stood out how?" he said, pressing for more information, and it was a question that made me sigh before answering.

"It was the only one that looked happy. So, who knows, maybe this was her safe haven."

"It's a good assumption and, let's face it, at this point we haven't got much else to go on," he remarked, prompting me to look down at my girl now paused on the screen.

"Well, we do now, thanks to you... Good job, Van," I praised, thankful for my friend's keen eyes for this shit. Because no matter how much he played around or how easy going he appeared to be about most things, there wasn't much you could get past him. Besides, when he was being underestimated, this was usually when my friend was at his most deadly.

"Now tell me, how the fuck do you know sign language?" I asked as I closed my screen, before rising from my seat so as we could leave my office. After all... *I had somewhere to be.*

"There are seven thousand languages in the mortal world, and I can speak at least three thousand of them, I thought at least to try my hand at the one where I don't need my tongue."

I laughed at that before pointing out the obvious,

"So, you fucked a deaf mortal, you mean."

"Yeah, and let's just say she benefited greatly from what else I could do with my tongue." I rolled my eyes at that as we made our way down to the lower levels in the elevator, after I first had to put in the code that allowed my people access.

"Did you know that despite a population of just 8.8 million, Papua New Guinea has over 840 languages spoken across the country. To put things into perspective, that's almost 12% of the world's languages spoken in an area that's roughly the size of California." I sighed at this and told him,

"I think I preferred it when you talked about eating mortal pussy." He laughed at that and said,

"You know, that's the first joke you've made since the heist." I tensed at this but then he told me,

"If she is your Siren, Ryker, then she is destined to come back to you."

I shook my head and admitted what felt like my greatest sin so far.

"I let her go."

"Yeah, but I'm not sure kidnapping is the best way to start a relationship, Ryk," he commented, using my nickname and one he hardly ever spoke in public.

"Yes, but at least doing so would have ensured her protection," I argued, causing his own argument to form.

"Yes, but at what cost? Look, I get it, your Demon is riding you hard and, well, she is the first treasure you have ever laid eyes on that has alluded you, stolen treasure not withstanding of course," he said, reminding me of the scepter.

"That is not the only reason," I admitted, and added more when his silence prompted me to do so. "That night, I felt it. I felt something for her and tried to ignore it. I fought against it, against the urge to claim her because I knew if I gave into what my Demon wanted, then I could have accidently hurt her. I would have, surely, fucking terrified her!" Van sighed my name,

"Ryker..."

"No, Van, there is no excuse. Because, in the end, I knew it was a chance I should have taken, as now she is out there alone and no doubt soon to be fucking penniless and, in truth... Van, I am fucking terrified, alright?" I admitted far more with this than I ever planned to. Which was no wonder why his eyes grew wide as his shock was easy to see. Because, in truth...

I had never worried about a fucking thing in my life before, let alone been fucking fearful.

I had my Greed. I had my power. I had my kingdom to

go back to anytime I wanted. I had it all up until this point. And now I was ready to give it all up just so as I could claim her. I would burn every last gold coin if all it awarded me was the knowledge that she was safe! All because I fucking worried for another living being. It wasn't me and, yet, *now it was.*

And truthfully… I didn't know how to fucking cope with it.

And neither did my Demon.

"Well, this should help ease some of the tension," Van said once we were down at the lowest level, walking into a basement people didn't even know existed. And for good reason too, as most of my private residences had a place where we could keep our prisoners.

Speaking of which, I was really going to enjoy this particular one.

Especially when I opened the locked door and found the fat bald man squirming on a hook, bleeding from the beating he had already received. The man that had given Hector Foley all the information he needed to send someone to go beat on my girl.

A perverted little prick. Which was why I said,

"Why hello, Bill, so glad you could make it." Then as I closed the door, I allowed my Demon out to play, and the sounds of Bill's terrified screams were cut off from the rest of the building the moment the doors sealed his fate.

A fate, he had dared to fuck with.

CHAPTER II
DELIVERING MYSELF
EVIE
TWO WEEKS LATER

"Miss... Miss?" I shook my head from the memory I lingered on and, this time, the daydream wasn't of him kissing me like usual. No, it was the one where he was demanding to know my name. A name I had foolishly given him.

"I am so sorry, Monday mornings, eh?" I said with a smile, one that went by unnoticed as the woman started to reel off her order for a second time. So, I scribbled down the sandwich and coffee she wanted before ringing it up in the till and taking payment. Then I told Wesley the coffee order as I walked over to the prep counter and started making her sandwich. Trying once again to get my head back in the money earning game.

To be fair, the job wasn't bad, and I would take making sandwiches and bagging up Danishes over working for that dickhead Bill any day of the week. Besides, my job came with a roof over my head as Denise, the lady who owned Destiny Coffee house, took the rent right out of my wages. Of course, it was also the first place I had stopped at when I had finally made it to Seattle and, well, the name had said it all.

It was fate.

But then she had taken one look at my face and after asking me if I was alright, she unknowingly opened the flood gates on my sad, dire life. Meaning she told Wesley to watch the counter before taking me upstairs to her own apartment, while she poured me something a lot stronger than coffee.

That's when I made my first friend, and what a lifeline she had been. But not wanting to repay her kindness with trouble I told her I was on the run from an abusive boyfriend. Something that most definitely went with the state of my face. I felt bad for lying, especially when it turned out she had experienced something similar ten years earlier. But I knew the truth could make her an accessory to harboring a protentional fugitive and I didn't want that.

I also gave her a different name as I had needed to fake my own ID's. Something I had done while making my first stop on my way in a shitty motel. Thank you, Arthur, for those extra nefarious life skills. Little did I know at the time that I would be needing them.

As for Denise, she was a lady in her forties, divorced from said abusive dickhead, and used some inheritance money to start Destiny Coffee. She was tall, curvy, and wore her hair in pinned curls like a 50's pin up girl. She was full of fun and would often be found dancing in the back kitchen, swishing her retro skirts and tapping a pair of cherry red heels I had no idea how she lasted in all day.

Naturally, I already loved Denise and owed her what felt like my life. So, I worked my ass off for her as she deserved everything I could give her. Which meant I was happy offering to open the shop early or close late just to give her a break.

Of course, her love for 50's retro had become the theme for her little slice of heaven on Capitol Hill. However, it wasn't cheesy or over kill with vinyl booths, jukeboxes, or a black and white checker floor. No, it was light hardwood siding to match the floor, with pale turquoise walls that held classy black and white photographs of old film stars. It was comfy, plush, velvet sofas in teal tones adorned with round pleated raspberry cushions. It was a single neon sign that spelled out the name of the coffee shop and hung from the large window on a chain. It was soft jazz playing from the speakers and a countertop that took up half of the shop, so as to display the epic pastries that Denise was well known for.

And I loved it!

Besides, my job helped keep my mind from everything that had happened... well, *most of the time.* But then after the dream I'd had last night, then today was most definitely an off day. Of course, most of my dreams lately included him... oh, who was I kidding? They all did! However, the main storyline my mind focused on was portraying my Thief as being the hero. The one that rushed into my apartment to save the day, killing the thug before I had been forced to do it myself.

Of course, the hero part was romantic and after he picked me up to carry me to my bed, the man bleeding to death would disappear quickly. However, it was the dreams where he didn't make it in time that were always the hardest to wake from. The ones where I would wake up screaming as the face of death would be found standing over me, covered in blood after stabbing the thug over and over.

A mask of death, back to covering his handsome face as he would just stand there like my judge, jury, and executioner. As if he was some Demonic God come to punish me and take me back with him to the darkest depths of Hell.

But why then did I always wake from these dreams clutching onto the mask I had stolen? I didn't know why I would hold it to my chest and cry, as if a piece of him was here with me. It was an irrational response, seeing as his presence had been the catalyst into turning my life upside down. Yet despite this, I knew this was not what he had wanted for me. That he had tried to do right by me, going so far as to pay for the lawyer.

Why had he done that?

Had it been to ensure I wouldn't say anything that could to lead to him or his men? It hadn't sounded like it on that phone call. He had told me he wanted to kiss me. That he wanted to know where I was and, well, half of me had been more than tempted to tell him. To see what would have happened had he showed up and saved the day. But then I knew to do so would only end up pulling me even deeper into a world I wasn't ready to step into. Especially not when he admitted that he was a dangerous man.

That had scared me.

To know that he could have been part of the mafia or something. No, I couldn't do it. I couldn't cross that dangerous line, even if it felt as if I was already tilting on the edge of it. It was clear he was a thief and seeing as he was stealing from an asshole like Bill, well this was one thing, but just what else could he be involved in? No, it wasn't something I was ready to find out. And, truth be told, this hadn't been the only thing that had scared me. The intensity of his words when trying to order me to tell him where I was terrified me.

So, I had run from far more than the murder I had committed. I had run from the strength of my feelings for him, knowing he had the power to break me. To utterly destroy me and, well…

I couldn't allow that again.

I had made myself a vow long ago never to give anyone that kind of power over me ever again. So, I had run, despite knowing that he most likely could have helped me. That he would have likely made it all just disappear. That he could have protected me. So instead, I had asked him about that kiss. I had just needed to know why. If it was because he felt even a slither of what I had.

Which was why I told him that it had been worth it. Because if it was the only moment in my life I would feel that way, then at least I could draw comfort from that. Despite what happened next. Something that didn't stop me lying in bed at night wondering what would have happened had I trusted myself with him. He had said that we would have experienced more moments like that, should I just tell him where I was? Christ, but the temptation was the reason my hand would snake under the covers and I touched myself to the thought of where our next kiss would have led to.

What would it have felt like being with such a man? If only for one night? Well, if one kiss could leave such its mark upon my soul then I knew precisely what it could have been like, or should I say how hard it would make me fall. He was the worst temptation, and he came with the kind of danger I knew could end me. And despite the kiss being worth it so far, then I doubted I could claim the same if it meant risking the rest of my life.

At least that was what I kept telling myself.

"Turkey on rye, no tomato, mayo and mustard," I said, handing over the wrapped sandwich at the same time Wes handed the customer her coffee, one that seemed far more complicated than the sandwich had been to make.

"Seriously, why can't they order the day before?" Denise said after walking through to the front and past the curtain of plastic that led from the back kitchen where she made most of her cakes and pastries.

"Last minute order?" I asked, making her sigh.

"An office on 5th Ave wants sandwiches delivering and my car's still in the shop," she said pursing her lips.

"I can do it. It's only a thirty-minute walk." She waved her hand at this, telling me,

"Nonsense, I'm sure Wesley won't mind you taking his car, will you, hun?" At this the twenty-one-year-old goth shrugged his shoulders before pulling his keys from his pocket, making the chains on his pants rattle. Then he tossed me the keys and winked at me. He was a nice guy and despite not being overly friendly with customers, he was all smiles for me and Denise. Of course, I also knew why it wasn't practical for either of them to make the trip as Denise was usually up to her eyeballs in cooking in the back. And as for Wes, he was a coffee making extraordinaire that customers couldn't do without, smile or not. As for me, I usually stuck to sandwich making and stayed as far away from the complicated coffee machine as I could get.

"Well, if he doesn't mind, then it's no problem," I

offered, making her grip my shoulder and squeeze it in thanks.

"You're a doll," she said, making me grin.

"Give me the list and I will get on making them," I told her with a grin. I was always happy to help and she knew it. Hence why she winked at me before letting me get to work, meaning that by the time the lunch time rush came in, I was ready to help with that before making my way to Wesley's car with the order.

Thankfully, nothing was supposed to arrive hot as the traffic was a bit of a nightmare, which meant by the time I got there, I had to park a few blocks away, leaving my bag in the car because I couldn't juggle them both.

So, I carried the boxes labeled with the Destiny Coffee logo, that was a swirl of fancy turquoise letters over a coffee cup. I then carefully made my way to the imposing office building that was a tower of black glass reaching for the sky. But then as I was making my way to the entrance, I lifted the boxes up high enough so I could try and grab the door, covering my head while I tried to juggle my load. However, someone got it for me, and I briefly saw a masculine hand grip the handle and pull it open. However, seeing as my view was of piled white boxes, I could only mutter,

"Thanks," from behind them before walking inside and making my way straight to the front desk. Then I placed my load down on the counter and told the guy in a suit,

"I have an order for…"

"Elevators are over there. Find your floor," he said before I could finish, clearly loving his job as a receptionist. I frowned down at the list on the desk, at the same time shaking out my arms that ached from holding the tower of boxes for so long. I would have also groaned aloud knowing I was going to have to cart the whole lot into a lift and to the right office. So, seeing a line of businessmen all walking their tall frames toward the bank of elevators, I quickly picked up my white tower of boxes and walked with speed, calling out,

"Wait! Please hold the... *lift.*" This ended when lowering my tower of boxes to find the doors closing in front of me and a dark-haired man turning my way just as they did. I never got to see his face in time but damn, I must have been having another daydreaming moment about my thief. Because I could have sworn my mystery man had hair just like that. He had been tall as well and built like he was made for a Marvel movie rather than sitting there in a board meeting wearing a suit.

"Damn... hey, could you press the button for me, please?" I asked someone passing by, who thankfully didn't ignore the delivery girl. I then got inside and seeing as this time I was the only one, I ended up pressing the right floor with my nose as I balanced the boxes to the side. I was then forced to take in my appearance as the wall of mirrors wouldn't let me escape myself.

I had taken off my black apron with the coffee shop logo on it and was now wearing a black hooded sweater with a light-gray biker style jacket over the top to try and ward off the late September chill. I was also wearing a pair of worn blue jeans and white sneakers because there was no way I was lasting my day in heels like Denise did. There was one thing doing so in an office where I had spent a great deal of the day sitting down, but being on my feet all day... hell no.

As for my hair, this was all tied back in a messy bun as it

usually was these days, because the side plait had to go once I knew I was dealing with food every day. However, after walking the few blocks, I could already feel the wavy strands that were trying to escape the style. As for make up, I had my usual foundation on only, this time, instead of it being used to hide my freckles, (something admittedly I hadn't wanted to do since he had told me not to) it was instead used to hide the remainder of my bruises. Blotches on my skin that were now an unattractive greenish, yellow color.

I turned back to face the doors just as the elevator dinged and after checking once more that it was the right floor, I walked out, hoping I could just dump these on the front desk and leave. However, when I found myself faced with a 'out at lunch' sign I groaned.

"Seriously?" I complained before making my way around the partition that announced this as being some company called RW Investments. I then stepped into a sleek office filled with a line of frosted glass door fronts, before it opened out into the main floor with cubical in the lines down the center. Finally, a woman looked up over one, popping her head over the dividing wall and finding me with arms full of boxes. I also had to say that when her kind eyes lit up at the sight of me, I was proud of Denise and the name she had made for herself.

"Oh goodie, lunch is here!" she exclaimed, making someone shush her from the cubical next to hers. Both girls couldn't have been more different, with the smiley one having a riot of dyed red curls piled high on her head and the one that had shushed her having a severe cut black bob, making me wonder if the hairstylist had used a ruler. She also had black rim glasses that looked as though they were too big for her and, therefore, being forced to develop the habit of pushing them up her nose.

"Oh, lighten up, Brit." The red-head complained with a waft of her manicured hand and, well, the bright green nail varnish matched her pencil dress but definitely not her hair. Although she would no doubt look great at Christmas with the festive combo.

"The owner is in this week, or did you forget how scary he is?" this Brit said, lifting her head over as she pushed her glasses up her nose for the third time since standing here. This was also while shooting fearful eyes toward what looked like the biggest office, where I could hear someone getting a stern telling off.

"Oh relax, Mr. Bigwig will be gone before we know it and then we won't see him for another year," the girl in the green dress said as I approached, something that prompted her to make little grabby motions with her hands, saying,

"Gimmie, gimmie... best damn Danishes and sandwiches in Seattle," she said, winking at me and making me grin, hoping she still liked the sandwiches after I had made them. Despite this I said,

"Thanks, I will pass that compliment onto the owner."

"You be sure to do th... oh shit!" she muttered when a door was slammed, and I made the mistake of looking, gasping the second I saw who it was now standing there...

My Mystery Thief!

CHAPTER 12
IN THE FACE OF DEATH

"Oh shit!" I said, echoing her statement before dropping the rest of the boxes on the empty desk, rushing behind her cubical and hiding down, pleading with her,

"Please let me hide here."

"Wait... why... oh my god, don't tell me you know Mr. Wyeth?"

"Mr. Wyeth?" Again I echoed her, asking myself could that really be his name? Wyeth? Damn, even that was sexy hence why it most likely suited him. But wait, why would someone who obviously looked like a rich enough guy, one who obviously owned a company, need to moonlight as a thief? Was this like a Thomas Crown affair thing?

"Erh yeah, he's... he's... an ex of mine." At this her gaze grew wide in utter shock, making me give her my best pleading puppy dog eyes. Thankfully this worked and she told me,

"Quick, get under the desk."

I did as she said, refraining from saying, 'yeah that didn't work out so well for me last time.'

"Oh shit, he's coming over here," the one call Brit muttered. "Along with our manager... Seriously, Mindy, *you are not getting me into trouble again,"* Brit added through gritted teeth.

"Take a chill pill, Brit," the one with the green dress said under her breath, and I had gathered she was called Mindy. I looked up to see her fake smiling at someone as I held my breath and tried to calm my fluttering heart.

"Mr. Stanton," Mindy said to who I figured was her manager.

"What are these boxes doing here?" a man demanded and one I, naturally, couldn't see.

"Oh, it's just lunch... a erm, girl delivered them, lovely girl, no trouble at all," Mindy said, making me want to groan because, clearly, she hadn't grasped the concept of playing it cool. Meanwhile, my heart was still beating a mile a minute just knowing who I was sharing my space with. Just who was in the same room as me!

Speaking of which, I heard a very masculine sound of someone clearing their throat, prompting Mindy to say,

"Erm, I think Mr. Wyeth is waiting for you."

Mr. Stanton sighed heavily at this before the sound of his retreating footsteps was joined by his groveling apologies for making his boss wait. Which was when I braved a peek out at the side and saw my once mystery thief now standing by the elevators. He also looked like he was trying to figure something out, his handsome gaze was narrowed, making him look totally formidable.

Of course, seeing him in a suit instead of tactical gear was certainly a sight to behold and would, no doubt, be playing as a main feature in my dreams tonight. As usual, he still managed to look completely intimidating, even in navy-blue slacks and jacket to match, this he combined with a lighter blue shirt and deep navy tie. His dark hair was style back as if all he had done when getting out of the shower that morning was run his hands through it.

I had worried that I had somehow overcompensated with my memories of him, making him out to be far more handsome in my mind than what he actually was that night. As if this helped when convincing myself it had all been worth it, as utterly shallow as that sounded.

But I had been wrong in another way.

He was even more handsome than I remembered and damn my brain's weak ability at retaining that important information. My memories hadn't done him justice!

He was breath taking.

As in literally, as in I couldn't fucking breathe!

Oh shit, now he was turning my way, making me duck down quickly. I couldn't let him see me again because that would just end up spelling disaster! But more to the point, what the Hell was he doing here anyway? Well duh, Evie, he owned the company I was currently hiding in the reception of, but still, what were the freaking chances?!

"Okay, the coast is clear," Mindy said, making me sigh back on the floor, needing a minute to compose myself.

"Whoa, okay, you are sooo gonna have to explain this one to us, girl," she said, giggling as she gave me her hand to help me up. Something I did as I was still feeling breathless.

"I… well, it's…"

"A long story, no doubt," Brit added, popping her head back over the cubical next to her friend's now it was safe to do so again.

"Yes, and definitely one we need to hear over drinks!" Mindy said, clapping her hands together and making her long nails click like some evil villainess.

"Erm…" was my answer to this.

"You might want to ask her name first, Min," Brit pointed out.

"Good point, so my new favorite Chica, what's the name of the woman who once dated the most eligible bachelor in any city he is gracing at the time?" I couldn't help but chuckle at her choice of words, before telling her,

"I, erm… well its actually Grace, Grace Stella," I told them, giving them my fake name just like I had done with Denise and knowing now it was more important than ever.

At the very least, he hadn't seen me, so I knew there was little need to panic just yet. No need to run, *at least not yet.*

"Well, it's nice to meet you, Grace, you have no doubt gathered by now that I'm Mindy, Min for short, and this beautiful neurotic mess here is Brit."

I gave the shorter, slim girl a smile, who had rolled her eyes at her friend.

"So, I need your number?" Mindy asked, making me clear my throat before I started with the excuses.

"Well, my phone died last week so I don't really…"

"Oh, it's okay, I will just call the Coffee place you work at, which reminds me, let me get what I owe you," she said, turning for the wad of cash that she had obviously gathered from the other office workers, seeing as she seemed to be on lunch ordering duties.

"That would be great," I replied, looking back at the elevators nervously, hoping he wasn't going to reappear anytime soon. Thankfully, I think Mindy got the hint and therefore it wasn't long before I was back on my way and, this time, I was on edge all the way back to the lobby.

My nerves were so jittery, I couldn't seem to stop my hands from shaking all the way down, half expecting every time the elevator stopped to pick someone up, that I would find myself facing him. Knowing now that it must have been him the first time and thanking the Lord that those doors had closed. In fact, I was forced to take my jacket off before tying it around my waist, because I was so hot and flustered it must have looked like my cheeks were painted on.

But then my heart couldn't help but leap at the idea of seeing him again. As if it wanted me to ignore every single good sense I had left and go in search of him. Thankfully, I didn't listen to this insane part of me and, therefore, exited the building after it looked like it was all clear. Although what I had expected, I didn't know, because it wasn't like he was going to be down here waiting for…

"Oh shit," I muttered the second I looked to my right and saw that he was currently on his phone talking to someone. Someone who clearly wasn't making his life any easier because I could see the tensed line of his sculptured jaw from here. Luckily, he hadn't seen me and for the second time today I was saying a prayer of thanks to the Heaven's above.

A thanks that was most definitely spoken too soon because the moment I started to walk away, I bumped straight into a handsome blonde who could have been some GQ model with the tag line, 'Boy Next Door Heartthrob'. I also felt as if I had seen the handsome blonde before and, well, from the shocked look on his face, I would say he definitely knew who I was.

"It's you!" he exclaimed, making me wince before looking back over my shoulder to see my thief start to look our way. My gaze snapped away before he did, giving him my back and now left me looking up at the handsome blonde man.

"I think you have me mistaken for someone else... sorry, I have to go and..." This trailed off when I saw something out of the corner of my eye. And that second sense I seemed to have hit me so hard, I found myself reacting before I could think. I suddenly turned and found myself running back toward my thief, knowing exactly who the danger was aimed at this time.

And it wasn't me.

So, I ran as fast as I could and before I could shout a word of warning, the last thing I saw was his eyes register the sight of me coming at him. My name became a barely heard whisper coming from his lips. But then it was one that was quickly drowned out by a loud popping sound as the gunfire from a drive-by shooter took aim.

However, he hadn't accounted for me launching myself in the air right at their target and, therefore, taking the hit in his place.

Pain tore through my arm but at the very least, I had a softer landing than that of concrete because I landed right on top of my thief, knocking him straight off his feet and onto the floor. I hit my head off to the side, feeling pain there too as it made contact with the sidewalk.

Which meant that by the time I lifted my damaged head, the last thing I could think to say was,

"We really should stop meeting like this."

Then seconds after this, I promptly…

Passed out on him.

CHAPTER 13
SAVING SIREN
RYKER

Two fucking weeks.

Two fucking weeks and other than finding Arthur, we hadn't come any closer to finding her. So how the fuck I was now sitting at her hospital bedside was still a mystery to me. I could barely believe it when I saw her running straight at me, only the panic on her face told me of the danger before I had a chance to react to it.

Then I scented the blood and, I swear, it had taken everything in me not to erupt into my Demon form and take on the fucking city like Seattle was the birthplace for this Earth's next Armageddon. However, what did stop me was the fact that I had my little Siren in my arms and to destroy the world would mean letting her go. Something I vowed I wouldn't fucking do ever again!

Especially not when she was injured, as she had taken a fucking bullet for me! Gods, but only if she had known that a bullet would have done fucking nothing to me, then she could have been saved the pain. I was at least assured that the bullet had only grazed the top of her arm and there wasn't any more damage. It wasn't life threatening, not like the bastards had intended, the ones that had tried to take my life.

Of course, Van and the rest of my men were dealing with that current headache, one I was very much looking forward to ending... *permanently*. However, for that, I would first need to find the head of the snake, one by the name of Hector Foley. And like my girl had been, he was also in the wind.

But this was one problem I would not be solving right now, as there was nothing that could have taken me from my Siren. Not now I had actually found her. As for her injuries, she had received eleven stitches on her arm, and was due to have a scan on her head to make sure she had no hidden damage after hitting it on the sidewalk before she passed out.

That had been three hours ago, and she still was yet to stir. I was also taking no chances. I didn't care what department of the hospital I needed to donate to or fucking buy outright at this point, to ensure my girl was getting the best treatment possible.

Of course, I had no idea how she had come to be there outside my building. My men had yet to have the time to investigate as, well, they were currently a little busy beating the shit out of the two gunmen that had been trying to execute the perfect drive-by. Something that getting away from may have worked better for them had Van not made their engine explode, so as they had no vehicle left to speak of.

But discovering how Evelyn came to be there wasn't a priority right now. It didn't matter, seeing as she was going nowhere. In truth, it had been the first time since the robbery that I had managed to fucking breathe easy, and I was no fool as to knowing why.

Of course, our leads after finding Arthur had quickly gone cold and it was clear he had no clue as to where she was. And even if he had, he wouldn't have told us. But, in the end, it was a moot point as I had read his mind and found my disappointing answers that way…

17 days ago…

"Are you sure we have the right place?" I asked the second we drove onto a beaten track in the Montara Mountain area.

"I asked at the local grocery store, and their words were, crazy guy in the woods goes by the name Arthur, smokes a pipe and has a sawn-off shotgun by his front door. Yeah, that's Arthur," Van replied, before tearing a piece of the red stick of candy hanging out of his mouth he got from a packet of something called Twizzlers.

"Really?" I asked, nodding at the sorry excuse that humans called food.

"What? I had to fit in with the locals."

At this Faron chuckled from the back seat and said,

"Then you should have bought some moonshine and a packet of jerky."

Van chuckled and said, "Yeah, I thought the blue slushy was too much, although I was leaning toward getting the trapper hat with fluffy ear flaps."

"Well, considering we are not out here hunting for deer or trying to imitate Elmer Fudd, I would say somewhere in the middle of a teenager's choice of beverage and a normal man in his thirties would have been a better choice," Faron said, only half the shit I understood.

"Damn, knew I should have bought the root beer," Van muttered.

"I think you are overanalyzing this. Now, did you get the information we needed?" I reminded him dryly.

"Damn straight, I did, but then with this charming, panty-melting face, who could blame the cashier?"

Faron gave into the urge to roll his eyes before I did, as I was close to losing my patience days ago. But then I had to remind myself that it had been Van's keen eyes and predilection for languages that had led us to this point. Which meant digging deeper for even more patience and trying to ignore the blue sludge dripping into my new cup holder.

Of course, as soon as we heard it was in the sticks, as humans called it, buying a big SUV to get us there had been the next logical step. And, well, it had been the right call as this cabin looked to be in the fucking wilderness. In fact, I couldn't help my surprise, wondering if this was another fucking wild HellHound chase, as I was doubting Evelyn ever living here. But then I would remember her painting, one I now had in my possession along with all her others, and I would feel better about the trip. Besides, we had nothing else to go on, so therefore had nothing to lose but time.

"Fucking knew she was a girl scout," Van muttered when the rustic cabin came into view and, seconds later, an old man holding a sawn-off shotgun in his gnarled hands.

"I thought this guy was supposed to be deaf?" Van asked before Faron answered,

"He is but, clearly, someone watches all the Rambo movies, as I believe we just drove over a trip wire."

I couldn't help but smirk as Van commented, "I think I am going to like this guy."

"I will like him even more if he can tell me where my Siren is," I added before exiting the car and, instantly, our welcome became that of the old man snapping shut the double barrel shotgun and pointing it our way. I held up my hands in the universal sign for 'we come in peace', knowing any moment he would force my hand at putting him unconscious. Something I really didn't want to do. Not when I wanted to know certain things about Evelyn and, unless he was conscious, it was a lot harder to probe someone's mind for shit that you didn't even know was in there. For example, even if someone didn't want to answer a question or even lied about it, they would still be thinking the truth when asked, therefore it would be easy for me to find.

"Van, sign what I say," I told my second before turning back to address the old man,

"We are not here looking for trouble." At this the old man showed his first sign of surprise before Van translated his reply back to me,

"And yet trouble is what you found, son." Van choked back a laugh at the term 'son'. This making me shoot my second a scathing look, and one that shut him up real quick. Of course, having heard me being called son under any other circumstances would have been laughable, especially seeing as I was far older than the country he was currently standing in. Hell, but I was older than a lot of them.

I nodded again for Van to keep signing.

"No, trouble is what Evelyn Parker is going to find herself in unless I can find her first," I told him, and the guy did the very last thing I expected him to… he fucking laughed.

"Not bloody likely but, sure, if you say so," he replied through Van, making me frown.

"Yep, knew I would like this guy," Van muttered, nudging Faron who nearly fell into a rusty boat engine, making me briefly wonder if there was a lake nearby.

"What did he say now?" I asked after the old man had finished signing.

"He said, he would ask if we're friends of Evie, but after hearing you call her Evelyn then he knows we're not." This certainly made its mark as I forced down a growl of anger. However, thankfully, my best friend knew me and knew me well, as he quickly took over, speaking while signaling so as I would know what he was saying,

"I call her Evie, but my friend here, well he's a bit more formal. No, Evie and me, are real tight." I tried my best not to frown at that or let my jealously get the best of me, seeing as I knew this wasn't true. Van laughed at his reply before repeating it for me,

"Well, at least you don't look like some fucking agent. But how do I know you speak the truth…? Tell me something about her."

"Other than her being a damn good artist, a fucking girl scout who thinks fast and acts quicker, not sure what else you want me to say," Van replied, but the old man still didn't look convinced.

"Well, my girl is all of those things but any jackass with half a brain can…" I cut Van off and told him to sign,

"She has a tattoo on her wrist, an Inguz Rune, one she plays with when she is nervous." Then I lied and told him,

"She told me about it and that you have one too," I said, nodding to what I knew was just the hint of one I could see on his arm. Of course, with my advanced eyesight I could make it out but for any normal man that I was trying to portray myself to be, there would have been no way I could have made it out from this far away. I also couldn't help but glance at Faron, as he had been the one to get me this information. He had printed off the image of her wrist like I had asked him to.

Of course, I was lying when I told him that Evelyn had been the one to tell me about it. But I knew it was a lie he would believe, seeing as the chances of me recognizing the Viking symbol would have been slim at best. Meaning he thought a moment, watching wide-eyed as Van translated before setting down his gun and telling us,

"The square in the suit better drink beer."

Again, I felt like telling him I had been there at the dawn of fucking time beer had been first made, perfected, and consumed. I was older than the first supper but, hey, I didn't dress like a fucking hillbilly, so naturally, I was a pussy that drank gin cocktails and didn't use my manicured hands to wipe my own ass! Once fucking more, I gritted my teeth, swallowed down the insult, and ignored my friend's knowing grin.

Inside, his home was actually surprisingly more homely

than I would have imagined from the outside. Of course, this had been made even more so thanks to the artistic talents of my girl, for there was evidence of my Siren all over the place. I couldn't even count how many pictures there were, ones she had clearly painted, and pictures Arthur had likely taken of her growing up.

"He said that she always had a talent... talent for most things, in fact. Gods, but that girl. I swear could turn her hand to anything... Obviously, I exchanged the Christ part of this sentence for Gods," Van said with a casual shrug, but his words were taken as they were meant to be taken, *like a proud father*.

"How did you meet her?" I asked, turning to find Van signing.

"Ah, well, she was this skinny ten-year-old trying to steal food out of my truck after I parked outside the hardware store."

The second he said this, even more of that ice my heart had been caged in for so long started to thaw. Prompting me to fist my hands in anguish, just knowing that she's had such a hard life. But then he continued, and it didn't get any fucking easier to hear, but more ice certainly melted away.

"I knew she was a good kid the second I watched her use her jacket to clean the dirt off my wingmirror, so as I could see out of it. As if it was her only way to thank me for the food she needed. Besides, she could have taken the whole bag, but she didn't. She only took what she could fit in her pockets... I knew then she was a good soul in need of a good soul to look out for her." After Van had finished repeating the old man, he spoke again while signing to Arthur and asking,

"You took her in?"

Arthur replied with the movement of his hands and I was too intrigued by what his answer may be to let it go, quickly prompting Van to repeat it.

"What did he say?"

"He said, he took her in and taught her all he knew."

I grumbled at that, knowing now that I obviously had Arthur to thank for my missing Siren.

"She didn't go to school?" I asked.

"He says, that he couldn't chance it. If the authorities knew she was running from the system, they would have taken her back and arrested his ass, no doubt. No, he couldn't do that to her. So, he taught her himself, and then when she was old enough, he faked her grades and she enrolled in art collage."

I looked back at her art after he said this and knew just as Arthur had recognized it, that she had a gift. Hence why I appreciated a man like Arthur and more so for what he had given my Siren… *A loving home.*

But there was more I still needed to know.

"Did you ever find out what she was running from?" I asked, knowing there was no need to keep the sinister edge from my dark tone, for it was one he couldn't hear. Van continued to translate, and this time word for word.

"Nah, she never once told me and, to be honest, I didn't want to pry into that stuff. If she didn't want to talk about it, I wasn't going to make her. I know all too well about burying bad shit and, sometimes, the importance of keeping that shit buried, no matter what these fucking Docs tell you to do. I figured her way of dealing with it was by not letting the past define her future and it was a life lesson she appreciated." At this he opened a door and showed me just what he meant. It was a piece of artwork that, simply put, completely took my breath away.

It was of another tree, but this time one blossoming with every color of the rainbow. A kaleidoscope of color touching every blossom to every leaf. However, the startling difference was what grew beneath the roots. A dark and haunting world lay trapped there. The twisted faces of monsters screaming and howling in anger as their Demonic hands were all trying in vain to reach the surface. One she had buried there under the colorful tree of life.

Of course, I also couldn't help but wince, seeing as I didn't need to look at my friend to know he thought the same thing as I. That this didn't bode well for the Demon in me that wanted to claim her.

"Her best work, I think, and from the look on your face I'm reckoning I'm not the only one who thinks so," Van repeated what the old man signed, clearly oblivious to my inner turmoil. But then I also had to tell myself that these Demons she had painted, they were only a metaphor for the real horrors she had obviously run from.

"I will pay you whatever you ask to own this." Van tapped Arthur on the shoulder as he was now standing next to me, and translated what I knew was a desperate message.

However, the stubborn old man huffed at me and looked straight at me before signing,

"I reckon you could an' all, what with your fancy new truck and your rich clothes. But look around you, money bags, does it look like I would sell a damn thing my girl has touched with that big soul of hers?"

I gritted my teeth after Van was forced to give me this

blunt reply. Which meant I was barely restraining myself at being denied what I wanted. It was also why I felt Van's hand on my shoulder, and it was the only reminder I needed to hold back and not to do what I was tempted to do. Which was force him to sell it to me.

So instead, I focused on something I wanted even more.

"Where is she?" I ordered and, naturally, Van asked this in a more polite way, at least from what I could gather, as the old man didn't bristle in his answer. Which he would have done had he heard the growled demand in my tone.

"Well, I would say if you can't find her, then she is doing exactly what I taught her to do and that is staying safely hidden." Now this reply did make me growl and, once again, it was one he would not know to take seriously as he couldn't hear it.

"And that doesn't bother you?" Faron asked this time, and the old man caught sight of this movement and turned his way to answer with his hands.

"Gotta let a bird fly and realize it doesn't always fly back to the same nest. As long as she is safe in the world, that's all I care about," Van translated for him, making me snap,

"And if she isn't?"

He sighed at the question Van asked for me before he replied with swift movements of his hands,

"Well, I reckon that if you boys can't find her, being as resourceful as you are by finding me, then no one else will manage it. Because she knows better than to reach out and tell me where she is, in case someone comes looking like you fellas have," he told us and, unfortunately, what Van repeated was the truth. Because in all honesty, I didn't know whether to be surprised or impressed. She clearly cared for the old man like a girl would a father, as you could see that in all the pictures of them taken together. The little trinkets she had obviously made him, whether out of clay or wood, they were all there, in different stages of accuracy and age. The details becoming more pronounced as her skills improved. Everything from little clay handprints painted in rainbow colors, to carved birds sat atop a rough piece of pine. The details so fine you almost expected it to turn its little head and start singing.

She was incredible and I understood why he wouldn't want to part with any of it, despite me wanting it all. Every single thing, she touched I would have exchanged it for Spanish galleons full of gold. For all the royal jewels a vault could hold and the biggest diamonds the world had ever seen.

I was greedy for it.

A new type of treasure of the likes I had never known.

A treasure trove of the soul.

CHAPTER 14
TO DREAM THE GOOD DREAM
EVIE

The moment I heard his voice, I thought I was dreaming again. But that would have been the most logical explanation because, these days, he only ever existed in my dreams. With that one perfect kiss I knew would cling to my soul forever and remain with me until my dying day.

But as for his voice, I had to ask myself why was he angry after such a kiss, because surely, he felt what I had? Then, if so, why was he so harsh now? Why so severe and unyielding?

"My patience is at an end! I want her results and I want them now!"

Wait, my results? Results for what? The moment I heard this, it was like the catalyst for my memories to all of a suddenly come rushing back at me at once. My dream-like memories of him were quickly replaced, and it was no longer the kiss or the sight of him driving away in a van but, in fact...

It was of me falling on top of him.

This was when I didn't need to open my eyes to know what I would find. That I was in a hospital. I had been shot. But more importantly...

I had saved him.

And he was still here with me. Okay, so this admittedly was when I really started to panic. I hadn't thought about the consequences of my actions at the time. Naturally, I had only acted on impulse. The need to save him overriding everything else. Every thought of what could happen to me gone in the moment, and all centered on the need to save him.

And I had.

But as for now, well it was time to save myself. Because the police could be on their way already. He could have told them who I was and, surely, the police were instantly notified any time there was a shooting incident. They would put two and two together and find themselves with a fugitive. Okay, so granted, you actually had to be charged with something and convicted of it before becoming that but, still, it wasn't a stretch to know they were most likely looking for me by now.

In fact, the only thing that stopped me from suddenly bolting upright and making a run for it was the sound of his voice, knowing he was nearby. No, I needed to be smart about this. I needed to wait and make my move when the time was right. As for now, well, they still believed I was unconscious, so that was an advantage, right? Of course, it was, because at least that way I didn't have to answer any questions. Questions my Thief, who also now went by an actual name of Mr. Wyeth, was sure to ask me.

Damn, why hadn't I asked Mindy if she knew his first

name? Mr. Wyeth, although admittedly sounded sexy, also sounded incredibly impersonable.

I heard the door open and purposely kept myself breathing steady so as not to alert him to the fact I was only playing at being asleep. Although this was easier said than done, when I forced myself not to flinch as I felt a gentle caress down my cheek.

"The doctors are dragging their feet." His tone was such a strong, stern timber, well, I almost flinched at that too.

It was clearly a frustrated kind of anger that I never wanted directed at me. I knew I would have most likely cowered. He sounded as hard as stone and as unmovable as a mountain.

"When do they not?" another voice replied, and I would have frowned in question had I not been faking sleep.

"When they are paid not to!" he snapped and, again, it took everything in me not to flinch, something I wasn't sure I achieved. But if I hadn't, then it was obvious he was no longer facing me because my little act wasn't discovered.

"Then throw more money their way, get her signed off or whatever else you have to do, and we can get the fuck out of here and our asses on a jet with your girl waking up in Canada."

I couldn't help but gulp at that... *they were planning to kidnap me!?*

What the fuck?!

Although, stupidly, this wasn't the only part my mind chose to linger on, despite it clearly being the most important aspect of their conversation. I couldn't ignore the way the other man had called me *his girl*. A voice I was now starting to recognize as being the blonde thief there that night, the one I had also bumped straight into on the street before diving into someone who was clearly his boss. And speaking of whom…

"And I intend to do just that, but only when I am assured that there was no damage when she hit her head," my thief said, making me swallow down the frightened lump that was getting stuck in my throat. I couldn't believe it, this was their plan? But how and, more importantly, why? Did they think I was involved somehow? Surely not… I was the one to save him. I just didn't understand.

"Did the police believe the story about the car backfiring?" he asked, making his blonde friend reply,

"Give me some credit, it was like child's play. Trust me, the cops won't be paying your girl a visit."

Wyeth's reply to this (because seriously, I couldn't keep call him Mister) was what I could only assume was a relieved sigh, one I would have mirrored had I not feared alerting them to the fact I was awake. Because as scary as it was to know these guys planned on kidnapping me, it was still the lesser of two evils because the very last thing I wanted was the cops showing up ready to haul my ass to a jail cell. And besides, their intentions were clear, although obviously sketchy at best. I didn't think they intended on hurting me.

Yet despite believing this, my plan of escaping at the first chance I got hadn't changed. I just needed to remain as calm as possible, play the long game until an opportunity presented itself and not lose my head until then.

Arthur had always taught me how to keep a cool head in all situations. *"Your heart will give you away,"* he always told me, and I knew that with these bad guys in the room, it had never been more true. Because there was one part of that phone call that had never left me, and that was when he had told me he was a dangerous man. The way he had said it. So relaxed and at ease with it. There had been no saying it for show or playing the big man. It hadn't been ego talking, it was just simply... *bad.*

Like a fact of life, one he had owned, mastered, and conquered long ago. It was an unapologetic statement made to let me know that there wasn't anything he couldn't handle.

Well, all except... *Me.*

"I don't like this. Call the pilot, tell him I want the jet fueled and ready to leave in the next few hours. Wrap shit up at the tower and tell Hades to get his people here by the time we are ready to leave. I want a full security team and a fucking convoy of cars, if need be, for I will not allow anything like this to happen again," Wyeth ordered and, again, if I had been free to do so, I would have sank further into the bed in a clear show of submission.

"Easy, Boss, that bullet was meant for you, not her, and the bastard didn't know we are fucking bullet proof."

I would have frowned at that... what the hell did they mean, they were bullet proof? Like they all wore armor under their clothes or something? Jesus, just what were these guys into for the need to wear bulletproof vests every day?! Well duh, Evie, executing million-dollar heists for one.

"Yes, and she got hit in the crossfire!" Wyeth practically snarled, and I felt my fist grip the hospital sheet, quickly forcing myself to relax before he saw this.

"No, she jumped into the fucking crossfire, there is a difference." I heard another angry intake of breath.

"Foolish girl, she could have been killed!" he snapped in

return, and I was glad I wasn't facing his obvious wrath, the ungrateful bastard!

"Yes, but she thought you would be... she thought she was saving your life, Ryk." I frowned at this, wondering if this was his first name? And if it was, was it short for something else, Ryker perhaps? Well, it was the only name I could think of.

At this, he took a few more calming breaths and told his friend,

"Yes, well, as noble and brave as it was, it will never happen again, for I will not allow her to ever take such a risk."

Again, I would have frowned, because since when did he think he could stop me from doing anything? Er, duh again, Evie, since the guy is seriously planning on kidnapping you!

"Then for that to happen, may I suggest telling her who and what you are, so as what you do never becomes a worry to her. Then next time she can watch as you simply push out the bullets like taking a crap," his friend replied, making me even more confused and right now, that was saying something.

"Nice, Van, great picture you just painted." he replied wryly, making his friend chuckle.

Meanwhile, I was still stuck on... well, most of it! What the hell did he mean by any of that...? *Push the bullets out?* Arthur had made me watch the Rambo movies enough times, so is that what he meant by it? Were these guys ex-military or something?

Well, it would kind of fit, considering how I first met them and what they had all been wearing.

"Well, what can I say? Rumor has it, you are a collector

now." This was obviously some inside joke I didn't get, and nor did I intend to stick around long enough to even try.

"Just go make the calls, asshole, or next time I get you in the ring, I will make an example out of you in front of Hades' men," his friend said, who was obviously the same one he had called *Van* that night of the heist. Because, really, just how many people could one person know that went by that name? And speaking of names, I now had two for my mystery Thief.

Ryk (most likely Ryker) Wyeth.

"Ah like those pussies could take me," Van scoffed before his boss, who was clearly not amused by this, countered angrily,

"No, but I can, so move your ass!"

He growled then... actually, real life fucking growled, astonishingly, making the one he called Van laugh, as if he was totally used to this type of reaction. Despite the fact that I was now shitting myself at the idea of being left alone with this terrifying guy!

"Going, going," he said in a way that made me imagine him with his hands up in mock surrender, before the sound of the door closed behind him.

After this, I heard, who I was now assuming was call Ryker, release a deep sigh, before I felt my hand being taken in his. Then he turned it over and started running his thumb over my tattoo, sending zings of sensation traveling up my arm. Because despite being afraid of him and, clearly, for good reason, I still couldn't help my reaction to him. Or should I say, his hypnotic touch.

"Hmm... A clear favorite of yours, I see," he mused to himself when finding the second one after I felt his fingers shift my hair from my neck, as I was faced away from him.

"I have to wonder if this is the only other one or if there are more hidden and ready for me to find."

Oh my god, but the sexual purr to his words had me near squirming and made playing the sleeping sandwich maker all the harder to do. Because, gone was the hard, pissed off man in charge, growling orders. No, now I was experiencing a whole other side of Ryker, and the same one who had been so gentle with me that night he stole more than just a golden bird.

The one who stole my thoughts and seemed to consume my every waking minute.

"Well, it is a treasure I look forward to discovering and a journey I hope to take soon, my beautiful little dove," he said softly, now brushing back my hair from my face and, I had to say, it was a side of him that was making my fear quickly melt away.

"Mr. Wyeth?" The sound of another person in the room caused him to sigh before answering with a clipped,

"Yes?"

"The hospital bill is ready to be paid and the doctor will be here shortly to discuss any treatment or after care." At this he rumbled a curse under his breath, before I felt him invading my space again, this time to tell me softly,

"I will be right back, sweetheart, so keep dreaming for me." Then I felt a kiss bestowed on my forehead before a sweep of the back of his fingers caressed down my cheek. It was the hardest part by far to remain still because I so wished I could have opened my eyes then and seen his face for what I knew would be the last time. Especially if I was able to slip away like I hoped.

But for that, I had to wait for the sound of the door closing and as soon as it did, I held my breath a moment longer before opening my eyes to check. Thankfully...

I was alone.

And soon to be in more ways than one, I thought bitterly because why oh why, couldn't he have been one of the good guys?! It was just too cruel and nearly way too tempting to stay. But then I remembered the guy was planning on kidnapping me and decided that, after this, I needed my damn head examining, again!

But to do that, I would first need to escape, which was why I was glad to see that most of my clothes had remained intact and were sitting on a chair folded and waiting for me. As for my T-shirt and sweater, these I knew would have been blood-soaked trash by now, so it looked like I was wearing this hospital gown for a while longer.

I was, however, thankful that I had taken my jacket off and tied it around my waist just before it happened because, at the very least, I had something to hide the hospital gown with. As for my jeans, these were also fine, so I quickly grabbed them and put them on, feeling a moment of dizziness hit when I did. However, I pushed past it and stuffed my feet into my sneakers before tucking my gown in my waistband, all the while watching the door like a damn hawk.

I vaguely looked at my arm, seeing it bandaged up and realizing now that it mustn't have been that bad. The bullet must have only grazed me. Of course, I knew it would most likely hurt like a son of bitch at some point, but for right now, I was still running with glorious drugs in my system. And speaking of running…

I pushed open the blinds and released a huge sigh of relief when I saw I was only one floor up and right at the corner of the building. Which meant I could easily shimmy down the drainpipe. Plus, it wasn't that far down if I was to fall, and well, I hoped those bushes weren't the thorny type.

Knowing I had no time to lose, I opened the window, having to release the safety catch so as it would go wide enough for me to fit through. Then I reached out and grabbed hold of the pipe, thankful for two things; one, growing up in the woods and always climbing trees and the second, that I wasn't afraid of heights. Which meant that despite the pain in pulling on my stitches, I managed to make it down the pipe, A) without falling and breaking my neck and, B) I made it down there in good time. Of course, my palms burned from sliding on the pipe but my feet were safely on the ground, so that was all that mattered.

After this, I ran around the side of the building and started waving like crazy when I saw an empty cab start to drive away.

"Hey, wait!" I shouted, feeling as if fate was on my side the moment it stopped. Even more thankful to find that I still had the wad of cash in my pocket from the sandwich order Mandy had paid for, and it was enough to get me back to where I had parked Wesley's car.

At the very least, I had to be thankful of a few things with, of course, the main one being that I was still alive. After that, came the fact that the cops weren't involved, thanks to Ryker's involvement with whatever law-breaking lifestyle he nefariously led.

The other thing was that I hadn't had a single form of ID on me as I'd left my bag in the car. So, this meant that not even he knew my new name and therefore now that I was far from that hospital, he had no way to track me.

I was safe.

For now.

Which meant all I had to do was lay low for a few weeks before potentially moving on, once I had enough money, that was. Perhaps I would try and find a way to get a new passport so I could travel further. Even, one day, perhaps get as far as somewhere in Europe. Either way, I needed money for that type of thing and right now I had barely anything to my name.

Which meant I just needed to sit tight and wait for all this to blow over.

Of course, the biggest mystery of all, was still…

Why had my Thief wanted to steal me?

CHAPTER 15
A GREED'S RAGE
RYKER

I paid the bill and unfortunately spent far too long arguing with Evelyn's doctor until I finally got my way. But this was at the cost of time spent first having to speak to the hospital's medical director. I had then been about to write an even bigger check when suddenly one of the nurses came running out the room asking where the patient was.

After this, *I lost my ever-loving shit.*

I raced back into the room and had to control the minds of everyone within a large radius, causing each to drop to the floor asleep so as they wouldn't see me as I burst into my other form. That was because, for the second fucking time...

My Siren was gone!

Needless to say, the room did not survive my attack. Which meant after the thirty seconds it took me to tear the bed apart, I ended up using parts of it to smash through the open window, where I now knew she had obviously escaped from.

At the very least, the sound of destruction was enough to

force myself back under control, knowing that she could have been under it at the time. Meaning that in my panic, by the time it took me to run to the now broken window, I was myself again. The relief at seeing she was not there and not in need of even more medical attention due to my rage, was so palatable I could practically taste it.

Of course, my brief moment of relief turned back to bitterness instantaneously, because knowing now that she was on the run again was something I could not ignore. At the very least I knew she could not have gotten far. Not without a vehicle to hand. I then noticed that her clothes were gone and cursed myself for not checking if there had been any money in there, for the nursing staff only mentioned her having no ID on her.

"I have nearly…" Van's voice was one I was happy to hear, despite the growl of my words that followed,

"Shut the fuck up and listen, I want you to check all cab pick-ups at the hospital." His eyes widened in shock as he took in the state of the room before they focused on the window.

"What the fuck happened now?"

"She fucking ran!" I seethed in my Demon's tone, one powerful enough that it rattled the doors in their frames and twisted anything left that I had not destroyed in my rage.

"Okay, I am on it," he replied quickly as he pulled his phone from his tan-colored jacket. While he did this, I paused long enough in my rage to look around at the destruction I had caused and said only two words,

"Damage control."

He nodded at this before asking,

"Where are you going to be?"

I snarled back at the window and told him in a dangerous tone, *"Out hunting."*

This before jumping from the broken window and quickly picking up her scent, hoping like Lucifer's blood I would find her before she found a car. Of course, when this trail went cold right outside the main entrance, I knew my worst fears had come to fruition. She had managed to get in a fucking cab! Seconds later. and my own ride turned up with Van behind the wheel.

"Faron got us an address," he said as way of hello, and I would have grinned or even praised my second for his quick response to my problem. That had been had I not still been killing mad.

"Good, then the net around her grows smaller."

My second grinned at that before putting his foot down the moment I was in the car. Then he was soon breaking every speed limit before traffic impeded the chase. However, it did us little good as by the time we made it two blocks away from the office building I owned, there was no car or, more importantly, no little dove to speak of.

"Faron, get me surveillance footage of exactly where she was dropped off," I quickly ordered after Van pulled over and parked. We both knew there would have been no point aimlessly driving around the city. Something it turned out, we wouldn't need to do either.

"Oh, but I can do one better than that, Boss."

I narrowed my gaze for only a moment before Faron's cocky tone told me something I would really want to hear.

"I know exactly where she is going." I jerked my head slightly, surprised by how swift he had been to discover this, as even for Faron, that had been fast.

"Explain," I demanded firmly, knowing there would be time to praise them but only after I had my girl back.

"Van asked me to try and find out what she was doing at R.W. Investments."

"And? What did you discover?" I asked, now looking at the fucking genius sitting behind the wheel looking smug and, for once, I didn't want to remove it with the use of my fist.

"She's a delivery girl, works for a place called Destiny Coffee house in Capitol Hill, address is 475 Broadway E."

"Fuck! But she was the girl trying to get in the elevator, the girl I opened the fucking door for!" I snarled, and mainly at myself for being too occupied to notice.

"Gods, but this girl just keeps finding you, doesn't she?" Van commented as he put the car back into drive and started off at speed toward the address Faron had given us.

"Yes, and then she fucking runs from me... well, no more!" I snapped in frustration before forcing myself to give praise where praise was clearly due,

"Well done, Faron."

"My Lord," Faron replied before hanging up and, as for my friend, well, he was sporting yet another shit-eating grin.

"And well done... oh come on, you know you wanna say it," Van said, making me groan.

"I will say it when I have my girl back," I retorted, but instead of the cocky ass reply I was expecting, he suddenly looked tense.

"Out with it," I said, narrowing my gaze on him.

"Yeah, about that."

As soon as he said this I nearly groaned aloud but instead snapped, *"What?"*

"Can I make a suggestion?"

This time I did groan before answering with a definitive, "No."

"Okay, well I am going to make it anyway."

I sighed and scrubbed a hand down my face in frustration.

"Ask yourself why she ran."

I was a little surprised by this. "Care to elaborate?"

"She didn't know you were there, unless she was faking being unconscious and neither of us picked up on that when we surely would have, so…"

"So?" I repeated, wishing he would just get to the fucking point already.

"So, the chances are she found herself in hospital and simply freaked. She still thinks she's a murder suspect on the run, remember?"

I thought on this and, admittedly, it did manage to calm me somewhat.

"Then what do you suggest?" I was forced to ask.

"Watch her," he replied, and I swear my head whipped around to look at him so fast, had I been mortal it would have snapped.

"Excuse me?" I asked, exchanging an exasperated tone for one of pure disbelief.

"Look, evidence clearly shows that we are not dealing with just any ordinary girl here. She's got skills and after meeting with her old man, then I am no longer surprised why. My point is, that if you watch her from afar, then you can make a better plan that doesn't involve her potentially slipping through your fingers again."

I fucking hated that his reasoning held strength but, despite this, forced myself to say,

"Go on."

"Stalk the woman, put a team on her twenty-four seven. And then when she is settled once more or, more to the fact, least expecting it, make yourself known in her life but in a way that doesn't include a traumatic event," he said as he continued to weave in and out of traffic with ease.

"Then what, are you suggesting exactly… dating her, the woman I would have been knowingly stalking beforehand?"

"Well yeah… look at it like any other hostile takeover. You discover all you need to know, mainly her weaknesses, and then you exploit them in a way she will give in to you. Make her need you, crave you as much as you crave her… she doesn't know she is a Siren, Ryk, she doesn't know of our world at all."

Okay, so this was another very good point he made and, no doubt, a rocky road I would navigate when the time was right, which clearly wasn't now. However, despite agreeing with this outright, I let my frustrations do the talking.

"Fuck me, you talk a lot," I complained which, in other words, was me admitting I knew he was right. Naturally, he chuckled at that.

"In a nutshell, make this girl want to rely on you, on your protection, rather than reverting back to her well-known defense mechanism."

"Which is?"

"To fucking run."

I released a heavy, weighted sigh, once again conceding that he was right.

"Look, I get it, the need to claim her is most likely riding you hard... no wishful pun intended..." I gave him a wry, 'not fucking funny' look at that.

"My point is, that if you try and take her by force this will only backfire... *again.* Because as much as I joked about kidnapping her and getting our ass back on a plane to Canada, I now think that the moment Girl Scout woke up, flight mode kicked in, and if she sees you again so soon..."

"Yeah, yeah, she will run again, I get it... but answer me this, what if she is already packing her bags and readying herself to leave?"

"Then, naturally, we will follow but I don't think she will do that," he replied, sounding confident and forcing me to ask,

"Why not, what makes you so sure?"

"Because it isn't the smart choice. She will think things through, knowing that she had no ID on her. Meaning the hospital doesn't know her name even if the cops did show up. If they interviewed you, then the name you know is one she has most likely changed weeks ago with fake IDs."

I granted him a disbelieving look at that, and one he was quick to argue against in her defense.

"No, you don't think so...? Come on, Ryk, we already know she is resourceful and can seemingly turn her hand to anything... or have you forgotten what Arthur said?"

I didn't reply to that one, but my heavy sigh no doubt said it all.

"Well, when you were busy fanboying over her art, I was reading the books her mentor had on his shelf, and let's just say it wasn't bedtime stories he was reading her." Now this got my attention.

"And?"

"And, I wouldn't be surprised if he had a hidden bunker in his back yard and those two were the last mortals to survive an apocalypse." Another fucking sigh later and, I had to admit, I was seeing where he was coming from.

"Besides, she also knows that she needs money to run, and I very much doubt that she would start stealing because we both know she doesn't have that in her, despite how he found her as a kid."

This, I could agree with, especially with what he had told us and, let's just say, it was one story that touched my heart enough that more ice melted from it.

"That is a fair assumption, yes," I agreed, something I seemed to be doing a lot of during this short car journey.

"Which is why I bet my Ducati she is going to play the long game and lay low while she waits it out."

Unfortunately, as much as I liked his bike, I knew to bet against my second was a fool's errand.

"Look, here it is now," he said, coming up to the coffee place and even from where we parked, I could see her inside and, finally... *I could fucking breathe freely again.*

"And there's our girl scout," Van said in a far more easy-going manner than what I was capable of, for now it was time to give my orders.

"I want a fucking team on her every Gods be damned second of the day."

"And you will have it," Van assured me, but I was far from done.

"I want cameras wherever she is staying, and her place bugged so as I can hear every damn thing."

"Okay, but I don't suggest the bathroom, as there is no coming back from that one if she finds out... okay, okay, I will get them on it," Van said, lifting his fingers from the steering wheel in mock surrender.

"Not a single thing she does goes by unnoticed, and I swear at the first sight, the first fucking twitch where she looks like she is going to run, I don't care about easing her into my world, she will find herself in it. Ready or not!" I snapped this time, already feeling my Demon riding me hard to just storm into that coffee shop and fucking take her!

"I wouldn't suggest that being written in a Valentine's card anytime soon but, yeah, I get you, Boss."

I growled low, allowing my Demon to release some of his tension now that we could see her and knowing that, deep down…

Our prey was finally caught.

CHAPTER 16
FROM THE SHADOWS
EVIE

A week later and I still couldn't believe I had gotten away with it. Because not once did someone show up at the coffee shop to question me. I had my bag packed and an escape plan in place but, so far, nothing. Of course, the moment I got back to the shop I had to explain why I was walking in four hours later with a bandaged arm, a lump on my head, and minus the money it took me to pay the cabbie.

But like I knew she would be, Denise turned into mother hen on me and brushed off my concerns or worries that I would be in trouble. She told me to take the rest of the day off and even got me some pain killers for my arm. Naturally, I had to lie and tell her that I was mowed down by a rogue cyclist and woke up in the ER. But then with the big lump on my forehead that looked like I had golf balls on the brain, it wasn't any wonder I passed out.

Which meant that by the time I dragged myself into the shower, I was feeling as if my head was going to spilt open.

So much so that I fell asleep wearing my wet towel, something I must have kicked off myself during the night.

Although, in my dreams, I woke to find my thief standing next to my bed. Or should I say, one incredibly handsome…

Ryker Wyeth

The natural response would have been to react surprised by this, even in my dream, but my mind was too foggy to respond with much more than a slight whimper. A sound that, in my dreams, prompted him to hush down at me, before he caressed my hair back from my face, taking care around my injury. Then that same hand found its way to the dressing on my arm where a gentle fingertip followed the line of the bandage as if trying to soothe the hurt.

"You ran from me again, Little Dove," he said softly, making me shiver because that was what the power of his voice did to me. Then that same fingertip left my injury, moving up my arm, over the curve of my shoulder, until dipping down again across my collarbone. He did this so slowly, as if not wanting to startle me, but also as if wanting to see how far he could travel before I stopped him.

But there was no chance of that. Not when I craved his touch and, well, if my dreams were the only way to receive it, then I wouldn't discourage my thoughts by being outraged. So, I silently watched him and, in turn, he did the same. However, the moment he reached the swell of my breasts, I held my breath. Something he watched with apt fascination when taking note of the way my body responded to him. My chest rising and staying there as if frozen and too afraid of breaking the spell.

However, instead of doing as I silently begged for him to do, he gripped the covers and pulled them further up, covering my nakedness beneath instead of exploring it. Then he leaned down and whispered, in gentle reprimand,

"No more running, my sweet, coffee shop girl."

I finally released my breath at that, doing so in a little gasp as I watched his shadowed form retreat into the darkness that seemed to surround him. It was an impossible sight that ended up giving more strength to this being a dream. One I quickly fell prey to when it dragged me further under, until there was nothing but morning light shining through my blinds.

But that had been a week ago, and every night since he had entered my dreams in one way or another. Sometimes he was merely a silent presence in the room. Other times he would touch me in some fleeting yet gentle way. Hushed words luring me deeper into sleep or some sweet endearment bestowed, making me feel safe and treasured. But with each time he spoke, he would always warn me of the same thing…

Not to run from him again.

However, last night was the first time he took these dream visits to the next level because, this time, he did more than lightly touch me. No, this time, he left me with an everlasting memory. I swore that by the time I woke, I was halfway to believing it had all been real…

⚜

By the time I had finished closing the coffee shop, I was beat. I had wanted to do something nice for Denise, so I did her weekly deep clean a day early so she wasn't faced with it tomorrow night. I also left a note and vase of fresh flowers in her little office so she would know it had been done for when she opened in the morning.

She had been so good to me, it was the least I could do for her. Which meant that by the time I was back upstairs in the apartment, all I wanted to do was run myself a hot bath, get in my cupcake and coffee cup pjs (because who didn't love to be reminded of the joys of coffee and cake?), and then curl up into bed.

As for the apartment, or should I say, the gift that was having a nice place to live… it was bigger than my last one and everything about it was a hundred times nicer. Denise clearly had an eye for decorating, which wasn't surprising considering how much care she put into her pastries and how perfect all her food always looked. She always said that you eat with your eyes first, and I happened to agree with her.

It was not surprising that her perfectionist streak translated over to the apartment she lived in, as well as the one she usually rented out. I was just fortunate enough that my arriving had been good timing because her last tenant had only just moved out after falling in love online and moving to Arizona to be with her new girlfriend.

I swear, when Denise showed me around, I had nearly wept for how nice it looked. It was bright and airy thanks to the large front windows that faced the main street and flooded the living room with natural light. An important aspect that all artists appreciate.

It was also made to feel bigger thanks to the tall ceilings, open plan concept and the pale cream walls. But that didn't mean it was sparse of color because this was injected into the room with the furnishings she had used. Like the emerald-green velvet couch that was adorned with big flower-print cushions, along with a rectangle one in the middle that was a contrasting mustard yellow.

The rest of the furniture was sleek and stylish, with a retro vibe I knew Denise adored. It was most definitely a far cry from my last apartment, that was for sure. For starters, this one had a dark, hard wood floor, meaning there wasn't any pealing or cracked fake tile vinyl in sight. As for my bedroom, this was both pretty and girly, with its pale pink walls and a cream bedspread that had a pattern of a cherry blossom tree creeping up from the bottom. Matching, light wooden furniture, rattan bedside lamps, and a fluffy thick pile cream rug, pretty much completed the room.

So, as I slipped between the soft cotton sheets, it didn't take me long before my eyes started to close, and I was soon dreaming of my Thief once more. Those incredible dark blue eyes accessed me where I stood, transporting me back to that night in Bill's office. It was as if he had been trying to strip me bare of my secrets. Of my past that had been well guarded for all these years… and a single moment with him felt as if it threatened it all. Adding even greater depth to the confession of him being a dangerous man, because I knew each minute spent around him would have been a risk, and not for the obvious reasons one might think.

No, it was how he seemed to be able to disarm my heart and consume my dreams that made him the most threatening of all. Dreams that seemed far too real, making me wake from one only to find myself in the throes of another. Which meant that, one minute I was squirming under his penetrating gaze with my back to the wall, and the next I was lying in bed only to find those same intense eyes staring at me from across my bedroom.

I gasped, jerking back and shifting my body further up the bed in sight of him now standing in the corner. His eyes were glowing with the reflection of light I couldn't yet find the source of, making me quickly look around the room as if expecting it to be somehow changed in my dream. But in the time I had turned my attention elsewhere, fumbling for my lamp and turning it on, these seconds had been all he had needed to make it to my bedside.

"Ah!" I cried out in shock. Now I could see more of his imposing figure looming over me. He was wearing dark clothes that had moments ago merged into the shadows he had been hiding in. But now, I could make out the details; the dark jeans and the black shirt he was wearing. One he wore underneath a thick woolen black jacket that was a long trench coat style. His short dark hair and dark eyes framed by thick lashes and dramatic sharp lines of his brows made him a truly fearsome sight to behold. However, he seemed to sense my fear as easily as if he had been able to taste it upon his perfectly shaped lips.

"Ssshh now, go back to sleep, my sweet little Evie," he cooed down at me, making me start to shake my head, something he put a stop to by reaching down to cup my cheek.

"You are safe now... *no need to run,*" he whispered before leaning closer and granting me a gentle kiss on my forehead. However, the moment he started to leave, I did a stupid thing. I ignored all my own warnings as I reached out for his hand and stopped him. He looked down at the contact as if shocked by it, before raising his eyes to mine.

"You wish me to stay?" he asked in surprised.

"It's my dream after all," I told him, and his reaction was a gentle grin before he removed his jacket and folded it slowly over a chair in the corner. He did this without taking his eyes from me and I openly drank in the mouthwatering sight of him. Because there was no need try to conceal my attraction. Not in my dreams. So I didn't bother trying to hold back my clear desire for him or allow myself to be embarrassed by it.

Although I knew the moment I rose up, ready to rid myself of my strappy top, one covered in childish cartoon cakes and coffee cups, that something wasn't right in this little fantasy of mine. Because instead of him appreciating the sexual intent, he stopped me. Naturally, I frowned in question before he told me,

"Offering such temptation is not wise, not when the limits of my restraint are but a single thread held against the blade you hold, and your body is a weapon I cannot fight against."

I swallowed hard, knowing that for a dream I was surprised I was capable with coming up with a response so perfectly executed. I didn't know my mind had it in me. Of course, I wished it had developed into a sex dream, but as far as romantic refusals went, then yeah, it was right up there with being near damn flawless.

It was so perfect, in fact, that it left me breathless and with the inability to say something equally as profound in return, I merely nodded. Then I watched as he prowled around to the other side of the bed, again not taking his eyes from me as he did so. He reminded me of some kind of predator stalking his prey and, boy, did I just feel like letting him eat me. Hell, if my mind would play ball, then he would be doing so right now. But that was the thing about dreams and our inability to control them. However, I guess beggars couldn't be choosers, because if this had been real, then I would have been embarrassed the moment he ran his fingertips down my cheek and purred my name in a soft reprimand,

"Evelyn... you keep looking at me like that and I will cross an important line, one I promised myself I would not cross."

Again, I almost begged him to ignore this rule. But then that thought alone painted itself as clear as day in my wide-eyed expression. Which was no doubt why he let his fingertips slip to the underneath my chin, before using pressure there to keep my face tipped up to his. Then once I was where he wanted me, he lowered his head and I couldn't help but hold my breath as his lips travelled closer.

"Perhaps it is a line I could push back slightly," he mused to almost to himself, despite speaking his thoughts aloud. So, I did the same.

"Or it is one you could dose in lighter fluid and burn all together?" I said, making him grin down at me and it was a pure sexy as sin expression. One granted before he suddenly gripped my chin and pulled me closer, eliminating the last inch between our lips so he could growl directly over them,

"Fuck the line!" Then he kissed me. Christ, I swear I didn't think anything could beat the original one we had shared, the one I obsessed over, but damn, my mind was good!

However, the second I started to reach for his body, now trying to run my hands under the shirt he wore, he moaned a deep and guttural sound when I made contact with his skin. Unfortunately though, it only lasted seconds before I found my wrists shackled in his large hands holding my hands captive in front of me.

"You play with fire, Little Dove," he warned, and the growl in his words was one I couldn't ignore, even though I continued to tell myself that this was only a dream. Because how could it be anything else?

"Well, I did tell you to burn the line," I reminded him, feeling his grin against my cheek. He opened his mouth as if he wanted to bite me but before he did, he chuckled, telling me,

"That you did, sweetheart." Then before I could question his actions, he lowered himself to the bed and, instead of resting his weight over me, he sat down next to me, with his back to the headboard. I was about to ask him what he was doing because this wasn't the way my dream was supposed to go. But then he placed a pillow over his lap and when I frowned in question, he motioned me down with his fingers.

"Come now, lie down, Evelyn," he said, easing me down and positioning me against him so my head was in his lap. Then he proceeded to untangle my braid, doing so with gentle, proficient movements that meant it was soon loose around my head. This seemed to please him as he continued to run the now silky strands through his fingers, and the action quickly had me losing myself in a different part of the dream.

Another dream within a dream.

The feeling of his hands on me, the hypnotic feel of his

continued caress, it was lulling me under, to a place I believed myself to already be.

A place he clearly wanted me to stay.

A place he clearly…

Didn't want me to ever run from.

CHAPTER 17
INVITATION

Naturally when I woke, I felt more than a little confused. Had the door not still been locked and with the extra measure of the chain hanging across, then I would have believed last night was real. I even found myself touching my lips as I did for days after our first kiss. Knowing that it brought me comfort to remember the feel of his lips against my own, as if this was enough to warrant the upheaval of my life. A sad realization if one perfect kiss was all it took to make this an acceptable excuse.

However, when I touched my lips now, I did so trying to remember the dream. One that felt far too real to be normal. It was as if I expected to wake with my head still in his lap. The feel of those strong thighs beneath me and the strength in his hands that still managed to handle me like fine China. It created such a contrast in the depths of my dream that the effect had left me feeling sexually frustrated.

Which was why I couldn't help myself. I got up, used the bathroom, then checked the locks, my next thought was to relieve myself of the ache the memory of him had left behind.

So, after getting back in bed, my hand found its way under the covers, snaking down my body and making sure to feel my breasts as I went under the top I wore. Then after tugging on my nipples, I could wait no more as I suddenly crossed my arms and lifted the top from my breasts, freeing them by tossing the material to the floor. Then with the covers still in place, I wiggled out of my shorts, now kicking them free of the bed. After this I let my fingers dance down my naked belly.

But this lasted seconds before I was getting to the main event as I played out my fantasy in my mind, exchanging my touch for his. Something I would have given anything for in that moment when my fingers dipped down and gathered the evidence of my frustration. I then dragged them through the folds of my sex, using my arousal to coat my clit, making me sigh in pleasure the second I did.

Then knowing I wouldn't last long, I tried to tease myself enough to prolong the pleasure. My body became too hot as the thought of his touch ignited something within me. So, I quickly tore the sheets from my naked body and let them join my pajamas, now arching up into my own touch, moaning shamelessly,

"Yeeess... oh... oh... more," I pleaded to no one, despite knowing exactly who it was spoken to in my fantasy. His hands teasing me, playing me like some sexual instrument of his, tugging at my strings. Christ, I wouldn't last, not even in my imagination was it possible. He was too much. Too intense. Too... *everything.*

Which was why I quickened my pace, soon calling out

my secret name for him as I felt the knowing build start from my toes. That fiery need that could easily burn me whole should I let it. Should I trust it not to consume me. Usually, I'd stop because I was too afraid of the intensity and that was always the problem when finding release by my own hands.

I was in control.

Control I wanted him to own.

Regardless of my wants I arched my back, thrusting my breasts up in the air as I opened my mouth and gasped his name.

"My Thief!" I cried breathlessly, followed by a silent scream I couldn't dare release for fear of who may hear below. So, with my energy spent, my body flopped back to the bed as I panted through the afterglow. Now wishing I was spending the time gathering my wits wrapped in his strong arms. Arms I knew, deep down, would make me feel safe enough not to question my being here with him. That the moment of clear, calm thinking wouldn't result in me tearing myself from his hold after giving too much power to my doubt.

Of course, I told myself this one minute and then the next, I was reminding myself of the reasons I ran from him in the hospital. Reminding myself of the warning he unknowingly gave me when confessing to being a dangerous man. But most of all, reminding myself that he had easily admitted to his friend about his plans to kidnap me. So yeah, it may have been the best kiss of my life, but that wasn't really a good enough reason to overlook the more life changing aspects of my future, the ones that screamed red flags.

So, with all the reasons why I ran firmly in my mind, I

got out of bed again, had a shower, and was just towel drying my hair when the apartment phone started ringing. I ran into the living room, holding the towel around my body while I fumbled for the phone. Then I answered it like anyone would when they never received calls.

"Hello?" I said in a tone that was definitely more questioning than welcoming.

"Hey, Gracie girl!"

I frowned when I didn't recognize the voice right away, not until it finally hit me…

"Erh… Mindy?" I asked, making her giggle.

"You got it! Oh, and Brit is here too. Although her hello is definitely quieter than mine."

I had to laugh at that, despite being slightly on edge by having her ringing me. Something that quickly prompted me to ask,

"Erm… how did you get this number?"

"Oh, I rang the coffee shop and told some guy called Wes that we were total besties, he then gave me the number for your apartment." I frowned, thinking me and Wesley were going to have to have words, because I didn't exactly want people knowing how to reach me.

"Way to go in coming on too strong," I heard Brit say sarcastically in the background, making Mindy shush her.

"Anyhoo, I just wanted to call and invite you out for Birthday drinks."

"Birthday drinks?" I repeated.

"Yeah, mine, silly, although for all I know it could be yours… erm… is it yours?" she asked, making me laugh this time and force myself to relax at how harmless this all was.

"No, don't worry, I will not be raining on your birthday

parade," I replied, this time in an easy-going tone.

"Oh thank God, only I don't share the lime light very well," she admitted dramatically, making Brit comment dryly,

"No shit, understatement of the year... what...? Just sayin', Jeez."

This made me giggle again. I could just imagine the look she just gave her.

"Anyway, you in or what?"

I winced at this, "I appreciate the invite but I..."

"Oh, come on, you haven't lived here long, right?" I frowned at that and asked,

"How do you know that?" At this she laughed and there was a certain edge to it, one I couldn't put my finger on. But then again, these days I was about as paranoid as Arthur was.

"Oh please, no offence, Chica, but it was written all over your face. You know, that fish out of water, in a new big city look. Oh, don't worry, it was cute, but I could tell you need some new besties to show you all the best places to be seen." I winced at this and admitted,

"Yeah well, being seen isn't really my thing, if you know what I mean."

"Oh, come on, what do you do on your days off? No, wait, let me guess, you tidy your apartment, do laundry, groceries and what-not... all those tedious, boring, grown up things life expects us to do... when really what you need to be doing is living it up and making the most out of your twenties, what are you, like fresh out of college...? Live a little, girl," she said, not letting me get a word in and I couldn't help it, but I smiled at her infectious energy.

Although I wasn't sure being shot at only a week ago

could be classed as not living it up or being boring but, whatever. In her defense, she didn't know this.

But then she kind of had a point. Because exactly what was the purpose of living, if all I was willing to do was play it safe all the time? If all I was going to do was hide myself away? This made me question, what was the point of survival if I wasn't living a life worth saving? Because she had unknowingly hit a nerve. Or hell, she knew exactly what she was doing by taking a sledgehammer to it.

Either way, she was right, it was another Saturday night and my plans had been to clean the bathroom, do laundry, and order takeout, so other than grocery shopping, she pretty much had my whole day pegged.

"So, you in?" she asked in a pleading tone and just before it was chased by an exaggerated 'pleeease', I told her,

"Okay, what time and where?"

She squealed down the phone, and said, "I will send a car for you."

I frowned at this before asking, "You will send a car?"

"Erm yeah, my brother owns a car business thingy or whatever."

Again, I found myself frowning, especially when I thought I heard Brit mutter in the background,

"Ooo good one."

"Erm yes, that spreadsheet should work... sorry, just Brit trying to remind me I have a job or whatever." I laughed at that, thinking these two were certainly a pair and trying to force myself not to be so paranoid.

"Don't forget the delivery bit," Brit said, louder this time, and I could just imagine her nudging her over the cubical.

"Yeah, yeah, so just in case you don't have anything to wear, I am sending something over."

Okay so, admittedly, this was getting weirder. I mean, had she really thought I was that badly dressed, or did she just assume I lived in jeans and sweaters? Of course, the fact that these days I practically did was irrelevant, especially considering I spent most my time working in the coffee shop.

But when I had worked in an office, I had enjoyed making an effort and dressing smart. It just meant that now I didn't have any reason for skirts and heels. Well, until now that was. So I quickly thought about what I had brought with me that may be suitable and told her,

"Oh… you don't have to do that… I mean I don't have anything too fancy, but I have something suitable for a bar at least," I replied, making her say,

"Oh, sweetie, when I tell you we are going out, we are… *Going. Out.*"

"Okay, not sure I understand what that means exactly," I admitted.

"Look, don't worry about it, just think black dresses and killer heels, besides, you would be doing me a favor. My sister designs this stuff and she wants all her line of dresses to be seen out so we can like… you know…" She paused and I wondered at this moment if she were rolling her manicured hand around the air as she tried to think of her words.

"Get feedback?" Brit offered helpfully in the background.

"Yeah, get feedback and what not" Mindy repeated.

"Oh, okay, so free dress for the night, I can do that. Do

you need to know my size?" I asked, accepting her reasons and rolling with it.

"Oh please, I am like a pro shopper, trust me, I have an eye for this shit and know exactly what will work with your body type," Mindy replied, making want to point out that she was clearly in the wrong job if that was the case, but I refrained.

"Okay, well that's great then but nothing too revealing, right? I'm not really into the whole clubbing scene and need to be dressed in more than a glow in the dark mini skirt and tasseled bra." At this she laughed before telling me,

"Oh don't worry, where we are going is the classiest place around, eeek I am so excited. It usually takes months to get on the guest list," Mindy squealed, and you could practically feel the waves of excitement coming down the phoneline.

"Min..." Brit said her name in a warning tone, making her mutter back a muffled,

"Don't... I... this." Mindy then hushed her back but I barely caught more than a few words, making me wonder what they were up to. Well, as long as it wasn't trying to set me up with anyone, I was fine for a simple girly night out. Which, after what she had said about this club, had me worried for another reason.

"Well, in that case, how will I get in?" I asked, making her say,

"Okay, so I had friends cancel on me and have spare tickets but please don't think you're second best, they canceled ages ago and I instantly thought of you and..." I chuckled light-heartedly at this.

"Mindy, it's fine, I get it and I appreciate you thinking of me. It's been forever since I have been on a girl's night out," I told her, thinking that forever was right because the last time was with roommates at college.

"Great! Well, it's all sorted then, I will get my... erh brother or whoever to pick you up at eight, you live at the coffee place, right?" Again, I didn't remember telling her this.

"Yeah, how did you know?" I asked, and before she even replied the obvious came to me.

"Oh, that Wes guy told me you were upstairs, so I just assumed... or if not and you live somewhere else, it's not a problem. I am sure he could come pick you up from any address in the city." Okay, so this made sense and I scolded myself for jumping to conclusions again.

"No, no, the coffee shop is fine, I just couldn't remember if I told you or not," I replied, trying to force myself to relax once more.

"Right well my boss is about to come this way, Mr. Stanford, not you know who," she said giggling, making me hold back a groan.

"See you tonight, Chica!" Mindy said sounding even more enthusiastic than before, making me wonder if my accepting the invitation had anything to do with it... *had she really wanted me to go that much*?

"Well, that went well, I think and..." I didn't hear anymore as she hung up and no doubt didn't realize I had heard the tail end. Something I found myself chuckling to myself about and my smile said it all. Because now I was feeling as if tonight was the first sign that a life here might actually work.

It was true that, growing up, I hadn't had many friends.

Running away before I could be put into the system meant it was hard to trust anyone. Like being some scary cat or dog on the street and being in constant fear of the authorities finding you and picking you up to take to the shelter.

But then suddenly I had met Arthur and, after that, I hadn't felt like I had needed anyone else in my life, just grateful that I had someone who finally cared about me. Someone I could trust.

Of course, this meant that when I had finally gone to college, something Arthur had paid for me to do, (despite me protesting for years) I felt as if making friends was a new life skill I had to learn. It took me a while to relax enough around new people. But, in the end, I finally came away with a few people I still spoke to, even to this day. Despite the fact that all of them had gone off in their own separate ways, making a life for themselves. Meaning the only way we kept in touch was through emails because I saw very little reason to be on social media. For starters, I gathered it actually required a 'social life', one I surely lacked.

Well, maybe tonight would be the start of something new. Perhaps Gracie was the new me and a chance to reinvent myself.

Although as soon as I thought this, with it came that slither of doubt and that even bigger portion of guilt because, in the end, they would never truly know me.

Never know what I had done.

Never know that they were really friends with…

A murderer.

CHAPTER 18
UNEXPECTED PLEASURES
RYKER

I had to say that watching my girl had quickly become my new obsession and, therefore, it was the only thing preventing me from outright kidnapping her. Not that I admitted this to anyone, as not even Vander knew the true depths of my depravity. Because as soon as she fell asleep, I was, in fact, breaking into her apartment every night.

I just had to touch her.

Just had to be close to her.

Close enough to take in her scent and breathe it in like I was drinking back the finest cognac. But I hadn't lied when I told her that I knew there was a line I would not cross. It was bad enough that on the few occasions she awoke during these times that I continued to make her believe it had still been a dream. Of course, discovering that I featured in them naturally had helped with making her believe this. But then it also gave me hope, knowing that her mind still lingered on our meeting. Which, at the very least, managed to alleviate some of the guilt I felt when intruding on her personal life and, well, basically stalking her.

Yet like I said, even *I* knew there was a line I would not cross during these times, despite how hard it had been last night. Especially, when such temptation constantly presented itself in the form of everything that was her. However, when it was clear that last night she had wanted to turn her dream into the erotic kind, by the Gods, it had been the hardest fucking thing I had ever done by denying us both the pleasure!

I had wanted her like no other!

It had felt as if I were bathing in the raging river of Phlegethon, as if my skin was being licked by the eternal flames that incessantly scorched the riverbank. In fact, I had never known my will to be so strong. For the urge to just take her and make her mine had my Demon waging war inside me, fighting against the admittedly thin veil of my morals.

The line I refused to cross.

One that I knew, if any more time passed between us, would be nonexistent, being set alight like she had asked for me to do only last night. Hence why I had quickly hit my limit on waiting, as now it was time to act. Of course, Van believed I was being too hasty. Well, that was until he found his throat in the hand of my Demon and pinned to the nearest wall, a foot from the floor. Then my Demon had snarled,

"Do you still think so?"

"Er, yeah, maybe not," he conceded after he choked back a breath, one I had forced him to take after first squeezing harder. Then I let him drop back to his feet and forced my mortal form to return, after now proving my point. Because, any longer, and I would lose the ability to get my Demon to back down entirely. Meaning I feared that the next time she awoke from a dream, she would find a very different version of me staring back down at her.

Of course, my Demon would never hurt her. I was assured of that now. But that didn't mean that he wasn't as ready as I was to claim her. He wanted her with just as much desperation that was building within the part of me that asserted control. It was why I had to visit her at night, for it was the only thing that kept me sane. Well, that and watching her days play out through a computer screen. I'd had my team place cameras in every inch of her place, apart from her bathroom. As I had taken Van's advice when telling me that this indeed was a step too far.

Even for a possessive asshole stalker like me.

My men had also broken into the coffee shop at night after closing and done the same thing so as I could watch her work. I was assured that, at the very least, this time, she lived in a place that was significantly better than the last. Something I discovered was thanks to the kindness of the owner of the coffee shop, who had offered her more than just a job. A fact that I couldn't have been more grateful for, because if I was yet unable to care for her the way I wanted to, then this was as much as a compromise as I could hope for. Hence why, in a few days, this Denise would find herself winning some 'random' prize money, as it was the least I could do to repay her for unknowingly taking care of my girl.

Gods, but I couldn't wait for the day I got to take on that responsibility without having to hide it. Evelyn was mine to care for and, therefore, it was my job to ensure that she had everything she ever needed. That she wanted for nothing.

That she had everything her heart ever desired and more. But above all…

I wanted her happy and safe.

Now, just how she was going to feel about entering into my world and how she would cope with discovering who I was at my core… well, naturally, it was not a part I was looking forward to. Because I knew the outcome would go one of two ways. She would either think me crazy and belonged in some mental asylum, or she would be utterly terrified of me and run again. Both outcomes prompted me to wonder just how long I could get away with keeping this side of my life a secret. But in truth, there was no good way in which I could see this side of things going. No, I could only see them being handled one way and, well, that included me managing the fallout.

In other words…

Eventual kidnapping.

Because, at some point, I would have to prove it to her and when I did, I knew that no matter how brave a girl she proved to be, as a mortal human, her fight or flight instincts would kick in. And well, most of me wished fighting would be her first reaction, as *that* I could deal with. Mmm, I had to say, the idea of restraining her on my bed quickly and unashamedly came to mind.

Gods, but how beautiful would she look, tied up in yards and yards of strips of silk, black or blood red against her lightly freckled skin. Shibari was the name of this particular kink and it was one I was particularly skilled in. Shibari was a Japanese word that broadly meant 'binding' or 'tying' and was therefore used in the BDSM world to refer to a particular style of decorative bondage.

It was an art form and, Gods, but how I would adore to have her body painted that way. Especially in her usual artistic style of shades of black and white, with the only color belonging to that of her parted lips and the blood-red silk that I would bind her body with. I would have the painting hung above my bed so as we both may look up at it every time I thrust into her. Every time I claimed her and made her scream my name. So as she knew who she was eternally tied to. To whom she belonged to and always would.

The thought that brought me back to last night when I had never wanted something so badly, something that, under the circumstances, I knew was wrong to simply take. For I could undoubtably be cruel. I was most definitely sinister. I was, at times, a sadist and always in complete and utter control. But with her, I could feel so many more things start to infiltrate my once cold, dead heart that only breathed an ounce of life when Greed had been the driving force.

But since she came into my life, I had discovered the birth of new emotions, many of which I didn't fully understand yet. However, there was one that I did recognize and started to understand well enough...

Morality.

The need to do right by her, which was why I had turned down her dream-provoked offer. Of course, I had been elated to know that she wanted me, even in her dreams. To know she had been ready to give herself to me freely had been like a gift, one I was sorely tempted to take. But my integrity held me back, despite it only getting me so far as nothing in this world would have prevented me from kissing her. Not when her large doe eyes were looking up at me in silent pleading for me to do so.

Just like the next morning when my scrupulous actions of restraint were put to the test once more. Only this time, they were also quickly destroyed the moment I saw what she intended to do when she woke to find herself alone. I swear, the moment her hand started to navigate a sensual journey down her body, one I was very much looking forward to taking myself, preferably with my tongue and teeth, well...

I was a man lost to the same desire.

Unsurprisingly, my Demon roared at me to claim what was ours and give her something to really moan about. How could I be so fucking jealous of her own hand?! I swear, the second my men entered my office I had roared so loud; the windows had shattered and would have rained down on the fucking street had it not been for the invention of safety glass.

But I didn't care, because the idea that even a single breathy, sexual sigh was heard by anyone other than me, had me wanting to tear fucking ears out! Every single inch of her belonged to me, which included her orgasms. I would have punished such a sin, to keep this one from me, if it hadn't been my name she had cried out for at the end. She saved herself and her ass from my palm with that one.

My thief.

That was what she had called me. It was ironic really considering the parts of me it felt as if she had stolen that night. The very first glimpse of her looking up at me from under that desk. It had been like being struck down by Janus himself. The God of Time laying the claim of my Fated on me and I had been too stupid, too fucking stubborn to notice it for what it was.

My Siren's call.

Just like when crying out her orgasm, the shock still evident but no less affective as I locked the doors with my mind before unzipping my slacks. Then I put the recorded scene on repeat, took my cock in hand and did something I hadn't needed to do in centuries…

I jacked off.

Naturally, just like with her own, it hadn't taken me long, not with the memory of her tongue dueling with mine and imaging it licking its way up my cock. Those pouty lips stretched wide around my girth as she was forced to take more of me. The feel of her gagging as I fisted her hair and punished her witty mouth to hold me longer, just to feel her panicked little swallows vibrating along my length. I just knew it would be unforgettable.

This fantasy played out, all to the sight of her finding her release as she did now on screen. I would demand that she finger herself while sucking my cock, ordering her to make herself come but only on my command. To feel her crying out with her mouth stuffed full of my length would no doubt make me explode, the thought tipping me over the edge now.

Yet, as long jets of semen landed on my desk and overflowed onto my fist, I knew it was a waste, as I wanted to feed her it, making sure she didn't miss a drop. I wanted her to gag on it, to watch her struggle to swallow me all down. To watch as my cum dripped to her beautiful breasts, a sight that she had awarded me with when tearing the sheet from her perfect body. I would lift one creamy globe to her lips and force her to suck her own tit, until it was clean of my release before I would inspect her work and praise her for such a good cleaning job.

Gods, the things I wished to do to her. It was a never-ending list that grew with each passing day. Not all of them sexual either, where once upon a time, that was the extent of all my encounters with females of my own kind. But as for last night, of course I had sexual thoughts running rampant in my mind, for I would be a liar to say otherwise. But this hadn't been the only thought, as I had wanted something I had never thought myself possible of needing before. I had wanted to experience the comfort of simply being with her. The pleasure in which is born from also offering comfort in return.

I wanted to lay her in my lap and play with her silky hair until she was resting sweetly. Content with just being with her, touching her, and not in a solely sexual way. And like I said, this was not something I'd ever had or experienced before. Something I had been morally free to act upon without the weight of guilt intruding on our private time.

Now, when I would get to do this without having to make her believe that I was just a figment of her unconscious imagination, was unknown, but I knew one thing…

I was losing patience and fucking quickly.

CHAPTER 19
A BARGAIN MADE

My temper.

Something I was quick to lose these days. A fact I wasn't exactly hiding, either, for I was making my frustration very apparent to all that had no choice but to endure it. Just like my outrage at being disturbed. I sighed in frustration despite the brief sexual release that seemed to do little in ways of calming me down. No, if anything, it only reminded me of what I didn't yet have in my possession. My greatest treasure found, and one I felt as if I did not yet own. Again, I gritted my teeth in annoyance as I cleaned away the evidence of my obsession before I finally rejoined the world in which I ruled. Something that started when Van braved to knock on my door this time.

"What is it now?!" I couldn't help but snap, with my vexations that seemed to be mounting daily, despite the release I had.

"You might be interested to know of a conversation I overheard between two of your office bunnies," Van replied with a smirk as, clearly, my foul mood had no effect on him whatsoever.

"Since when was I being mistaken for someone who ever gave a shit for office gossip?" I practically growled, but again this had no influence on his cocky demeaner, as he replied in that annoyingly easy tone of his.

"Oh, I don't know, maybe since this particular office gossip is about that little mortal girl scout of yours." Now this, of course, got my attention, and I felt myself rising out of my chair before I even knew my mind was dictating my actions to do so.

"Tell me!" I ordered, making the bastard's smirk deepen. But of course, it fucking did! The guy hadn't seen me lose my shit like this since first coming to the mortal plane and getting drunk from the fears of others. It had been like an alcoholic waking in a distillery.

"Turns out that the day you were shot at, your girl delivered sandwiches to a couple of girls in accounting and made quite an impression."

My face said it all, which of course was to hurry the fuck up and finish telling me the rest of what felt like vital information.

"And by 'making an impression', I mean when she saw you and freaked out enough to hide in their booth so as you wouldn't see her."

I frowned at this, knowing that none of this could be that much of a coincidence as our paths continued to meet.

"Bring them in here," I told him, knowing that I wanted to hear this account of events for myself. But once again, the smug bastard must have known I would say this, as all he had to do was open the door and jerk a couple of fingers at the two girls he must have kept waiting there outside my office.

Both of which walked inside and the first thing I noticed, like most people would, was that they were the total polar opposites in appearance. One had an overabundance of red curly hair that was currently pushed back from her face with a black and white zebra print band. It was one that matched the pencil skirt she was currently wearing and was of a style that showcased her hourglass figure. A figure that I could tell, instantly, Vander had not missed. In fact, he was still basically eye fucking her from behind; he liked a woman with curves and this one was showing off both. What with her tight-fitted black see-through top that did little to hide her bra or the breasts that filled it.

Now as for her friend, well she looked like all she wanted to do was run into a little hole in the ground and never come back out. Not until I had vacated the building, that was for damn sure. But despite appearing terrified of me, she was clearly the more professional of the two and looked as if she took her job more seriously.

Her hair was a stark contrast to Miss Firecracker, as it was black and cut short to just in inch below her jawline. This matched the thick black-rimmed glasses that seemed too big for her slim face. She wore a full, navy-blue suit, so as not an inch of skin was showing.

Like I said, they both looked equally petrified of me and, well, I guess that my reputation preceded itself. But then I wasn't surprised. When it came to business, I was known as being as ruthless as I was when it came to a very different type of business. This known fact, despite being here only once, perhaps twice a year at most.

But then I had offices all over the world, so this wasn't exactly surprising. No, the only place I found myself staying in long enough to call home was Toronto. Making me wonder, for not the first time, how she would feel about relocating there. Of course, she had already uprooted her life once before and had barely had enough time here to form a foundation strong enough to stay. A foundation I was soon to crack like foolishly choosing to build your home upon the ice. And well, I was the creature lurking underneath it, circling her like prey she was unaware lived there, watching her. But speaking of shattering her fake little world…

"Come closer, girls, I wish to speak with you." The unsure looks they gave each other spoke volumes.

"You heard him, ladies," Van said firmly, and it was enough to get them moving closer.

"Did we… erm, do something wrong?" the curly redhead asked.

"Sir…say sir," the quieter, shy one said, nudging her friend.

"Sir, yes of course."

"Be at ease, ladies, I merely wish to ask about your encounter with my… well, shall we say, a friend of mine," I said, correcting myself before I let slip just who Evelyn was to me. After all, she had chosen to hide from me and did so with the aid of these two. A thought that still stung and was a bitter pill to swallow or, should I say, one grinded between gritted teeth.

"Oh, you mean Grace," the redhead said in acknowledgement.

"Yes, Grace," I replied with a knowing smile, as of

course hearing the name made me want to chuckle. She would never be my Grace but always be my Evelyn.

My Evie.

Now it was time to get her to understand this too. Which was when an idea started to formulate quickly.

"Well, she brought us the food we ordered but it was over a week ago now," she continued, as it seemed she was more at ease doing all the talking, whereas little miss shy was content to simply nod.

"I mean, we didn't know it was your ex-girlfriend and if it helps, I thinks she was just as surprised to see you."

I frowned at this making the redhead add, "I don't think she knew this was your office, sir."

"She told you that she was my ex-girlfriend?" I asked, making them once again look to each other before answering me in a way of both nodding.

"Is she not an ex, sir?" she enquired, and no doubt because of the dark look I was now expressing.

"No, *she is not,*" I stated firmly before clarifying. "She is not an ex of anything and very much still my... em, girlfriend," I said, never once using such a term for any other before. It seemed so... *insufficient.* Too weak a phrase. Too unbefitting for someone who was my soul mate. My Electus. My Chosen One.

My Lost Siren.

"Oh... oh, okay erm, well she seemed to..."

"She was wrong," I reiterated once more and, again, my tone said it all. Or perhaps not enough, as both girls looked at each other and their confusion was easy to see. Even Van thought I needed to add something to this statement as he started to roll his hand around behind them, as if trying to

prompt more of an explanation from me. I therefore refrained from rolling my eyes and instead told them,

"I won't bore you both with the details..." I started, and their faces looked like it would do anything but bore them, as I imagine these two lived by office gossip.

"...But we had a disagreement and... and..." This was where I started struggling and, therefore, giving Van what he must have taken as the green light to intervene.

"They were on a break."

"Like Ross and Rachel," the one with the glasses said, speaking for only the second time, but the statement was so confusing to me it made me frown and she instantly looked to regret making the sound.

"I have no idea who they are," I informed them, and as such, it seemed to surprise them, making me wonder if they were a famous couple or something.

"Anyway, I wish to make my intentions known and force..."

"Surprise her," Van said quickly, now coming to stand next to me and grinning, making the two girls do the same in return, as clearly, he had the ability to put them both at more ease than I did.

"Yes, *surprise her,*" I said, despite this being somewhat stilted in its delivery considering I had no idea what Van was doing by adding to this. But then again, I suppose the word 'force' did imply that she would be my girlfriend once more by exercising that pesky little mortal thing called *free will*. Because even *I* had to recognize that this situation was not what conventionally happened when you intended to date a girl... or in my case, *tying them to you for all eternity.*

"Ah, I see, and you need our help?" the redhead said, nudging her smaller friend as if this was a good thing.

"Of sorts, yes," I admitted, making them grin.

"Well, we did get chatting and I did say we would have to take Grace out sometime, especially considering that she's obviously new in town."

"Yes, we did say that," the shy girl agreed, and again my mind started forming a plan.

"Excellent. Have you heard of club, 4Gold?" At this, both girls reacted the same way, with wide eyes and open mouths.

"Of course! It's like impossible to get in there on a weekend, that is unless you're on the guest list, and it's even harder to get upstairs to the VIP lounge."

This was good news, considering I now knew I had something they both wanted. I conveyed this to Van with only a look.

"Then I will make you a deal. Tonight, there is to be a masked, red-carpet event to launch Stolen Gold, which as you know is the new vodka brand we invested in." The event was one of many and not something I usually took the time to participate in. However, now it gave me the perfect excuse to execute my plan.

"Oh yes, we know... I mean, the marketing team has been making all the preparations," the shy one said while pushing up her glasses and making Van smirk down at her, causing her to blush.

"It's all the office is talking about," the redhead said enthusiastically.

"Well, how would you like to have your names on the

guest list?" I asked, which given their excited expressions, I now realized was a foolish question.

"For real?!"

"Seriously?!" they both said in unison.

"Get Grace to accept an invitation to the club tonight and I will provide all three of you with not only your names on the guest list, but one that will get you all up into the VIP with all expenses paid for, including a driver for the night." This must have been the right thing to say, as both girls actually squealed, a reaction that caused the same confused look to be exchanged between myself and my second.

"You can count on us, sir; we will have Grace with us," the redhead said assuredly.

"Good, then I will leave all the details to Stanford, he will provide you will further instructions. As for the details you give her, that I will leave up to you. The complication of course will be forming the reason I will be sending her a dress to wear that doesn't implicate me as being the one behind the gift." At this both girls grinned before the redhead took charge, telling me,

"Leave that to me, I know exactly what to say."

"Very well, but please remember that this is to be a surprise, so I would prefer my name be kept out of our little arrangement," I said, trying to convey once more the importance of this fact. Because if she knew I was behind it then it would most undoubtably make her run again. Which was why I would have to have a team in place watching her and at the ready in case this happened.

"In other words, Ladies, mention the boss and no 4Gold," Van said, making the terms as clear cut as they could be.

"We understand and won't let you down," the redhead said with a comical little salute, and one that looked to have embarrassed her friend.

"Then I believe you have a phone call to make," I told them, making them both nod rapidly at the same time and doing so like shaken little dolls. This was something they were still doing as they were being ushered out of my office.

"I hope you know what you are doing," Van commented as soon as the door was closed behind the girl. As for me, I looked to where I had not long ago had to rid my desk of my release before telling him,

"I know exactly what I am doing and pretty soon…" I paused so as to run a finger down the face of my girl on screen, then I finished my sentence directed straight at her…

"…She will be right where I want her."

CHAPTER 20
LOCKED TO THE NIGHT
EVIE

"Grace, there was a delivery for you, a rather large box." I heard through the wood after Denise knocked on the door. I rushed to open it, not wanting her to struggle for longer than she had to. She twisted her way through, surprising me with how big the box was. She also looked as stylish as ever, with her flared tartan skirt and cute little black sweater with its collar of pearls and puffed-cap sleeves. She was also wearing heeled black boots that had leather buttons up one side.

"I would have come down for it," I told her once she had put it down on the couch.

"Oh nonsense, besides, I was curious," she said, winking at me and making me chuckle. As soon as I told her that I was going out for the night, she had seemed so excited for me. So happy, in fact, that she had demanded that I take Sunday off, telling me that everyone needed a hangover, junk food, pajama day. I told her she was an angel and also pointed out that she was the best boss I'd ever had.

Well now she was hovering next to me as I looked down

at the big black dress box. It was tied with a glittering gold bow, and I couldn't help but wonder who Mindy's sister was exactly. She must have been someone very high up in the fashion world, especially to have her own fancy packaging.

Then, as I removed the lid we both gasped in unison. Even before I lifted the dress from its box, we both knew it would be exquisite, just from the fabric alone. A stunning damask pattern with acanthus leaves, feathers, and scrolled fan shapes all encrusted with sparkling gold sequins. I finally lifted it from its bed of black tissue, feeling the weight and, therefore, obvious expense of the dress, before holding it to my body.

Denise gasped again shortly after I did, knowing the dazzling gold pattern on top of clingy black material would hug my figure like a glove.

"Who did you say this friend of yours was?" The look I gave her was enough to say without words, 'I don't know anymore'.

"Now I have to see this on you," Denise said, and I couldn't help but smirk.

All of a sudden, I felt giddy and excited about tonight. It felt like being invited to a prom I never got to experience. As for the dress, I knew the second I finally put it on that I had never worn anything as beautiful, and most definitely never had an occasion to. Of course, Denise's reaction certainly helped make me feel as if I belonged in it, because she gasped the moment I stepped out of the bedroom.

"Wow… just wow, Grace, you look incredible."

I blushed at this and brushed my hands down the tight material in a nervous gesture.

"You really think so?" I asked, already feeling as if it was too much. I looked more like I was going to the Oscars than a nightclub. But then Denise scoffed at my fears before reassuring me,

"Oh, my girl, I know so, and it was like I thought, a dress like that is made for you."

I grinned big at this, unable to help myself as the confidence in me started to bloom.

"I think it might be a lucky guess, but Mindy did say she was good with getting people's sizes."

"Then she should take that gift to the circus because it looks damn near perfect."

I couldn't disagree. I had never worn something that fit me so well.

It was a cross between a maxi style dress and a mermaid. It started with a sweetheart neckline, with off the shoulder strap sleeves. This then fitted the curves of my body, being tight from my chest, all the way down to mid-thighs, where the skirt flared out into a dramatic mermaid tail of even more sequins. The design and shape made me look like some priceless vase, painted in liquid gold.

"Now may I suggest a sexy little up-do? Maybe even some pinned curls off to the side?" Denise said before ringing down to the coffee shop and asking Wes to close up because she had important fairy Godmother duties to attend to. I couldn't help but giggle at this as she started to sing bibbidi bobbidi boo from Disney's Cinderella.

Before long, she was doing my hair and make up for me, giving me little tips as she worked and informing me she used to work the cosmetics counter at JC Penney's. Meaning I now knew how to achieve the perfect golden eyeshadow without looking like a drag queen. It looked more on the seductive side, thanks to the flawless flick of black liquid liner and the natural curl of my lashes that were made longer thanks to the expert use of mascara. I also knew how to accentuate the perfect cupids bow of my top lip by using a dark red liner to match the lipstick she leant me.

This all meant that, by the time the car turned up for me, I was literally a whole new me. I was also full of nerves, despite Denise trying to boost my confidence enough that I actually made it through the door. But I wasn't sure if the dress helped with this or if it was in fact the thing that made me more nervous than I would have been.

Of course, the dress hadn't been the only thing I had found. The box had been so big, it also had a separate compartment at the bottom. A smaller box within a box that had contained black, thin heeled sandals, that tied with a gold strap at my ankles. The box had also contained a black and gold sequin bag that matched the pattern on the dress and hung from a long gold chain. One that I swear looked real enough you could have worn it around your neck and bought it from a jewelry store.

"Wow, fancy," Denise said in reference to the black stretch limousine that made me wonder if Mindy's birthday party started here.

"I honestly was just expecting a fancy cab."

At this Denise laughed before telling me, "Well, these friends of yours must have high paying jobs if they can afford to send a car like that."

I frowned at this and told her, "I don't think so. I mean, they work in accounting I think."

"Well, whatever the case, enjoy the luxury while you can, that's what I say. Oh, and enjoy the night, obviously." I smiled at this before lifting up the bottle that now had a bow around the neck, telling her,

"Thanks again for the wine," I said because I had nothing else that I could give Mindy for her birthday, seeing as it was so last-minute notice.

Denise waved off my thanks and ushered me out the door quickly as if she was afraid the driver would get fed up with waiting and zoom off. But then the driver got out of the car and came and opened the door for me, surprising me with the level of service. I had never had any door opened for me, let alone been in such a luxury car before.

"Oh, thank you… but you didn't need to do that, it's only me," I replied, looking up at the handsome black man that had perfect skin and long lengths of even more perfect dreadlocks. They were half tied back from his face into a knot, granting me an unobstructed view of the high cheek bones and a chiseled jawline speckled with dark, day-old stubble. But it was the smile in his light-blue eyes that danced with mirth as he told me,

"We wouldn't have it any other way, miss."

I felt as if there were some hidden meaning behind this. Like a joke I hadn't yet been privy to.

"And who is we?" I asked after getting in the car and glancing around at all the empty seats, because it was just me.

Luxury wasn't a strong enough word for the inside of this car. I had never seen so much hand stitched leather in all my life. Of course, I aimed this question at my driver, once he had situated himself behind the wheel and started the engine.

"Just the collective we," he replied cryptically. However, before I could say anything more, he told me,

"I am Kenzo by the way."

"It's nice to meet you, Kenzo, I'm Grace." He smirked at me in the mirror and told me,

"Yeah, I know, babe."

I blushed at this because the look he gave me would have had the power to disarm any woman with a healthy pulse. Damn, he was gorgeous! Plus, having him call me babe just wasn't fair and if I hadn't still been obsessing over my thief then I would have needed to have start fanning myself!

"So, you work with Mindy's brother?" I asked, trying to make conversation and, for a second, he frowned as if I had caught him off guard. Something I thought was strange until he replied,

"Sure do, but I just started a few days ago, so I haven't met this Mindy yet." Well, that will explain having to take a second to think because he, no doubt, hadn't heard her name said all that much.

"Will we be picking up the others on the way?" Again, my question seemed to catch him out in some way. But this time he simply replied with a clipped,

"No."

I would have pressed for more, like why would they send this statement ride just for me, one that was clearly big enough for at least eight people. But then before I got a chance to ask, his phone started ringing and despite the laws, he answered it without hesitation.

"I sure do, Boss," he replied without so much of a hello, or hey. No, it was like the person on the other end started the phone call with a question.

"Five minutes out," Kenzo said with a glance to me before adding something in a foreign language, something I didn't understand.

"Gergin." (Means, 'Nervous' in Turkish.)

After this he responded to another unheard question, telling whoever it was,

"No, I don't think so." Then after a short, "Understood." He hung up the phone and silence fell between us, making me start to fidget nervously. Something he seemed to notice.

"Relax and help yourself to a drink," he said, making me look to the champagne on ice that had already been popped.

"Oh."

"I took the liberty of opening it for you, just in case."

My eyes widened in surprise before I told him,

"That was very kind of you, but I feel with only me in the car that the whole bottle is going to go to waste... unless, of course, you have another pick up after me?" At this he smirked again, and I swear it made his eyes seem as if they actually glowed.

"Nope, I only had one important pick up tonight and I was told to treat you well, so please, help yourself and don't worry about the waste," he said with a genuine looking smile.

It eased my worries enough to do as he suggested and I poured myself a glass. Then I lifted it up to him in the mirror before saying,

"Cheers."

He nodded in acknowledgement as I took my first sip,

unable to help but moan a little as the delicious taste first bubbled across my tongue.

"Good?"

I smirked back and nodded before telling him, "Oh yeah, the best I have ever tasted." And, well, granted, my experience with champagne was limited but he didn't need to know that.

"Good to know," he replied, making me question why this was good to know as it wasn't like I would be making many more trips in such luxury again. It was bad enough that I already felt like some imposter, just in this short limo ride. Like I was just pretending I was used to such lavish attention, something that wasn't helped when pulling up to what was very obviously an exclusive nightclub. One that had a sleek black carpet with a swirl of gold letters that spelled out the name of the club:

'Gold 4'

This matched the poles of polished gold that were linked with the twisted black rope Kenzo had pulled up in front of. As if I was some celebrity about to get out the car. Of course, my eyes automatically homed in on the mile-long queue, one that spanned the full length of the street until it disappeared around the corner.

"Oh my God, I can't do this… I can't do this…" I muttered to myself as I started to panic, seeing as we had pulled right up to a place that was clearly for the mega rich.

"I think there must be…" I never got to finish this as my driver got out of the car and started making his way around to my side.

"...A mistake!" I practically squeaked the end of this sentence the second Kenzo opened my door, forcing him to bend to look at me now with a questioning frown.

He then released a heavy sigh before pulling his phone from inside his jacket pocket. I frowned in question and tried to ignore all the stares and whispers coming from the audience of people queueing. I debated whether or not I would get arrested for suddenly scrambling through the small dividing window and making a quick getaway. But I also didn't think it was wise to add grand theft auto to my growing list of felonies, despite this one being on the slightly lower end of the crime scale compared to murder.

So instead, I simply tried to shrink down into my seat, wondering if I could slip out of the other side and call a cab before the driver noticed. Besides, it looked like he was busy on the phone, once more talking in a foreign language.

"Erm, I think I will just..." I was about to tell him that I would make my own way home, when he took matters into his own hands and told me,

"One moment, Grace."

Then he shut the door and I swallowed hard when I heard the distinct sound of...

The doors locking.

CHAPTER 21
THE MASK OF NERVOUSNESS

Okay, so if the crowd had freaked me out before, now I had a whole new reason to panic. What the hell was going on?! In fact, after waiting a full minute, I knocked on the window. However, my only response in return was when Kenzo held up a finger to tell me to wait. Which meant that panic turned to being pissed off in a heartbeat. But then before I could start ranting and making a scene, he suddenly opened the door.

"Sorry about that, Grace, but I wanted to ensure your friends were here so as you weren't walking inside alone," he said, blowing the wind completely from my angry sails because, seconds later, and there they were, now approaching the car giggling like teenagers at prom. Naturally, I instinctively relaxed while still trying to calm my pounding heart when I was helped from the car by the handsome driver. One, that admittedly looked to work out enough that he should have been on the security team for the club because he was as big as the two doormen keeping people back and firmly in line.

Of course, the crowd of people were still staring at me like I was the imposter I felt I was most days. Because well, that was exactly what I was, wasn't it? Most of my life, I had felt like I had been in hiding but this was different. This was the kind of terror that didn't just rip you away from the life you were desperately trying to cling onto. But the kind that then threw you in a jail cell to rot for the rest of your days, making it a different type of fear you lived with. The type that had you waking in the night whenever you heard a sound and believing the cops were at your door. The one that had you flinching whenever you heard a siren. Christ, a cop had come in for coffee the other day and I swear I had nearly passed out from anxiety.

"Grace!" Mindy said, coming to hug me like we had been lifelong friends since kindergarten. She was wearing a skimpy, strappy black dress that had panels of see-through material in geometric patterns that managed to hide any rude bits. As for her hair, this was worn down and was a mass of spiralled red curls around her face that bounced as she walked on her gold platform shoes.

As for Brit, she was wearing a strapless, empire-waist dress that had a gold belt of sequins under her breasts and a skirt of sheer material over satin. One part flared out around her legs and finished just above the knees. Her hair had been swept back at one side, held there by a gold feather clip that matched her belt and strappy gold shoes.

Both girls looked me up and down and gasped.

"Oh my God, that dress is to die for!" Mindy exclaimed, finishing her statement by clapping her hands and Brit nodded before telling me,

"You look stunning!"

I blushed a deeper shade than the blusher Denise had used before telling them, "Thank you, you both look beautiful too and as for the dress, well, it's gorgeous. Your sister is so talented, please tell her I say thank you." This made Mindy react strangely at first, and she showed a moment of surprise before shaking it off, something she did after first looking to Kenzo who was still behind me.

"Oh, you might not have met Kenzo yet but he works with your brother, I believe," I said, moving aside and letting Kenzo say hello.

"Oh, yeah, I erm… I think I heard him mention you, my brother that is," Mindy said in a slight strained voice.

"You're welcome, Mindy," he said and, again, I couldn't help but feel as if something was off. It was all very stilted, and I was sure I was missing something, although what, I didn't know.

"Oh, my bag and…"

"No worries, Grace, I have it right here," Kenzo said, making me smile up at him.

"Thank you. Oh, but I brought you a bottle of wine for your birthday Mindy and…"

"Aww that's so sweet of you!" She shouted, pulling me to her and giving me a hug, taking me off guard.

"May I suggest leaving it in the car, so as she may pick it up later," Kenzo said, coming to stand next to me, and it was done in a strange way as he placed a hand on Mindy's arm, as if alerting her to the fact she was still hugging me. Meaning she quickly stepped back, shot a nervous glance to Kenzo, and said,

"Yeah, that's… that's a good idea."

I had to say, the whole exchange was an odd one, but I tried to shrug it off as being none of my business.

"I believe they are waiting for you," Kenzo said, nodding to the entrance and to the doormen there.

"Okay great, thanks again for driving me here," I said, causing him to beam down at me and send me another dazzling smile that would make any girl fall madly in love with him. Or should I say, girls that weren't already infatuated with someone else's smile, that was.

"You're most welcome, Grace," he replied with a smirk before nodding again to the club and telling me,

"Now go and have fun."

I grinned in response before turning around to face the large, black glass doors that showed nothing of the inside.

"Eeek, I am so excited!" Mindy said before linking arms with me and Brit, walking us down the black carpet.

"Hello, we are on the guest list," Mindy stated, and naturally I was shocked to hear this, now eyeing the long line of people warily and flinching when I saw the looks of jealously being aimed our way.

I hated standing out.

"Of course, ladies, please wait inside and someone will hand you your masks. Just tell the host your name."

Mindy and Brit nodded their thanks to the smartly dressed doorman, however, I was left wondering why he hadn't even asked for our names before letting us in. Was it because I had arrived in a limo? Did he mistakenly believe I was someone important?

He opened the door for us, and we walked into a tall, circular lobby that was all black, thanks to the long lengths of material that shimmered under the oversized, hanging glass lanterns above.

A blonde woman in a stylish black pencil dress stood waiting for us behind a polished black marble plinth. One that held what I guessed was a list of names in the little black guest book. She was also wearing a black masquerade mask that was feminine in its shape and curved around half of her face perfectly.

"Good evening, ladies, can I have your first names please?" she said politely, looking at us one by one as we each gave our name. However, when I told her mine, she grinned down at the book before informing me,

"Ah, congratulations, as our 40th guest on the list you have won our exclusive package for you and your friends. Wear this and drinks will be on the house and get you into the VIP area."

The girls squealed with excitement, whereas I just looked to the woman with wide eyes. She turned to face the wall and moved some of the fabric aside to reveal a recess. She then grabbed two black masks in the same style she wore and handed both to Mindy and Brit. Then she turned again, only this time she pulled out a dark wooden box engraved with gold edges.

She then placed this down on the top of the plinth before opening it up and producing a gorgeous gold mask from inside the satin cushion. It was stunning and looked to be made from real gold filigree that was overlaid swirls on top of stiff black velvet. If anything, it seemed to match my dress perfectly, as if each had been made with the other in mind. Of course, I knew it was pure coincidence but, still, it was shocking enough to cause me to hesitate.

"I... don't erm... I can't take..." I started to say, knowing that accepting it would mean standing out even more because, so far, it seemed like everyone was wearing mostly black.

Everyone...

But me.

"Of course she will," Mindy said, taking the mask from her and passing it to me, giving me no choice but to hold it for fear of dropping it. I looked down at it in awe, seeing it now in more detail and realizing instantly that it was definitely more extravagantly made than the other plastic ones.

However, my indecision was taken out of my hands once more as I felt Mindy's arm being linked with mine for the second time.

"Have fun, ladies," the hostess said just as she pressed a button and the material ahead of us was being lifted to reveal a set of curved double doors. I felt like I was about to walk out onto a stage and it had to be said that the place wasn't lacking in its theatrics.

Meaning I was soon being walked inside with Mindy and Brit either side of me, as if even *they* expected me to run a mile and try to escape this night. But even as I looked back over my shoulder to the closing doors, I got a glimpse of the hostess on the phone looking directly at me.

A shiver rolled over me and I suddenly had the very distinct impression that her phone call had been about...

Me.

CHAPTER 22
GOLDEN CAGE

I couldn't help but gasp the second I stepped inside the club. I'd never seen anything like it before. It was incredible and reminded me a little like stepping inside some modern-day palace. The circular room was huge and rose four stories up, with different balconies framing the whole way to the glass-domed roof above. The center of which hung the biggest glass chandelier I had ever seen.

It was made up of what looked like hundreds upon hundreds of black tear-shaped glass lights that extended down the center like an upside-down Christmas tree. It must have been at least fifteen feet long, but from down here it was hard to tell exactly because its length could have easily exceeded that.

I suppose, only those on the upper levels would have been able to tell as the balconies surrounded it. However, I could only see people looking down over to the first two floors as the other two upper levels looked completely empty. Perhaps they were reserved for private parties or something. No doubt only the elite and mega rich could afford to be up there. I wouldn't have been surprised as the rest of the place looked made with millionaires in mind.

What with its plush black velvet booths that framed the circular room and its gold and black checker tiled dance floor that was directly under the grand chandelier. Off to one side was the fancy glass bar that was also etched in gold, with the club's logo sparkling across the front.

Even fancier gold champagne flutes were lined up and being handed out to guests by smartly dressed waiting staff wearing all black suits. However, each were wearing their own masks that were bone white with gold swirls at the cheeks. This, no doubt, was a way to differentiate between the guests and staff because every single person in the club wore a mask. As for the staff members, they also had on gold gloves that matched the theme perfectly.

On the other side of the black marble bar top was an ice sculpture of the club's logo, and surrounding it were black shot glasses being filled by some type of black and gold bottle.

"Their new vodka, said to have actual gold flecks in it," Brit informed me as she started to fit her own mask, tying the ribbon around the back of her head. I looked to Mindy when she started to add to this, only to find she was also doing the same.

"Yes, tonight it the launch of it, it's how we got on the guest list." At this Brit shot her a dirty look, making me about to ask more when, suddenly, we were being ushered over to the bar by one of the staff who looked ready to hand us our free drinks.

"Quick, put on your mask so we can get into the VIP area," Mindy said, making me look down at the half golden face of what could have easily been mistaken for some goddess. I found myself running my fingertip around the elaborate curls of gold filigree with its cushioned black velvet behind, making me wonder if this had been added to make it more comfortable to wear.

Well, there was only one way to find out and, at the very least, no one would ever recognize me behind this thing. Not that I knew anyone in this city. Although after what happened a week ago, I could only hope that was still true and my rich thief had moved on already.

Now if I could just get my heart to follow in that same logic, I would finally be able to move on with my life.

So, with this thought, I followed suit and put on the mask just as everyone else had in the club. As for the men's design, this was simply a male version of the woman's, being that it was slightly bigger to fit better and therefore held more of a masculine appearance.

One look at the new vodka brand and I knew why the theme had been chosen for the launch party because I could see the same twin masked faces of both female and male on the fancy vodka label. Both of which were entwined with a golden ribbon that then spelt out the name,

'Stolen Gold'

The words beneath the masks matched the rest of the launch party branding as there were golden ribbons attached to all the glasses, three of which we took with thanks from the waiting staff. But I couldn't help but be a little taken back by all the men in masks. It sent my mind to only one place…

The past.

Or should I say, back to only one man, because shamefully I still held onto a fragment of that night, being foolish enough to bring it with me when I ran from San Francisco. It was a mask I had stolen from the scene of the crime and still had tucked away, hidden under my bed. It was the last piece of him that I had, and originally the only proof I had left that none of that night had been a dream.

Of course, now it wasn't the only piece because I couldn't help but reach up and rub the few stitches left in my arm. Most had thankfully dissolved by now, leaving an angry red line of freshly healing flesh. One I had covered up tonight with a few skin-colored band aids.

"Let's go check out the VIP," Mindy suggested, and I froze at this, knowing it was bad enough being down here. But then as I looked up at the black marble staircase that wound around the edge of the room, and one that was guarded by two more big security guards, I couldn't help but gulp. Intimidated wasn't a strong enough word.

"Maybe we should stay down here for a bit, you know, get the vibe of the place," I proposed, but even before I had finished speaking, I knew I was dragging out this losing battle as their faces said it all.

"Nonsense, the vibe up there will be even better... come on, ladies, let's go party, VIP style," Mindy argued with a giggle, and this time they both linked arms with me, so there was no escape on both sides.

Which meant I had no choice but to down my drink just as they did, hoping the liquid courage would help. Then after we left our empty glasses on a nearby table, I readjusted the chain of my bag more firmly over my shoulder, before I let them walk me to the intimidating staircase. And with each step I took, I did so at the same time praying that the security guards there would turn us away.

However, they took one look at my mask and unclipped the rope that hung across the first step before we even needed to say a thing. Again, the girls thought this was brilliant and giggled even more as we made our way up the staircase.

We then reached the first level and the luxury continued with slightly more gold on show than the ground level. Something that made me wonder if, at the very top, the floor was just completely covered in gold. Like some dragon's horde stashed away in a mountain.

However, I didn't know if I was surprised or not to find that it had been done so tastefully, it was almost surprising because it wasn't gaudy in any way. Simple touches of gold, like on the seating that instead of all black like downstairs, here they were upholstered in a richer material, one with contrasting thick and thin lines of gold. This matched the tables which were gold leaf painted tops with black marble bases. The walls also held fancy artwork that was not exactly my style, as these were just interlocking geometrical shapes.

But what I did find surprising was that I was still the only one up here who wore a gold mask. I would have thought most people up here would have been gifted one too. Although I then started to remember the hostess saying something about being the 40th person to arrive, which must have meant they had a competition of sorts. Of course, this also meant that all heads turned and looked at me just as they had done downstairs. I was just glad that no one could see my blush or the shame in my eyes. Although it didn't manage to get rid of my awkwardness entirely, which was why I suddenly blurted out,

"Bathroom!"

"Oh… erm, okay I guess we could…" Brit started to say when I cut her off.

"Oh no, that's okay, you guys go to the bar, I'm sure I will find my way," I said, nodding to the smaller version of the bar that was downstairs. I could also tell the girls were happy about this because, clearly, they didn't want to miss a second of this night. As for me, I would have rather had my freak out/mini melt down alone, so this worked for me also.

So, I walked away and started looking for the ladies, when I first felt as if I was being watched. I frowned and turned, catching a very tall man turn away from me but, I swear, for one second, it looked as if he was wearing a different type of mask. Perhaps he too, like me, had won his mask by being the right number to walk in here.

Perhaps they picked one male and one female?

I didn't know, but either way I spent the next few minutes trying to shake the feeling that I was still being watched regardless. And to the point that the moment I made it to the fancy toilets, the first thing I did was to stand over the sinks, grip the sides of the gold basin, and told myself,

"Stop, Evie, stop being paranoid. No one knows you here." Then I swallowed hard and looked up, finding the face of a golden goddess staring back at me. Which was when I started to relax at the sight. Because no one would ever recognize me. No one would ever know who it was that was really behind this mask, so why couldn't I have one night? Just one night to enjoy myself and let my hair down.

"You can do this, girl, that's what Arthur would tell you."

So that was exactly what I did. I walked back out of there, pulling the pin from the twist in my hair and releasing the curled locks so they cascaded down my back. Then I walked with confidence. Meaning that, this time, when all the masked faces turned my way, I embraced it just as the band started playing some confidence boosting number. It felt like fate. Especially when I strutted across the club floor with my head held high, flicking my hair back with a barely contained grin on my painted red lips.

"Whoa, look at you, sexy Chica," Mindy said whistling.

"Yeah, so glad you decided to let your hair down, looks so pretty with your dress." I smiled at that and instead of shying away from the compliment, I let it empower me.

"Thanks, ladies… now who is up for giving this vodka a try? After all, it would be rude not to," I said with a grin, making the girls look to each other as if to ask silently who this new girl was and where had the shy unsure one gone.

"Hell yeah, let's do it!" Mindy said, making Brit agree with a nod.

"Yeah, and then after, we can make our way through the cocktail list because, look, the new vodka features in every one," Brit said, showing me the sleek black and gold menu where one name stood out above the rest;

'The Gold Goddess'

"Sounds like a good plan," I agreed and now… *I just hoped I was right.*

· · ·

About two hours later, I wished that plan had been a good idea. But with only a few cocktails left on the list, I was starting to wish my tolerance to alcoholic had improved with age. Unfortunately, after too many shots of vodka to remember a number, and chasing them down with the 'far too easy to drink' cocktails, my inhibitions were far too low not to resist when Mindy suggested the dancefloor below.

When my bladder started to cry out, I told them I would meet them there, deciding my newfound confidence would only get me so far. Because no amount of hair flicking or sexy strut walking could mask pissing yourself on the dancefloor. But then, as I made my way back to the bathrooms, I got that same feeling of being watched again. But this time, when I looked over my shoulder, I ended up bumping straight into someone.

"Oh, I am so sorry," I exclaimed, holding my hands out to save myself and finding them clutching onto a pair of hard biceps that were barely kept restrained under the confines of a designer suit.

Of course, when the owner of what admittedly felt like impressive muscles had a pair of hands that were currently gripping to the sides of my waist... well, *I couldn't help but feel the flutter in my belly.* One that worked its way up my throat before getting stuck there like a restrained sexual sigh.

But this feeling didn't come with a face, because the masked man just looked like all the others and, suddenly, I found myself hating the secretive theme of the night. This despite praising it only hours ago. But as for now, well the depths of his eyes were intensified by the black paint around his eyes, creating a darker picture. In fact, it suddenly became far too close to home, and that home being the secret crevices of my mind where I had tried to contain my thief to.

"I am not," the man said and his voice was so deep, so seductive, it made me shiver. In fact, I felt as if my imagination was playing tricks on me, or more like six cocktails and a copious amount of vodka was.

"Please excuse me," I said before pulling myself from his hold and, for a single, terrifying moment, I thought that he wouldn't let me go as his fingers pressed harder into my flesh, like he hadn't *wanted* to let me go. Christ, some insane part of me even wished that he hadn't.

Fuck, what was wrong with me?!

When he actually did let me go I quickly rushed to the toilet and, this time, used the facilities instead of just using the mirror to give myself a little pep talk. And after wrestling with the heavy weight of my long dress, I flushed the toilet and left the cubical to check my makeup. I lifted my mask and checked that I didn't look like a gold painted raccoon under there, despite knowing it didn't really matter if I did. Because I didn't intend to take off this mask again until it was time to leave.

But as for my lips, well these were on show, so I opened my bag and grabbed the lipstick Denise had leant me. Then I reapplied the red stain that was impressive enough that it hadn't transferred to any of the glasses I had drank from. Long lasting was right and I wondered if it meant that I would have red lips for a week after tonight. I grinned to myself as I twisted my hair back up from my neck, knowing it would undoubtably get hot while on the dancefloor. I also dipped my head under the chain of my handbag so it remained at my side without constantly slipping off my shoulder.

But then as I did this, I also couldn't help but think back to the man I had bumped into. It had been the first time I had found someone else attractive since my Thief. One that I knew came with a name but a name I refused to use in my mind all the same. Because doing so made him more real somehow and killed the fantasy, leaving me with only the terrifying side of him I knew was very, very real. And as for now, well, after my encounter with whoever that man was back there, I was no longer feeling quite so confident. I don't know why but it was as if the single touch was all it had taken to completely disarm me.

Perhaps I should find the girls and tell them that I wasn't feeling well and needed some air. Instead I could just call a cab and explain to them once I was home, not giving them the opportunity to convince me to stay.

"Yeah, I should do that," I told myself, before facing the door and briefly wondering why I hadn't encountered anyone else both times I had been in here? But then this question quickly left me, as the moment I stepped back out into the VIP, I did so only to find a mask on the floor as if waiting for me.

Had someone dropped it?

I quickly looked around as if searching for a face, but then the second I saw the same man I had bumped into walking away from me, I knew it had been done deliberately. Because now I could see that he no longer wore his mask. However, with his back to me, I still couldn't see all of his face, making me quickly start to follow him, after first picking his mask up. I don't know what compelled me to do this, but I found my feet moving regardless. I swear, at one point I saw him even look back ever so slightly, just enough for me to see the slight hint of a smirk. But then the crowd soon blocked anything from view, and I was forced to try and crane my neck to keep watching him.

It felt almost as if he were playing a game with me and, suddenly, I felt a bit like Sarah did in the labyrinth when the Goblin King was toying with her. I couldn't explain this need I had to find him, even as he started to disappear fully. The music drowned out the sound of my frustration as I looked down at yet another mask in my hand, wondering if this meant I would soon need to class it as a collection.

By now I bet the girls were wondering where I was so, in the end, I found myself with no other choice but to give up my search and instead I started to make my way down to the dancefloor, mask in hand. But why I still had hold of the mask, I had no idea.

Well, that wasn't strictly true. I knew that if I did manage to see him again, then I would, at the very least, have an excuse to speak with him. But even with the thought of this, I couldn't help but feel something for my Thief. As if my loyalties should have been with him and him alone. As if I was doing something wrong by being attracted to another man. Which made me shake my head a little because it was ridiculous. A completely irrational feeling to have considering what had happened at the hospital.

He was a dangerous man, Evie.

I needed to remember that.

Then why was his mask yet another I refused to let go of and still kept under my bed like some dirty little secret I would sometimes clutch onto at night? Again, I tried to shake the reality of these shameful thoughts out of my head as I tried to make my way through the dancefloor. One that was now packed full of people, all with their own piece of the floor claimed and, therefore, with very little room for me.

Which meant that I was, once again, craning my neck to try and see if I could spot my new friends, searching through the forest of bodies. However, what I saw was the very last thing I ever expected to see, making me quickly gasp,

"Impossible." This was just as the music started to change to a slower tempo, as if all dancers had sent out a collective thought to the DJ. A slow and sexual beat brought couples together like someone had just flipped a switch named Lust.

And as for me, I was left standing there in the middle of it all, staring at the unbelievable sight slowly coming into view. Because there was my masked stranger looking straight at me. However, he wasn't looking for what he had lost, but now he was staring at me like I was someone he very much… *wanted to find*.

He made his way through the crowd in such a way, it was as if he owned everything and everyone in the room. Cutting the distance between us with such ease, it made my attempts and struggles at getting through them earlier, now almost laughable.

But none of this was what I really focused on. No, it was all centered on the new mask he now wore. The near mirror image of the one I had picked up that night. The one I still couldn't let go of, despite trying. It was near identical, if not for the crude gold brush strokes over the horns and three lines of spikes at the forehead. Those Demonic features that startled the breath from my lips as more details came into view the closer he got to reaching me.

However, unlike the mask I had stolen and had spent far too many hours studying with my fingertips, this one had a big difference. Because it wasn't a full mask that covered all of his face. No, this time it left the lower part of his face on show as it finished with sharp lines down the sides of his cheeks. Which meant that I could see the knowing smirk at his lips, one that was as handsome as it was alarming.

I swallowed hard as the DJ's light cast a white beam along the floor and up the figure of the man that was a powerful sight to behold. Light flashed against the gold on his face, casting those Demonic lines aglow and painting a frightening picture I wanted to run from. But with the strength of that dominance cast over the room, one that at the moment, was very much aimed solely at me, then I felt my whole body become a prisoner to my fear.

I wanted to flee. I knew that I should, while there was still space between us, but I was frozen to the spot. I was like a small creature caught in the lure of the hunter, far too terrified to move. Which meant that the moment he jerked his head to someone behind me, I was released from the spell long enough to look. Which was when I realized that any attempt at escaping would have been pointless. Because this had been a signal to security that I hadn't noticed, and each of them guarded a section of the dance floor.

He had been prepared for me to run.

I swallowed hard and it was a sound that was quickly chased by another. Because the moment I turned back to look at him, he was suddenly right in front of me making me gasp. I instinctively took a step back but little good it did me, because he took a much larger step into me. This time hooking me around the waist and doing so much more firmly than when in the VIP. Then with his other hand, he let it stroke down my arm before finding my fingers that were clutching his other mask in what was most likely considered as a death grip.

He managed to pry my hand open with startling ease and, clearly, I was no match for his strength.

"You won't be needing that now. Not now I finally have you..." He paused long enough to lean down and whisper the rest of his sentence in my ear, making me shiver when he said...

"...In my golden cage."

CHAPTER 23
AS THE WORLD FALLS DOWN

"Ah ah... easy now," he cooed down at me the second I tried to fight myself free of him, something he countered by pulling me even more firmly against him. He also did this in a way that made it look like we were about to start dancing.

"How... how are you here...?" I stammered like this was impossible.

"Isn't it obvious?" he asked, nodding to the side where I could now see the girls watching us and waving at me like this was some big surprise. And well, they weren't wrong. Especially not when I felt my masked thief lean down closer, so his lips were once again at my ear.

"You should really be careful who you trust in future, Little Bird."

I shivered against him, feeling that warning making its way down my body. But then he was right.

I kept making the wrong choices.

"It was all a lie," I muttered to myself in a pained way, knowing this had been his plan all along. Of course it was.

As they both worked for him and, somehow, he had found out that I had delivered sandwiches to them. That they had been friendly to me. Friendly enough that perhaps I wouldn't question why they would ask me to join them for a night out.

But it hadn't been real.

I had been so foolish.

"No, the only lie was the one you told yourself when you believed you could run from me," he told me firmly, making me start trying to struggle to free myself again. But it was useless. He only held me tighter and tried to soothe away my need to escape.

"Easy, Little One… Now relax and dance with me," he suggested and, again, the sound that escaped me was neither classed as a word of protest nor was it a sound of acceptance. But clearly, he didn't need either one, because he turned me in his arms so I was back to facing him. This meant that my panicked gaze went by unnoticed as, clearly, my friends totally missed the obvious 'help me please' look I had been giving them.

Although, in truth, I had no one else to blame but myself because I certainly knew the risks coming out with them. They worked in his building for Christ's sake, how could I not have feared this would happen?!

Of course, if I had even entertained the idea of him being here tonight then I would have run a mile. But if I had, then standing here now, dancing with him, was the very last thing I thought would have happened. Here in the middle of the dancefloor, where people were clearly giving us a lot more space than they had when it had been just me.

Then again, I think we both knew I was clearly in shock, because I had stopped struggling against him and instead let him take me through the motions of the dance. It was a gentle sway before he turned me around in a spin, yet all the while making sure to keep a strong hold of me, telling me without words that I was going nowhere.

"Do you like my mask, little Evie?" he asked, making sure to not only remind me that he knew my real name, but that he actually knew my nickname as well. One I had never given him.

"I wore it for you," he told me and, again, the only thing I could think to ask was a whispered,

"Why?"

"I wanted us to match," he told me, and a moment after was when he spun me again, giving me the time to look at all those that surrounded us seeing that he was right. We were the only two people in the room with gold on our masks other than the waiting staff. This then prompted me to ask a very stupid question.

"Do you know the owner?" At this he laughed, and I didn't have long to guess why when he told me what now seemed obvious.

"I am the owner."

I swallowed hard and muttered to myself in what I knew was a foolish and hopeless tone,

"I didn't have a chance, did I?"

However, it was only when the song was coming to an end that he slowed us to a stop before tilting my head back so he could look down into my eyes. Then when he knew that he had my full attention locked to his own intense gaze, he told me what I already knew.

"No... *no you didn't, little Siren.*"

I frowned at the name he gave me, wondering what he meant by it.

"I don't understand why... why do all of this?" I asked, ignoring the name Siren for questions that were far more important.

"Your answers will come soon but not now," he told me firmly, making me frown in annoyance.

"But why? I want to..." The moment I said this and started to make my own demands, his dominant look was enough to get me to stop speaking. Because I didn't know which side of him I found more intimidating, the one I was looking at now or the one I knew lay behind the mask.

"Now come, I think you could do with a drink."

I frowned at this, but it was lost on him, and it had nothing to do with the mask I wore. But then when he took my hand in his, I started to pull back against him. Something that, in return, made him tug at my hand, and it was hard enough that it sent me tipping on my heels and I fell into him. This was so he could then growl down at me,

"If you wish to make a scene, then you merely have to say so and I will make one you will not forget, nor will anyone else, for that matter."

I shuddered at the clear threat and decided it was most definitely best for me to do as he said... *for now.*

After all, I had no idea what this man was capable of other than pulling off the perfect heist and getting away with it. Besides, he also knew that he had a murderer on his hands, so the cards he had to play were far higher than what I held. No, he had an ace up his sleeve, whereas I felt like all I had left was the Joker.

So, I had no choice but to let him pull me from the

dancefloor, with the space we left behind being swallowed up by oblivious bodies taking our place. But then my eyes lost focus of them and instead took note of the men in suits that fell into line behind us as if this whole thing had been choreographed. The dangerous dance known as securing the asset. Stealing away the witness and kidnapping the fugitive. And with a line of guards now behind us, I felt like I had lost, whereas he had won the game only one of us ever wanted to play. The one that meant that my life had been thrown into chaos the very second I first laid eyes on him.

And to think of all the treacherous dreams I'd had about this man. The man behind the mask, who was nothing but a thief in the night getting ready to steal just another thing. Because I was a nothing. A nobody that would be missed by the grand old number of one.

Arthur.

The one man on this earth that truly knew me. Christ in Heaven, how I would miss him. The thought made me nearly shatter as a sob desperately wanted to break free. To the point that my steps faltered, and my captor noticed.

"Not far, Little Dove, be brave for me a little longer now," he told me, and I shook my head a little as if trying to understand him. Be brave for what? For him to get me alone so he could kill me? So he was free to put a gun to my head and pull the trigger?

I just didn't know. *But one thing I did know, and that was that I was utterly terrified.*

However, as he led me firmly up the stairs, I noticed that we continued past the VIP level and headed straight for the next floor. I wondered what would have happened had I just stopped and started screaming? What could he do about it?

But more importantly, what would *they* do about it? All these people who were rich enough to be allowed up to the next level. One that was now filled with even more wealth than the one Mindy, Brit, and I had been in.

And I had been right, because even more gold was on display here. Gold that played an even bigger part and, therefore, drawing the lines between the rich and the richer. However just when I thought he would drag me to some private room or something, he shocked me. Because he did as he said he would, now leading me over to a bar that was basically a replica of the one below. A bar that cleared pretty damn quickly. Especially when the guards fanned out and started ushering the richly dressed elite back.

"That's better, a little privacy is what we need," he said before spinning me and making me yelp at the sudden movement. Of course, when I was back to facing him, it was the last place I wanted to be, feeling far too vulnerable. Especially when he started walking me backward, with his hand rested at my hip as if to steer me where he wanted me.

But then as my heel slipped again and for fear of falling, I couldn't help my reaction as I suddenly reached out and gripped onto him. Of course, I would have been a fool to miss the growl of approval he granted me after I did this. Or the way he added another hand to my waist to steady me, at the ready to prevent my fall.

"What's happening?" I whispered, feeling lightheaded and knowing it had nothing to do with the drinks. At this he smirked and lowered his head before telling me,

"Well, if I didn't know any better, *I would say that you're falling for me.*" At this obvious flirt, I couldn't help my reaction as my mouth dropped open a little. An action he definitely didn't miss because his eyes fell to my lips before becoming hooded in the darkness of his painted skin around them.

This was when I knew I had to take some power back, even if it was only a slither. So, I quickly let go of him and turned around so I was facing the bar instead of him. Now taking a much needed step out of the danger line of what being in his arms did to me. I also had to ignore the knowing chuckle coming from behind me as he obviously knew the power and effect he had on me.

"Why am I here?" I asked firmly, something that came a lot easier now I was no longer looking at him. Of course, this easy task quickly took a turn for the complicated when I felt him stepping up behind me. A move that meant he was now caging me in, locked to the bar with his hands resting at the marble bar top either side of me. He was huge and towered over me with frightening ease.

"To get a drink of course," he told me before motioning with his hand for the barman to approach.

"And I believe there is one cocktail you are still left to try." At this my eyes widened before I hissed in an accused tone,

"You were watching me?"

"But of course," he replied unashamedly, and again it was an easy admission that made me shiver.

"Golden Goddess," he hummed after dipping his head closer to my ear and, this time, my breath caught.

"Wh-what did you...?"

He interrupted me with an order this time.

"Now drink up, Miss Parker... or is it, Stella?" he said in

a knowing tone and, therefore, snapping me from the spell he cast.

I wanted to shout at him, scream at him and demand why he was doing this. But then, in the end, I seemed to blink twice and seconds later I saw the drink he now referred to sitting in front of me like magic. A fancy martini glass swirled with gold shimmer. In fact, it now looked like a spell I was expected to drink, and everything in my mind screamed at me to turn and run. A feeling he must have recognized with the way my body tensed so close next to his own.

"Easy now, Little Dove, I promise not to hurt you."

"Then why am I here?" I asked again, and the frustration was no doubt easy to hear in my untrusting tone.

"Because you are right where I want you to be, that is why," he told me resolutely, making me gulp.

Then suddenly I was reaching out for the drink just for something wet to help push the lump he had created down my throat. It tasted sweet with an aftertaste of sour bitterness to it that seemed to mimic the theme of the night.

"Good girl," he praised, at the same time his fingers danced down the length of my neck, starting under my chin.

I could then hear his slight chuckle the second he felt the way I finally swallowed a sexual lump known as stupid fucking lust! Christ, why did I feel this way around him? Why couldn't I seem to help myself?

I was about to put my glass down when he covered my hand in his own and brought the glass back to my lips.

"I think you will need it," he warned close to my ear and unless I wanted to wear it, I had no choice but to drink down the rest of it. Especially with the way he tipped up the glass,

forcing it down my throat until I had consumed every last drop. Only then did he allow me to place the glass back to the bar. I then noticed the barman hold up five fingers to the dominating Thief at my back, making me turn to look at him in time to see him nod the once in acknowledgement.

Then without another word, he took my hand in his once more and started to lead me away.

"Where are we going now?" I asked, feeling as if my world had become a whirlwind with only us at its center.

"Somewhere more private," he answered, and the moment he started toward the next staircase, I began to pull back once more. However, this time I was able to snatch my hand from his... *something he didn't look too pleased about.* Not with the way he narrowed his gaze down at my hand, as if annoyed it was no longer in his grasp.

"I don't want to go anywhere private," I told him, hoping it came out more forceful than it sounded. His gentle sigh told me that it hadn't but, at the very least, he was no longer looking angry.

"And I don't think this is the type of conversation you want to have in front of others," he countered, making me frown back up at him. Damn him for being so tall!

"And what type of conversation is that?" I braved to ask, now folding my arms and standing my ground.

"I believe we both have our secrets, Evelyn, but there is only one of us who can control what happens to them once they are spoken, so by all means, take that chance... although I must warn you, there are always a few high-ranking officials in law enforcement that make the guest list."

I swallowed hard at this, and his sharp gaze told me he

didn't miss it. Because he knew the threat would work and, to prove it, he stepped closer. After tucking a lock of hair behind my ear, told me,

"Better the devil you know, sweetheart."

Then he retook possession of my hand and, this time, he did it knowing that when he started to lead me from the floor once more that he would do so without finding resistance. Because he had me between a rock and jail cell. Which was why the moment we made it to the third floor and I saw that it was empty, I pulled my hand from his and demanded,

"Why are you doing this to me?!" At this he took pause and closed his eyes in what looked like frustration.

"You may not understand this yet, but everything I do is for your benefit. Mainly, it is for your protection."

I started shaking my head and told him, "I don't need your protection."

At this he raised a brow, and before crossing his arms over his chest, he asked me in a condescending tone,

"Is that so?"

"I have done well enough on my own so far," I argued, stomping away from him and making my way to the bar, one that this time, wasn't occupied by anyone. Not even a barman, which was why I reached over the top and grabbed a glass and the first bottle I could find. A bottle which just so happened to be the celebrated vodka this whole event was for.

Of course, he followed me just as I was downing a much needed shot, making me hiss at the burn. He then poured himself one into the same glass I had used before telling me,

"What you think you know and what you do know, are

two very different things, Miss Parker." Then he necked the shot and, unlike me, it didn't look like it affected him at all.

"Then explain it to me, because from where I am standing, it seems like all my troubles started ever since I met you," I snapped, making him narrow his gaze at me and I was surprised I didn't back down from such a dark look. I could even see the tense set of his jawline as if he was gritting his teeth to stop himself from lashing out verbally.

"I suppose to you it would look that way," he said regretfully.

"It would look that way to anyone with half a brain cell!" I shouted and, again, the tick in his jaw jumped making me focus on it, deciding now that I should be wary. Which was why I lowered my eyes, and reminded him softly,

"I saved your life."

At this he reached out and ran the backs of his fingers over where I had taken the bullet, one that no doubt had his name written all over it. I tried not to flinch at this but then what he told me next had my eyes flashing open with defiance.

"No, Little Bird, you didn't."

I frowned so hard at this, it felt as if my brows would snap off like some pissed off Mrs. potato head!

"Are you fucking serious right now? I jumped in front of that damn... ah!" I ended this little rant when he suddenly pushed me back against the bar and covered my mouth with his hand, his eyes glowing in an impossible change of color for merely a spilt second. It was enough to get me to comply pretty quickly and I held my breath as if waiting for him to strike. And strike he did, just not in the way I would have thought, because he growled down at me,

"That bullet had never been intended for me." At this my eyes widened in shock, but just as I started to fight against him, his other hand shackled the back of my neck, gripping it more forcefully as his palm remained tight against my mouth. His body pressed harder into mine and I felt caged like the bird he kept calling me. I could feel it closing in around me, and instead of just his fingers creating a living cage over me, it was his entire body.

"So now you see why you cannot continue to be left to your own devices, little Siren." I tried to shake my head, murmuring my arguments into his palm and making his lips quirk up in amusement. But then something strange started to happen as my vision grew fuzzy and it became hard to focus.

"Not long now," he muttered to himself, but even this told me that he knew something I didn't. I also felt as if the fight was being forced out of me as my limbs grew unexplainably heavy. As if someone was dragging me down by them... *dragging me under.*

But the important question now was... *to where?*

"Easy now, just let it happen," he said softly, and instead of holding me prisoner against him, he eased his hold on me. It became one of aiding rather than disarming. His hand left my mouth and instead stroked up my cheek before smoothing back my hair from my face. Then the hold on my neck slipped lower so he could take more of my weight. This just as I started to slump back against the bar I had moments ago been pinned to.

"What... what did you... you do to me?" I pushed out, just as my lips began to feel funny. I tried lifting my hand up

to break his hold on me, but it was useless. It simply brushed against his arm with the strength of a kitten.

"What I had to do, I am afraid," he told me with little to no remorse.

"What... what's happening... to me?" I asked, feeling each word as if dragged from me, despite my mind going back to that drink and finding my answer...

He had drugged me.

However, this wasn't the answer he gave me. No, instead he wrapped both arms around me just before my legs were about to give out. Then he looked down at me and with a deadly, handsome grin, he told me,

"I'm afraid that this time..." His pause ended over my lips as he whispered the rest,

"...You're definitely falling for me."

CHAPTER 24
TAKING NO CHANCES
RYKER

I released a sigh the moment my girl passed out in my arms, just like I had intended for her to do. However, what I hadn't intended on was drugs being the cause, nor had I intended to admit so soon what I had only recently discovered. As the last thing I had wanted to do was frighten her. But it seemed as if she had the uncanny ability to push my buttons like no one ever before. Hence why this night had not exactly gone how I initially had planned for it to go.

No, in fact I had been planning on wooing her, despite how juvenile such word was to my own mind. Especially considering I had never had to 'woo' anything or anyone before in my entire existence. But that was all before my Siren and, well, I was willing to try anything. Just like approaching her and asking her to dance, keeping up the illusion it wasn't me until I was forced to reveal my true self.

I had even come close to achieving it as she seemed enamored by me at first. But then when I heard Van in my mind, asking to speak with me urgently, I had no choice but to let her go to the place she intended. At the very least knowing I had my men stationed everywhere just in case she thought to run again.

Of course, it was hard to keep my mind on anything else after I was gifted the first sight of her beauty. By the Gods, she was magnificent. In fact, I was not ashamed to say that she had taken my breath away. The way that dress clung to every exquisite line and curve of her body, it had me itching to hold her. To run my hands down her sides and grip her hips before pulling her more firmly to my body. One that ached to be naked against her, *to be inside her.* But I knew the moment I saw the dress I had to see her wearing it. So, I had purchased it with her in mind and had it adjusted for her body so as it fit her as well as it did, for she a fucking feast for my greedy eyes.

As for her beautiful face, I was half cursing the theme of the night as I didn't want even an inch of her being hidden from me. Although the use of the golden mask did mean it was easy to find her. Despite also knowing that she stood out well enough on her own among the crowd and without the need for so much gold covering her face.

She was the most beautiful creature in the room and the hungry eyes of men knew it. In fact, it had taken all of Vander's persuasive skills to keep me from wanting to commit mass murder. Every eye that followed her, I wanted to tear out and step on.

The girl was mine!

Thankfully, the conversation between my second hadn't taken long. However, through conducting his own investigation he had discovered some alarming news. As the bullet hadn't been intended for me after all.

It had been intended for her.

Needless to say, after this, all my plans of wooing her had gone out the fucking window. I decided now was the time that she knew of the wolf's lair she had willingly stepped into. And, in short, a little bit of theatrics on my part certainly did the trick. In truth, I wanted to see what she would do and, well, she hadn't disappointed me. Because I knew as much as she wanted to deny it and most likely would, she felt the pull between us just like I did. The only difference was that she was fighting against it, whereas I had long ago willingly embraced it.

The quick decision to drug her had been the part I had battled with my own guilt, as I knew it was hardly the best way to gain her eventual trust. But then I also knew my options were limited. Because calling a Demon a Demon, I intended to kidnap her and knew the way of achieving that without causing the most amount of stress on her part was to put her to sleep.

My golden goddess.

Gods but she was utter perfection and the moment I first laid eyes on her, there was nothing in this world, or the one I was born from, that I wanted more. I couldn't keep my damn eyes off her!

Even now, deep in her forced slumber, I found my gaze focusing on the gentle slope of her neck meeting slender shoulders that were bare. Then my lingering gaze landed on her arm and took note of the band aids she had used to hide what would no doubt turn into an eternal reminder of that day. Of course, I had also been furious to know that she had endangered her life to save mine, but her bravery couldn't be denied. The scarred proof that she had risked her life to 'save me' and the proudest moment of my life so far.

Something she now knew had been a miscalculation on her side. For that bullet hadn't been for me after all. Yet despite her not knowing this at the time, the outcome had remained the same as her actions had unknowingly saved her own life. For the wide spread of bullets had meant for at least one of them to hit her. Something that would have no doubt happened had she not made the rash decision and jumped for me, believing my life in danger.

Which was why I had to act now and steal her away from the danger still lurking around the corner. In fact, the only reason I believed another attempt hadn't been made was because my own security detail had been seen keeping her safe from afar. Too risky considering I was having her every move monitored and recorded, meaning there would have been footage there to catch them in the act.

Vander believed this meant two things; one, that they were the acts of humans and two, they most likely believed my men to be undercover cops watching her. This made sense, as I doubted they could see any other reasoning for it and, well, Demonic overlord turned stalker would have been the very last reason in their minds. Hell's gates, but even rich billionaire stalker was a stretch.

Now, how I was to explain all of this to my little Siren was an answer that still alluded me. But then she was now safely in my care, and that was all that mattered. So, I walked from the third floor with her in my arms and, for the first time in weeks, my Demon calmed. Now if I just had a way to shackle her to me permanently that didn't constitute as being barbaric, then I would find this peaceful state something to look forward, instead of the fleeting moment I feared it to be.

Because I couldn't foresee an easy time ahead, not after experiencing the bite of her tongue and knowing that she would be no push over. I couldn't help but smile at this, as it would be challenge accepted and one I was eager to win. In truth, I had been glad to see her standing up against me, it wasn't something that happened often, if ever. No, only those closest to me in my council dared try and, even then, they knew my limits.

My little bird did not.

But she would learn them soon enough.

And I couldn't fucking wait!

"Ah, so your golden goddess turned into Sleeping Beauty quick enough." I growled at Van the moment he said it and would have had his throat in my hand had I not been carrying my girl. Of course, my reaction couldn't be ignored as he held up his hands and said in his defense,

"Easy, Ryk, the girl is yours and speaking of her obvious beauty doesn't change that."

I rumbled at this, with my Demon's heckles rising. I also knew that if he had been free to make his presence known, the spikes on my skin would have rattled before filling with poison.

"Yes, well, until I have claimed such beauty, I suggest you refrain from speaking of it so freely or you may not find me so forgiving next time," I warned, making him reply with a sure,

"Duly noted."

"Now, have my orders been carried out?" I demanded as I walked toward the private apartment on the top floor reserved for when I was in the city. I preferred to own the places I stayed in, or it made my Demon feel uneasy. Think of a fabled dragon curled upon its horde of gold and treasures. That was how my Demon felt about the things we owned.

Although as I looked down upon the face of pure beauty, then I had to admit that our priorities on what we classed as treasure were quickly blurring the lines of importance.

Would I really be prepared to light a match to it all and watch it burn just to have her? To watch everything I had built and all the riches I had accumulated over the centuries, as they crumbled to black dust and fell through my fingers like soft sand?

Yes.

Yes, I would.

Because there was no other treasure greater or more important to me. Now I just had to get her to a point where she felt the same for me. Of course, how I was to do that, I didn't know. Not when I knew I could have laid all of my riches at her feet, and she wouldn't have cared for any of it.

Oh, the irony of it.

The famed Prince of Greed fated to someone who cared little for money or personal possessions. For she had run from everything. Granted, it hadn't been much in the first place. But still, it had been *her something.*

The anger I had felt seeing that shit hole apartment she had called home, had me want to wrap her up in the most luxurious things life had to offer. It made me fantasize about making love to her on a bed of gold, about wrapping her body in golden silk and fucking her senseless. Tying her up in the softest rope and forcing her to accept my gifts, promising her release only when she did. Covering her naked body in glittering jewels and the biggest, clearest diamonds. Decorating her from head to toe in the rarest of gemstones that were the very best that filled my crofters.

Better yet…

I would fuck her in my hidden vault.

This Greedy Demon's Horde.

Something I had never shared with another living soul. Yes, she would be the first but before I was granted the opportunity to do so, I needed to plan.

"Your council awaits, as per your orders," Van told me after entering my apartment.

"And the plane?"

"It will be fueled and ready to leave when you are… *for a second time I might add,"* he added, making me grant him with another scathing look, and one that told him I would make him pay for it soon enough in the training room. Because yes, once before we had tried to execute this same plan back in the hospital. But unlike then, I now knew more about her or, should I say, her uncanny and continuous ability to evade me.

Vander continued to follow me as I carried her into my room, a place where the black and gold theme continued in my private space, only done in a more masculine way. Hints of gold were everywhere but it was done so as not to be seen as overpowering or garish. It was all sleek black lines of polished dark wood, or marble with black glass reflecting the room back in on itself. But despite liking this room, I couldn't help myself when hesitating as I lay her down on the black silk sheets, knowing that a beauty like hers needed color in her life. She was too vibrant a person to wake in this dark, colorless room with only the hints of the gold I liked so much.

However, seeing as I had very little choice here, especially given that the rest of the rooms in my home followed the same theme, I lowered her down. Then I removed her mask and placed it down next to her, before running the backs of my fingers across the freckles I knew lay hidden there under her make up.

I remembered our first meeting and asking why she would hide such beauty. I almost laughed at the memory of her asking me if I was flirting with her. I also recall thinking that I had never had so much fun before, feeling foolish now for not recognizing what was happening between us, who she was to me, the pull at the center of my very being.

It was a Siren's call tugging at the soul of her Enforcer.

I released a deep sigh before reaching up and removing my own mask so as I could lay it down next to hers. I hoped when she awoke that she would not miss the symbolic gesture, for now it was time we both showed ourselves for who we were.

There would be no more masks worn between us.

No more hiding.

So, wanting to get this meeting over with, I kissed her forehead before standing straight and facing my second.

"How long did the doctor say the drug would work for?" I asked, already being assured it would not harm her long term.

"At least an hour, two at most," Van replied, making me sigh as I looked back down at her.

"Good, then be sure the meeting does not extend thirty minutes as I want to be here when she wakes."

"Better you than me," he commented, making me raise

my brow. "Oh, come on, she is going to tear you a new one and you know it!"

I grumbled at that, knowing he was right and there was no point arguing against it.

"Then we better get this meeting over with so as I have time to think of the right thing to say."

"The right thing to say... to what, her kidnapping?"

I growled this time, "Not helpful, Van."

"Okay, so you want my help?"

I nodded, making him smirk before answering, "Make sure to lock the damn door or Girl Scout there may end up getting creative again."

"She is four flights up and the windows don't open, what is she going to do exactly?"

His answer to this was to grant me only a look.

As for me...

I locked the damn door.

CHAPTER 25
THE MASKS ARE OFF
EVIE

You know when you have one of those moments when you know you're asleep, yet you continue to dream the same thing, over and over again? Well, that was me right now, only instead of it being of my thief... a man who I usually prayed before bed every night that I would dream of... it was actually a moment from my past.

I was out in the woods as a kid, Arthur had turned his back for a second and not knowing much about the outdoors back then, I had grabbed a handful of berries and started eating them. It had also been in the early days of us living together and a time where I was still clinging on to when I had been living on the streets. Therefore, if I saw food, I usually ate it. This deep-rooted need to survive had stayed with me and impacted me enough to believe that, at any moment, I would find myself back out there again. As if I needed that fat on my bones ready for the day.

Arthur had also found me hording food under my bed, with other things I must have thought I would need. Like my favorite book. A blanket. My warmest socks. All of it in a bag under my bed as though I was at the ready to run the second that a knock came at the door with someone asking my name.

Of course, when Arthur found it, he had said nothing. Not a single thing. He just let me keep it there until, one day, two years later, he came home and found the bag empty and hung up near the front door. It had been the sign he had been waiting for, the one that said that I finally felt safe. It was an unsaid word about the comfort he gave me. Which was why I had gone to bed that night wearing those socks, with the blanket on the bottom of my bed and that book sitting on my nightstand.

But as for those berries. I hadn't yet known the vast and extensive knowledge of the outdoors that I learned as the years went by. All the stuff that Arthur had taught me. I hadn't known those berries were poisonous. The small purple berries had been too much of a temptation to resist and, after swallowing the blue nightshade, Arthur was quick to act. He had promptly stuck his fingers down my throat and forced me to be sick before making me drink copious amounts of water down and forcing me to be sick again. Then he had finally forced me to drink so much I felt my belly would burst. He had flushed the poison out of my system. Although I had still felt the effects of the poison for three days after.

But why was I focusing on that now?

Why was I replaying that moment in my life over and over again on an incessant loop? But then suddenly, instead of Arthur's hand cupping that metal camping cup, it was now a fancy cocktail glass and long gone were the pair of weathered hands I knew well. No, they were the large hands of a man that looked more fit to wield a sword in battle than the wrinkled and worn hands used to chop firewood or fix generator engines.

That's when that clear water transformed into a swirling gold elixir and, I swear, if I had seen my own reflection, it would have been with wide eyes mesmerized at the shimmering twister in my glass.

My Golden Goddess.

This was when my eyes suddenly flashed open and I forced my body to move, falling from the bed. I willed my blurred vision to focus long enough to make out some of the features of the room, despite it spinning. But I tried to focus on a door that I was hoping belonged to a bathroom. My body barely felt like my own and now I knew why.

I had been drugged.

So, with that poisonous memory clear in my mind, I continued to find the strength and determination in me so I could drag myself across the room. It felt a lot like being shit-faced drunk. You were somewhat there, like a small piece of you left in the back of your mind telling you what needed to be done. The need to make it home. The need to make it to your bed. To make sure you were safe before passing out. You willed your mind to focus as much as possible and that was precisely what I did now.

Thankfully, the lights must have been on some sort of sensor, because they came on in the bathroom the moment I finally managed to get the door open after I had missed a few times, reaching for the gold door handle and, in the end, gripping it long enough to push it open. Then I dragged my barely cooperative body through the doorway and over to the toilet. After this came the not so joyous task of sticking my fingers down my throat and bringing up the contents of all I had drunk the last few hours.

Of course, I had no idea how long I had been unconscious. I barely remembered what happened after I had consumed that drink. No, I just knew the cause or should I say...

Who was to blame.

I would have gritted my teeth at the thought had that not defeated the current object. So, I tried to bring everything up, doing so until nothing was left. Then I lifted myself enough so I could drink down some tap water, taking great mouthfuls with my hands. After this, I purposely threw it all up again, only to drink and repeat until I was assured it would be safe to keep down the water this time.

I then drank until my belly begged me to stop, knowing I needed it to do the same as with the berries... *to try and flush the drugs from my system.*

After which I then slumped down on the floor, knowing this wouldn't work instantly. Which was why the next time I opened my eyes, I was once again faced with having no clue just how much time had passed. I only knew that my head started to feel clearer, and enough that I was finally able to get to my feet. However, I still needed to hold on to the door frame because I nearly stumbled back into the bedroom. That's when I noticed that I still had my small handbag clinging to my side with the gold chain still across my body. In fact, with so much gold on the dress, I wasn't surprised that Ryker had missed it. Especially considering it matched the dress perfectly and kind of camouflaged in with the rest of the sequined fabric.

"Great, one problem solved," I groaned quietly in case someone was outside the door.

I was just glad I wasn't contending with the darkness because my handsome, asshole kidnapper had obviously left the lights on. Which meant that after first taking in aspects of the room, which didn't surprise me with the continued black and gold theme, I acted. Meaning I got down on my hands and knees and looked under the door to see if I could see feet. But after having no joy in this, I decided to try the handle.

Once it was obvious it was locked and I didn't hear any voices from the other side asking me what I was doing, I gathered they hadn't need anyone to keep an eye on me.

More fool them.

Because another crazy life lesson Arthur had taught me…

How to pick locks.

I quickly scanned the room before realizing I had everything I would need on me, so I quickly pulled the pin from my hair. I then straightened out the thin metal and got to work. Thankfully, I could see that it was a lock that had a twisting mechanism. Meaning that all I needed to do was insert the end of my hairpin and sweep it around in a twisting motion until it caught on something. Then I applied a bit of pressure and voila, the lock clicked. I then tried the door and let out a big sigh of relief.

However, I knew that unlocking the door was only the first part of my escape plan, because this wouldn't be the only obstacle standing in my way of freedom. I knew that seconds after I fled from this room I would in all likelihood be recognized. So, I made a quick mad dash to the walk-in closet and after scanning the shelves, I grabbed what I knew would no doubt look ridiculous on me.

I grabbed his clothes.

The first thing I did was strip out of my gorgeous dress, one I now knew he had most likely bought for me. Especially considering he had clearly orchestrated this whole thing. But despite how angry and hurt I was for being fooled this way, I still couldn't find it in me to just leave the dress discarded on the floor. After all, it may not have been Mindy's sister who had made it, but that didn't mean that whoever had, hadn't put a lot of work, love, and effort into it.

So, with this in mind I lay it gently on the bed, only now taking notice of the two masks that had been placed there. This had been done in such a way, it was almost like he had been trying to make a statement. Some symbolic gesture to remind me of the lies we both wore like armor. Because, clearly, there was more to Ryker Wyeth than just being a successful thief. And obviously, he already knew that I was no Grace Stella.

Which meant that now, *the masks were off.*

It was time to run again.

So, with this in mind I put on was one of his black shirts, having no choice but to knot it at my belly because it currently looked like a dress on me. After this I grabbed a pair of dress slacks and groaned when I saw the length of them.

"Christ, why did this guy have to be so big?!" I rolled them over and over at the waist but, in the end, was forced to run into the bathroom and search the draws for a pair of scissors. But of course, the ones I found were the smallest ones in fucking existence and therefore would have taken me a small age to hack them to size.

"Okay, think, think!" In the end the idea came to me as I ran back into his closet and grabbed a pair of dress shoes. I then yanked out the laces and used these to make a hem, tying the folded length up my leg and securing them there. I also made sure my own shoes were mostly covered so as not to draw attention.

Then I used one of his silk ties as a belt so the trousers wouldn't keep falling down. After this, I tucked the sleeves of his shirt back in on themselves and grabbed a black suit vest from a rack of many. I knew that this was the only thing I could use to hide a multitude of sins with this makeshift outfit of mine, so I put it on and used one of his leather belts as a way to loop it at the waist and pull it in tight. Then I emptied the cash from my bag, took my fake ID and my apartment keys so anyone finding the bag would assume that was where I was going.

Because, really, who left home without the means to get back inside the place you lived? After that I tossed it on top of the dress and pocketed the things I had taken.

After this came the even trickier part. I had already spotted the black shoe polish in one of the draws, as well as my gold mask on the bed.

It was time to get creative.

Which meant that, minutes later, I walked out of the room looking like what I could only hope was one of the waiting staff I had seen downstairs. Okay, so the mask was now all black unlike the ones they wore but, at the very least, it was no longer gold and standing out like a beacon of lies.

Thankfully, as soon as I made it out of what was

obviously Ryker's apartment, the lights were a lot lower out here and matched the club vibe on the ground floor. And a good job too, because the second I heard a shout at me from behind, I knew running was out of the question. Because that would raise an alarm quicker than anything else. No, the only shot I had at this was to wing it.

"Hey! Stop right there!" I froze in place and turned around at the same time, telling him,

"Oh please, my boss is going to kill me! I was brought in by Ricky's boss who assured Daniella that I could do this job. But then I got lost and now I am going to let Ricky down and I owe him so big after helping me out with my rent." I yammered on and on, hoping the bombardment of words would help with him wanting to just get rid of me.

"Okay, okay, just calm down, lady," the security man said who was dressed like all the others. One who thankfully didn't pay too much attention to how I was dressed.

"I didn't mean to come up here, it's just that they mentioned something about the Vodka and I thought the spare bottles might be up here, but now I am thinking they meant a left on the main floor and…" I started ranting again and could see his features lose all suspicion.

"Look no one has to know, just go back down the stairs and make sure not to come this way again. There is a storeroom through the door behind the main bar and next to the back exit, you will most likely find the crates of Vodka there," he told me, obviously feeling sorry for me now in my panicked state.

"Oh, thank you, thank you!" I said, gushing over the fact that he had just helped me out in more ways than one. Because now I knew where the back exit was.

"Yeah, yeah, go on, getting going before they realize you are missing," he said, waving me on and making me try not to look too obvious as his choice of words sent a panicked jolt into my heart. He had been closer to the mark than he obviously realized.

I nodded my thanks again and rushed down the stairs, glad that Ryker had cleared this space when bringing me up here. I also managed to slip past the guards unnoticed because they just assumed, like the other guy did, that I was part of the hired help.

But then, it made sense because I was no longer the girl in the golden dress. Which also meant that being dressed like this, I also had no problem getting to the back of the bar area. Because I wasn't stopped or even looked at when I came across the heavenly glowing green sign illuminated over the back door.

The one that said exit.

And the one that led straight to the street.

But more importantly, led straight to…

My freedom.

CHAPTER 26
THE PAIN IN PLANNING

Okay, so getting out of the club was only the second part of the plan, and now it was time to put stage three into action. Because, of course, I had anticipated that the worst might happen. Therefore, I had planned my next getaway the day after I was shot and escaped from the hospital. But then I also knew that despite my succuss at running, it was only a matter of time before I was caught again. And well, the next time my thief managed to find me, then I doubted I would be held in a comfy bedroom with a basic lock to pick.

No, at this rate he would be putting me in a barred cell with twenty-four guard rotation. Although, to be honest, I still had no idea what he really wanted with me. Of course, he had hinted at telling the cops, getting me to comply with going with him without making a fuss when mentioning who could be within hearing distance. But then once we were alone, he hadn't mentioned anything that had happened, nor had he made any demands of me.

So, what was his end game exactly?

I had no fucking clue.

I just knew he was dangerous, both in the very physical sense and mentally, because I swear, every time I was close to him I just couldn't be trusted. I had never wanted someone to kiss me so much in my entire life. Just being near to him had me practically melting against him, instead of my instincts taking over. And all of this while knowing that he had been ready to kidnap me!

But then I wasn't stupid because I knew there must have been something I had that he wanted. Now all I had to do was figure it out. Obviously, he could have just killed me if he was that concerned that I would go to the cops and tell them what I knew about the robbery. Because if he wanted me dead, then he could have done it numerous times already because, clearly, he knew where I lived.

Which meant I couldn't go back there. The pain this caused pinched at my chest knowing I wouldn't get a chance to say goodbye to my friend. Wouldn't get a chance to thank Denise or tell her how grateful I had been for her friendship, no matter how brief.

It truly saddened me to leave.

To be honest, Denise had been my first real friend in what felt like forever and I hated that she would be left worrying, not knowing what had happened to me. I should have written her a letter or something that she could have found in the apartment she let me live in. I guess I could buy a burner phone as soon as I was able, that way, at least I could thank her and let her know not to worry. I knew it was the not knowing that was the worst part.

As for Arthur, I had sent him blank postcards a few times now knowing he would know who it was from without needing to write a thing. Just so as he knew I was still alive and even though I was clearly on the run, I was doing everything he had taught me to do in order to stay alive.

Speaking of which, I ripped off the mask, dropped it to the floor and started walking down the street until it was safe for me to hail a cab. Thankfully, I had the money from my purse and a pair of keys in my pocket I would never get to use again. But Ryker didn't know that. Which was why I needed him to waste his time looking there. I was just hoping that he left Denise out of it because I didn't want to bring trouble to her door, despite it already being too late for that.

I could only hope that if he did go there, then he would realize she didn't have anything to do with this and hadn't helped me escape in any way. That she didn't know a thing. Yet despite knowing in my gut that he was dangerous, I just couldn't imagine him being the type to hurt innocent people.

He wouldn't.

"Yeah, like you know the psycho who is hunting you that well, Evie," I muttered to myself before feeling safe enough to hail a cab. Thankfully, the club life was still very much in full swing. Meaning it wasn't late enough for them to be coming out in the masses and all swarming the streets looking for a way to get home. So it wasn't long before I found an empty cab and was on my way to the next part of my plan.

"King Street station, please," I said when the cabbie asked me where I wanted to go. I then let my head fall back to the headrest and couldn't help but wonder what Ryker's reaction would be when he found me gone. Would he try and find me again? Fuck, why my treacherous heart wanted him to, I didn't know! It was stupid… so stupid, in fact, I started signaling in sign language with my hands just so I was free to speak to myself and not have the driver think I was a crazy lady. Although the bald man did glance nervously in the mirror, catching me do this.

Oh well, if he thought I was crazy, then clearly he wasn't wrong. Not when I was still thinking about Ryker. Questions like, had he walked back into that bedroom by now? Or had he hoped that the drugs he gave me would have worked for longer.

Damn it, I was so angry that he did that, that he violated me in that way! I couldn't help my reaction this time as I punched my hand down on the seat, purposely ignoring the strange looks from the driver when I did.

Tears stung at my eyes as my situation started to sink in once more. I didn't want to be on the run again. I didn't want to have to worry about money. To worry when my next job opportunity would be or how long it would take. I didn't want a life on the streets just to survive this mess. But then something he had said to me suddenly came back to me, and it was such a powerful memory, that I gasped aloud.

He had told me about that bullet.

The one not intended for him at all.

But one that had been aimed at me.

I couldn't help but frown, now questioning the truth of this. Because he could have just been lying. Just another way to try and manipulate me into believing what he wanted me to believe. But like I said, without knowing what his end game was, then I was at a loss to know why he did anything at this point.

There were just too many questions and with no way of

getting the answers, I was left with nothing else to do but slip into survival mode. Questioning his motives could come later and, no doubt, would. As for now, well I had limited time here. A small window of opportunity to escape.

So, the second the cab stopped outside of the large brick building with its large clock tower, I paid him in cash. Relieved at the very least that the station wasn't too far away from the club. Then I walked inside, wishing it was bursting with people, so I didn't feel quite so exposed.

But unfortunately, at this time of night, it was mainly people heading home early after calling it a night. It also wasn't helped that parts of the station were closed off for renovations. Naturally, it being as empty as it was, only managed to put me even further on edge.

Yet despite my concerns, I still had an escape to accomplish, so I made my way over to the bathrooms knowing I couldn't stand being dressed like this for much longer. Because now in the bright lights of the station, I knew how ridiculous I looked. Plus, I stood out more wearing this man's suit than if I had been wearing a glittering golden dress. So, I decided to take everything off other than his shirt, one I shamelessly couldn't help but lift to my face and inhale, hoping to get even the tiniest hint of his amazing scent.

Of course, he hadn't worn it, so I wasn't in much luck. However, there was the hint of something, and it was enough to tell me it was his. Another thing I didn't want to be parted from was my mask I'd had no choice but to leave behind. Well, at least I still had a piece of him left.

"Argh!" Why would I want a piece of him, I had no clue!

It was maddening. I wish I understood it. I mean, we had shared only one kiss for, God sake!

I shook these thoughts from my mind and got back to the task at hand. So, I rid myself of the trousers and the waistcoat, unknotting the shirt and smoothing out the creases. Then I used the belt I had stolen to tighten the shirt, so it looked more like a dress. Of course, I still had to roll up the sleeves, but it didn't look quite as ridiculous as it had before. Thankfully it wouldn't have to be for long because I came to this station for a reason... my planned get-away was on.

All I needed to do was grab a ticket and then get to my bag that was stashed in the locker I had paid for. I had a jacket in my bag and a few other pieces of clothes that I had stashed away in there. Along with almost all the money I had earned, a new ID, and other bits I might need, like food and basic toiletries.

Then I would be on my way.

I walked out of the bathroom and toward the ticketing booth, looking up at the board and seeing for myself which train was due to leave the soonest. Because despite having no idea where I was going, I knew it wasn't safe for me to hang around here for too long. Ryker might think to look here, so the sooner I was gone, the better.

After buying my ticket to Eugene, I walked to the lockers that thankfully weren't that far from where I would need to go to catch my train. I headed to the section that said baggage above the opening, then to the wall of lockers I knew would be there, thankful this wasn't one of the areas that were closed off to the public. Not like the main part of the building, where they were clearly doing something to the tall ceilings.

Whatever it was behind those boarded sections, I knew it would be grand, that was if the white marble pillars were any indication. Finding the right locker, I opened it and grabbed my bag and my jacket stuffed in there.

However, the moment I slammed the door shut, I let out a cry of shock as the man leaning up against the other side of it was waiting for me. A man I recognized as being one of Ryker's men. The handsome devil called Van from the robbery. He was also the one that had been with Ryker in my hospital room right after I had bumped into him just before the shooting. His was a voice I also recognized the moment he said,

"Hello again, Girl Scout."

I sucked in a quick breath before turning suddenly and trying to run out of the baggage room. But then I was brought up short because just before I got there, an even more dangerous sight stepped out from behind the wall. One that now blocked my escape.

But more importantly, it was a threat that was now striding toward me with clear intent and a single purpose. And with that burning look in his eyes and a name I hadn't heard before, one now spoken from his friend, well I had to say that in this very moment, it suited him.

For the look he gave me now, held every ounce of...

Greed.

CHAPTER 27
OWNED HEARTS AND STOLEN KISSES

The second I saw him stalking toward me, I dropped my bag and jerked out of my frozen state of shock enough to turn and run. However, the problem with this was that I didn't have anywhere to run to. Not only that, but Ryker's blonde lacky, Van, was still standing there looking smug, with his arms folded and the side of his body still casually leaning against the lockers.

I was trapped.

"You wouldn't get far, Girl Scout," Van said with a cocky wink. However, it was the reply to this I was more concerned with because it was one that came directly behind me.

"No, *she wouldn't*," Ryker said, making me whip my head back to the real threat that had now reached me.

I couldn't help my eyes from scanning the full length of him, despite him now being only an arm's length away from me. He no longer wore his midnight black suit he had been wearing at the club and, of course, he was now minus the mask. Yet the dark gray jeans, heavy duty boots, black shirt, and long black overcoat with its raised lapel collar, didn't make him any less intimidating. He simply looked as formidable as he always did. The only difference now was that I could see his painfully handsome face in the well-lit station.

However, I hadn't been the only one to take this time to assess what the other one was wearing. I knew this when he told me,

"Well, it has to be said, you are most certainly resourceful, sweetheart," he commented, cocking his head to the side a little as he stroked my body with his heated gaze. One that took in every inch of me and not missing the fact that I was wearing his shirt, his belt, and nothing else but the shoes he had bought for me.

"I... I... I am sorry I stole from you," I stammered out, making him smirk before asking,

"Are you now?" I nodded, swallowed hard, and answered,

"Yes."

Again, he grinned, almost as if he enjoyed my nervousness.

"Don't be, for it looks far better on you... I am just sorry that the occasion to see you wearing it came off the back of you running from me... *again.*" He added this last part with a low growl that, admittedly, scared me. It wasn't exactly a sound I was used to hearing from people. Yet despite this fear, I still told him,

"I am not sorry I ran."

"We all make mistakes, but I must say yours are adding up." His hard tone said it all because, clearly, he wasn't happy and nor would he be, all things considering. The lengths he had gone to were obvious when orchestrating this plan.

"I..." I started to speak but was quickly cut off.

"*You* are making quite a habit of running," he said, emphasizing the word 'you' and taking a step closer to me when he did so.

I, in turn, took one back, knowing I would run out of them pretty quickly with Van still standing behind me, watching this exchange play out.

"What did you expect I would do? You drugged me and kidnapped me," I threw back, and it looked as if it took everything in him not to just grab me so he could rattle me to death.

"Yes, I did," he said unapologetically, making me scowl back at him.

"But then I thought I had explained the reasons for such well enough," he added, and I had to scoff at that.

"Well excuse me if I am not ready to trust the man that is clearly hunting me!" I snapped angrily.

"And have I hurt you?" he asked with confidence, seeing as he already knew the answer.

"Well, forcing myself to throw up all the drugs in my system wasn't exactly fun for me," I told him and, this time, that usual tick in his perfect jawline jumped because, clearly, he wasn't happy with this answer.

"That was your choice, for mine was to have you sleeping peacefully until they wore off naturally." I gritted my teeth at that.

"And then what exactly? What were your plans for me, if not to kill the only witness to your crime?"

At this he actually laughed but more so in a bitter,

mocking tone. This before throwing the same accusation my way.,

"And what of your own crimes, Evelyn? Did you really expect you could just keep running from them for the rest of your life?" I couldn't help but jerk back a little at that, because he honestly didn't know how spot on he was. Nor did he know the depth of the nerve he just hit.

"I have been running for my entire life," I snapped as tears threated to rise.

"Ah yes, so you have." This made me angry enough to lash out,

"You know nothing of my life!"

At this his features finally softened and I hated the pity I saw there. But then he stepped up to me and I couldn't help but flinch as he cupped my cheek, telling me,

"I know a lot more than you think I do... after all, I visited your cabin." At this I cried out,

"NO!"

After which I tried to fight my way free, having him quickly take me in his arms and hold me to him.

"Calm down, Evie," he commanded softly.

"No! Arthur... what... what did you do to him!? I swear, if you hurt him, I will kill you!" I screamed, making him hold me tighter before growling down at me,

"I would never hurt those dear to you! Now calm the fuck down!"

At this I was suddenly pushed against the lockers, making them rattle against my back in the aftermath of him shouting at me. I started shaking my head, trying to calm my pounding heart, because all I did now was worry about the only father I had ever known.

However, it was the assurance that came from behind me that made me want to believe what Ryker said was true.

"It's true, Evelyn, I was there, we only went to talk to Arthur and nothing more," Van said, quick to back up Ryker's claim.

"And how can I believe you?!" I snapped, now fighting harder to free myself and banging my elbow in the process. Something Ryker didn't miss and it obviously prompted him to act.

The way he did this was to collar my throat, pressing my head back against the lockers and holding me there in a gentle, yet firm hold. One that told me that if I continued to fight him, the next time I got hurt would be by my own making.

"I have no reason to lie to you," Ryker said in a much calmer tone.

"Then tell me, why do you keep trying to take me, why can't you just let me go?" I asked, and the pleading in my voice was easy to hear. At this his gaze gentled and he released a heavy sigh before he dipped his head to my ear and told me,

"How could I ever let go of that kiss?" I frowned at this, despite his words having more power over me than I ever wanted to admit.

"I never told anyone about you," I said softly, making him pull back so his dark blue eyes could burn into my own.

"I know," he told me in an affectionate way.

"I never would, you have to believe me," I pleaded, thinking this was the only reason he would hunt me down the way he had done.

"Oh, I believe you, Little Bird," he said, reminding me of

the nickname he had given me that night. Making me now wonder if I would also receive 'little dove' before the night was through.

"Then why... I don't understand... I... I am nothing to you." This turned out to be the wrong thing to say, because suddenly his hand tightened and he growled down at me, making me close to peeing myself at the obvious threat.

"Easy, Ryker, you are scaring her," his friend warned, and it was enough to snap him out of his anger, but not enough to stop him from snarling,

"You are *everything to me*... never say that, ever again... do you understand?" I swallowed hard and nodded with tears in my eyes.

I then watched as he took a calming breath, and then another, before easing his hold on me. It hadn't hurt but it had done enough damage to have me even more terrified of him.

But then he eased back, giving me a little more space so he could now frame my face with both hands, using his thumbs to swipe away the tears that had overflowed.

"Don't be frightened, Little Bird, I am sorry I got angry," he said as if he truly felt guilty about his outburst.

I didn't reply to this because what was there to say to that? I just didn't know. In the end, my silence didn't matter and it turned out that Ryker knew exactly what to say.

"Now this is what is going to happen, sweetheart. You are going to come with us without making a fuss, then once I know you are safe *and secure*, I will explain to you why you have no choice but to stop running." I tensed in his hold, making him coo down at me,

"Ah ah, keep calm now. For I swear to you, I do not

intend to hurt you in any way. My only wish is to keep you safe, for there are men out there who wish to hurt you, do you understand?"

No, I didn't understand and that was the problem!

"But why? I haven't done anything wrong," I argued, making him raise a brow.

"Haven't you?"

My expression said it all and, suddenly, the face of the man I killed flashed in my mind's eye, making me wince. A guilty action he didn't miss.

"You worked for a dangerous man, Evelyn," he told me, and I bit my lip before pointing out the obvious,

"You're also a dangerous man." At this he didn't try and deny it, instead freely agreeing,

"That I am."

"Then why shouldn't I run from you?" I asked him, looking to my only exit behind where he stood.

"Because like I said, I am not a danger to you, nor would I ever be." It was at this point that I decided to be honest, no matter how much I knew I would regret it afterwards.

"That's not true," I told him.

"How so?" he asked, and half of me wished that he hadn't. But then I had started this, and I knew that I needed to be brave enough to finish it. So, I dared to answer, doing so barely above a whisper.

"You're a danger to my heart."

At this he responded by inhaling a quick breath in surprise and before he replied, he jerked his head to the side as if giving Van a silent order. I glanced to the side in time to see his friend passing us, now walking from the baggage area and giving us both the privacy that Ryker felt we needed. Then once we were alone, he turned back to me, giving me his full attention once more. Something that started with him humming my name in a sigh.

"Oh, Evelyn." Then he stepped into me, and this time hooked a finger under my chin, forcing my shamed face to rise to his. Then once I was looking up at him, he ran the backs of his fingers down my cheek and his other hand came to my side, as if at the ready to curl around my back.

This was when he told me,

"Not if you choose to gift it to me freely."

I couldn't help but gasp in response, because this had been the very last thing I expected him to say. In fact, I should have stopped there and left the ball in his court. But regardless of what I knew I should do, or in this case, *what I shouldn't do,* I found myself asking nevertheless.

"And what of yours?"

The question of his heart was one that had me paralyzed and I continued to question myself as to why? Why was I so invested in the answer? But more than that, why did I even ask the damn question to begin with? Nonetheless, I still held my breath despite these internal questions I asked myself. Even more so when he leaned closer as his hand pushed through my hair, over my ear, so he could whisper his response just as he closed the distance between our lips.

"It belonged to you after that very first kiss." It was a declaration made that he sealed with our second.

I swear, the moment his lips connected with my own, my little cry of shock ended up being taken as an invitation for him to deepen the kiss, taking me straight to nirvana. His arm banded around my back like I knew it wanted to and was soon being used as a way to tug me into his towering frame, fitting me tight against him. His head angled down to mine as I, in turn, arched back, open and willing for everything he wished to give me.

His other hand made its way to the side of my head, embedding his fingers in my hair before pushing it back and gripping a fistful of strands at the base of my neck. Something that made me cry out in surprise as the bite of pain managed to heighten my pleasure. It was also giving me the tiny glimpse into what a night with this man would truly be like. Just like the one that always seemed to enjoy dominating me in my dreams. How I had managed to get his character so right, I just didn't know.

But after only our second kiss, well, it was enough to know that I had been spot on. To know that he would strip me bare by ripping my clothes from me. To know that he would dominate my body, using it for his pleasure while simultaneously giving me my own. That he would hold me down and take me for hours any way he wanted to.

But then how could I think this way?! The guy had drugged me, for fuck sake, what type of relationship would that be!? And with this thought, my mind suddenly clicked into gear. Meaning that despite how amazing it felt to be in his arms, or the incredible taste of him, or even the feel of his tongue stroking against mine, I quickly tore myself from the kiss. An action that made him growl his displeasure.

"We can't... shouldn't... I..." I panted out my excuses and, in response, felt his fist curl in his shirt I wore, as if he was seconds away from ripping the stolen item from me.

"That didn't feel like a can't to me, *nor did it feel like a shouldn't,*" he growled but before I had chance to agree or disagree, I wasn't sure which one, we were suddenly thrown into chaos.

Chaos that came in the form of bullets flying.

Bullets that this time…

Were aimed at the both of us.

CHAPTER 28
THE DEVIL... YOU DON'T KNOW

The moment the threat became known, I suddenly found myself once again fearing for Ryker's life because he covered me with his body and became a human shield. I screamed as gunfire erupted around us, ricocheting off the walls and the lockers behind, pinging against metal.

"We need to move!" I shouted above the chaos, but Ryker was too busy shouting orders to his men because, clearly, there was more than just his friend Van. I knew that when I glanced toward the opening, seeing for myself at least five men now all taking positions with their backs to us.

"Find the shooters, they want to injure the girl!"

I frowned at this, considering I was pretty sure they wanted to do a lot more than just injure me, seeing as they were shooting at all of us. But there was one man in particular I was most worried about, and that was the man who would end up sacrificing himself for me, if we didn't find cover.

"You will get hurt!" I shouted at Ryker this time, with

my fists curled at the edges of his open jacket, as if gripping on for dear life. Like, any moment, I expected him to fall to his knees from being shot in the back. At this he finally turned his concerned gaze down at me and actually grinned.

Fucking grinned!

"Are you worried for my life again, Little Dove?"

"Seriously!?" I screeched.

"Answer the question," he demanded, despite the mayhem ensuring in the background.

"Yes! Okay...? Yes! I am worried about you, now please don't get shot!" I shouted, ending this by flinching when a bullet hit something close by. But then he soon left me speechless as he turned and in movements that seemed too fast to track, he suddenly ripped off one of the locker doors and held it up to use as a bigger shield around me. Useful then that the lockers were the type big enough to hold suitcases, as it was like having a small door to shelter behind. At least it was something, although how he had managed to do that was beyond me. He must have been crazy strong.

"Don't fear for me, my men will take out the threat and I will not let anything happen to you," he assured me and after the stunt he just pulled, then I was more inclined to believe him. However, despite this I still told him,

"Don't fear for you? Are you crazy?! You're using yourself as a human shield! You could die!" I shrieked and, again, my panic and fear for his life weirdly made him smile.

"I am not a *human* shield, Evelyn," he said, emphasizing the word human in such a way like it didn't apply to him or something. But of course, that was ridiculous, did this guy think he was fucking invincible or something?! But then the shooting stopped and after a few seconds, his friend Van shouted out,

"The threat has been neutralized."

Of course, it didn't take a genius to know what that meant, and those bloody flash backs came at me with a vengeance. Ryker must have realized this, as I started finding it hard to breathe when I tried so hard to push the haunting memories back down to where they came from.

"Hey, it's okay, baby, you're safe now," he told me gently and when he brought my face up to his, he saw there the haunted look of a girl with too many secrets to count. He narrowed his eyes down at me, as if trying to see them for himself.

"I... I can't..."

At this he pulled me into him, cradling my head to his chest as he hugged me. And I swear, just one breath was all it took to calm my panic and banish away the nightmares that threatened to take me under. Just like they had all those years ago.

From a past that threatened to expose me for the fraud I was.

Because I was so far from innocent.

But perhaps that was why I was so obsessed with the man in front of me. Why I had clung to him more than anyone else ever before. Because I knew he was bad. I knew he was a criminal. That he had broken the law and, therefore, his moral compass was cast in the shadows of gray.

Just like my own were.

But what if I was wrong about him? What if when he found out what I had done, he judged me? Judged me enough to tell someone? What if I was ready to put my trust into the wrong man? He had told me my boss was dangerous but how did he know that? Had he had him under surveillance?

Oh god, what if the heist hadn't been a heist at all? What if it had been some secret op or something? What if they were really undercover cops, and this was all a ruse? What if the guy's shooting were the real bad guys and these guys were just the cops protecting a witness? Or should I say, someone they were hoping to get a confession out of?

"Evelyn?" The way he said my name, it drew me only partially from my inner turmoil. My mind was still running amuck with all the possibilities and reasons not to trust him. He pulled back and took a step away from me so he could see me better.

"Are you wearing a bullet proof vest?" I asked quickly.

"Excuse me?" he asked in a surprised tone.

"Are you wearing a vest, like the ones the cops wear?!" I asked more frantically this time. It was stupid to ask. I knew it was, but I just couldn't seem to stop myself.

"No, why would you ask… wait… what are implying?" he questioned as his frown turned from concerned to accusing in a heartbeat.

"I… I…" I couldn't answer that. No, all I could do was take the first step away from him.

"Evelyn." He said my name in warning this time, as I started to back away further toward the opening.

"How did you know I would be here?" I asked instead, and he crossed his arms over his chest because it was clear he was getting impatient with my interrogation.

"You've been having me watched, haven't you?" I accused further.

"Now is not the time for this," he stated, but I ignored his intimidating stance and his hard tone.

"That's how you knew to come straight here. How you were only minutes behind me. You didn't need to check if I was at my apartment, you just came to the one place where I had my back up plan."

He released a heavy sigh after this and told me,

"I knew about the bag as soon as you left it in the locker."

I swallowed the hard lump in my throat, one that went down like a lead bullet.

"But how... how did you...?" I started to stammer.

"I found you almost instantly after you fled the hospital," he admitted, making me gasp.

"You've had me watched, all this time and then tonight... you planned to kidnap me."

"That hadn't always been the plan, no, but that didn't mean that my time at keeping my distance from you wasn't at its end." I narrowed my gaze at that, trying to come up with any answers that would make sense.

"I don't understand... what were you hoping to achieve? That I would lead you to someone...? To the bad guys?" At this he looked shocked, even going so far as to jerk back a little and I had to give it to him, his acting skills were second to none.

"I don't know what you have in your head but..."

"Were you planning on integrating me? Is that it?" I asked, interrupting him and, again, he showed his shock before his expression turned hard.

"We are not doing this here," he declared before jerking his head and, this time, it was to signal his men closer. I cast fearful eyes their way before reaching down for my bag, getting ready to run. I also wondered why no one in the station seemed to be in a crazed panic when hearing the commotion. Gunshots had gone off and there were dead people on the ground. Where were the police sirens? But why would be on their way, if they were already here?

"Oh God, that's it... I'm right!" I gasped.

"I very much doubt that, considering you have been right about nothing so far," he snapped in a bitter, mocking tone.

"You're cops!" I shouted, making him truly look astounded this time. A look that made me quickly add, "Don't even try and deny it!"

"To deny it would be to even entertain the foolish notion, and I have time for neither. Now, are you going to come with us quietly and be a good girl or do you wish to do this the hard way?"

I swallowed hard and gripped my bag to my chest tighter.

"I'm not going anywhere with you!" I scoffed, making him sigh before letting his folded arms drop to his sides.

"Very well. Little Dove, have it your way." He then motioned with his hand for something to happen. But then as I bolted back toward the main part of the station, I ended up screaming when someone suddenly grabbed me from behind and held a gun to my head.

"Please, I...!"

"Shut the fuck up!" was the only reply to this.

When the man forced me to turn and face Ryker, I suddenly realized that this hadn't been his doing. He hadn't given this order to one of his men. I knew that the second I saw his face. A sight that turned my blood cold.

He was furious.

He looked ready to commit murder.

But most of all... *he looked scared.*

I knew then that the man at my back wasn't one of his. No, it was one of the bad guys. The guys with guns.

"Let. Her. Go." Ryker said in such a dangerous tone, it was no wonder why I felt the gun shake a little.

"We will be taking the girl... our boss wants a little word with the bitch," the guy said as he started to walk backward. I looked to the rest of Ryker's men who also looked concerned... *one in particular.* His friend Van slowly made his way to Ryker's side and said something strange.

"I can't access their minds, Ryk." However, his reply was even weirder, as he told him in return,

"No, nor can I."

"You know what that means," his friend pointed out, and it was something only obvious to Ryker's inner circle, because I had no clue.

"We can't risk it," he agreed, and my panicked eyes became ones of pleading. Something Ryker didn't miss.

"It's alright, Evelyn, remember what I said," he told me, and I frowned at this. But then my mind went back to him telling me he wouldn't let anything hurt me. So, I nodded slightly, telling him I understood.

"Préparez-vous à emménager quand je vous le dis. Ils ne nous verront que lorsqu'il sera trop tard. Je vais sauver la fille, tu lui fais signe de se baisser." (Means, 'Get ready to move in when I say. They won't see us until it's too late. I will save the girl, you signal for her to duck.') Ryker started whispering something to Van in what sounded like French, making me wonder what he was planning.

However, I didn't have long to wait because while the gunman was preoccupied issuing orders to his men, Van shocked me when he started signing to me with his hands. And, well, that was one language I was a pro at.

'Duck when I get to three.'

I nodded and watched his fingers count down by his side. When he got to three, I suddenly dropped my weight and, seconds later, chaos erupted. I held the bag I still had in my hands over my head for a few seconds as fighting broke out and guns were being shot. I felt myself grabbed and I screamed when arms snaked around me. I felt myself behind lifted and, in what seemed like an impossible speed, I was transferred further into the main part of the building and behind a thick marble pillar.

"Stay behind here until I say it's safe. Don't come out again until we have dealt with them all... *don't even look,*" Ryker told me, but because I didn't respond quick enough, he gripped my chin and forced me to look at him.

"I mean it, Little Bird, *Do. Not. Move. From. This. Spot.*" He stated this order firmly, like he was laying down a sacred law or something. I nodded this time and told him a quiet,

"Okay." Then unbelievably he kissed me quick, before stepping out into the fray and making me wish I had told him to be careful. That I had begged him to stay with me behind the safety of this pillar.

However, the second I saw more of the bad guys rushing in, I knew the odds weren't looking good. Especially considering Ryker's men didn't seem to have guns and the bad guys did. But then that was odd, because why wouldn't cops have guns?

Something I didn't need to question for long as it seemed as if they didn't need them. Because I disobeyed one order of Ryker's by looking and after witnessing the petrifying truth of who these guys really were, I knew I would be quickly breaking another.

Because I did the only sane thing any person would do…

I ran.

Because these guys weren't human! They couldn't be. They moved at incredible speeds, making it to each gun man and snapping their bones like they had been made from burnt kindling. Bullets didn't even slow them down. Some of them even moved like they were half made of vapor.

Whereas others jumped impossible heights, before landing directly in front of the next bad guy. This was so they could be grabbed by the neck and lifted one handed at least two feet off the ground before they were then tossed aside like empty scarecrows. One of which smashed into a pillar hard enough that he obviously died on impact. Hearing the crack of multiple bones from where I stood made me want to throw up.

But it was the sight of one man that scared me the most, because Ryker now looked to have astonishingly grown in size and, for some reason, he was back to wearing his Demonic mask. He also moved with deadly grace. One second, he was choking a man to death up against the wall before snapping his neck one handed. And then he was disappearing into a shroud of shadows that seemed to appear from nowhere!

A dark, thick cloud that consumed the next gun man who started shooting beyond it; I could see lights flashing from the end of his weapon. Shots stopped being fired after a terrified scream could be heard as the man tried running for his life. However, he only made it a single step from the fog of shadows before he was then dragged backward into the dark void once more. After this I gasped in horror as the sound of death was quickly followed by the sight of his bloodied severed head rolling out from the mist.

It was like something from a fucking horror movie!

I gripped my bag in a death grip and ran for the nearest door that would get me the fuck out of here. This thankfully led me onto one of the platforms where there was miraculously a train that looked ready for leaving. In fact, I made it to the doors just in time before they closed, and I soon found myself in the carriage by myself.

And thank Christ that I did because I couldn't stop myself from shaking, trying to make fucking sense of the horrors I had just seen.

"No, that… that couldn't have happened!" I started shaking my head, asking myself what the hell I had just seen and if I had, in fact, just suffered a complete and utter mental breakdown. Had I just imagined it all?!

"Impossible… it's… impossible," I told myself over and over again, before the darkness of the night filled the window and I was left staring at my own reflection. One that, this time, not only looked like a woman on the run.

But more importantly, a woman now running from…

The Devil.

CHAPTER 29
LOSING CONTROL
RYKER

I was *furious*.

Yet again, *fucking furious*.

Because she had run once more, and I was starting to feel as if the Fates were fucking laughing at me. As if this was just one big fucking game to them and I was the butt of their joke! I swear to the fucking Devil that if this shit happened one more time, my Demon would crawl out of my fucking skin and burn my vessel so as there was no hope in ever being contained again.

It wanted to torch the earth with its rage and wreak havoc on every inch of its path until we found her. Which was why I knew that I was on borrowed time here before my Hellish rampage began. I had eliminated the threat, leaving only one survivor to be interrogated before making my way back to the place of hiding I had left her. However, the second I saw her not standing where she should be, I punched a chunk out of the supporting structure until it looked like a toothless mouth mocking me.

In fact, I would have started to try and destroy the whole fucking station had Van not intervened.

"We can track her but if you lose yourself now then we will have no hope when all our efforts are spent containing your Demon," he had told me with his arms holding me in a bear hug to prevent inflicting any more damage. To which I had snarled at him to release me.

"Let me go."

"Are you in control?" he asked, making me grit my teeth before growling,

"Yes, now fucking release me, you prick!" At this he did as I ordered. And not that I was ready to admit this, but I was thankful that he had been in his right mind to contain me. To not only try to calm me, but to do this out of the view of my men, so as to not let them see this weakness in me.

Thankfully, Hades had created a barrier between the pandemonium and the rest of the world surrounding. Which meant all humans within radius of the station would turn away, no longer feeling the desire to travel by train. Nor would they have heard the gunshots within. Of course, it helped that I had given the order to have the station itself emptied of all travelers by taking hold of their minds and making them leave before approaching Evelyn at the lockers. Which meant that no mortals were caught in the crossfire of the fight that ensued shortly after. Of course, it was concerning to know that the gunmen couldn't be controlled this way, making me realize now that supernatural forces were behind the attack.

"Get a fucking clean-up crew here and get every fucking man on tracking down that train she left on!" I ordered when

I was able to push my Demon down enough so as not to speak for me.

Faron made his way to me, doing so already with a tablet in hand as he started tapping furiously on it.

"I will hack into the security systems and get all footage of the stations it may stop at. We will track her," he assured me.

"Don't worry, Ryker, we will find her again soon and, this time, at least we know what name she will be going by," Van said, and it was enough that I managed to uncurl my fist at the very least. Because he was right, for we hadn't just tracked her movements here not long after she fled the hospital. But we had broken into the locker after she left and found the contents of a makeshift new life. It was everything she would need to run again, and the sight infuriated me as much as it saddened me.

To live each day on the edge of upheaving your life at the slightest of hints that she had been found. It was a heavy burden to carry, one filled with worry and anxiety. It was why I had taken Van's advice to take this slow with her, starting with the nightclub. But then only hours before, proof had made its way to Van's desk that she had been the intended target for the shooting. Well then it had been all bets off and taking it slow was no longer a fucking option!

Of course, they had been aiming to hurt her, not kill, as tonight confirmed that they wanted her alive. The question now was simply *why?* What could she have that someone would want? Well, at the very least I had someone to torture that information out of, but even this didn't ease the pain I felt.

She had thought I was a fucking cop?! I tried to tell

myself that she hadn't been in her right mind at the time she threw this allegation at me. But then I started to try and think of things from her point of view, and I could understand some of her reasons to assume as much. Especially now she knew there were men after her. But then did she really believe that I would have used her as fucking bait to get to them?

Did she really think so little of me?

It was maddening.

"You're growling again," Van commented days later when walking into my office, one that was becoming sparser by the hour as I had destroyed all but my desk and a few chairs. All decoration long ago smashed against a wall, with pictures cracked, punched, or clawed at. My sofa, I had torn apart with my bare hands seconds after watching the footage of her train hopping from one station to the next. Faron had pieced it all together for me and, unfortunately, she was too far ahead for us to catch up. Meaning that I had been forced to give into my second's advice and wait until she settled again. And like he had pointed out, at the very least we knew her new name.

Matilda Cameron.

Where she kept conjuring up these names from, I had no idea.

"Tell me you have something useful for me," I pushed out, trying to control the growl in my voice after Van spoke upon entering.

"Well, she rang the coffee shop owner like you suspected she would."

"And?" I snapped.

"I didn't get much out of her, only that her mind told me

of her worry and sadness, as she misses the girl. The conversation was swift and gave nothing away of her whereabouts. Only to say that she was safe, running from her past and that she was sorry and thankful for the cute woman's kindness." I frowned at that.

"Cute... please tell me you didn't then sleep with her."

He smirked at this but when I started to growl again, he slumped on the chair opposite me, looked at his nails, and said,

"As delightful as that distraction would have been for both of us, especially considering her dreadful and shitty taste in men... alas no, I did not fuck the curvy mortal delicacy."

"Alas?" I repeated with a raise of my brow.

"I'm thousands of years old, Ryker, give me a break... fuck but I even said, 'come hither' the other day." I scoffed at that, for nothing could make me commit to a full laugh these days.

"I bet that still got you laid, you horny bastard."

At this he smirked, and it was a look that said it all.

"So, another dead end." I sighed not knowing how long I would last for. It had been three days and I had felt every single fucking minute of them, as if I had lived three centuries without her.

"You know she is safe at the very least."

At this my look spoke for me, despite adding a bite of bitterness to my words, *"Yes, but for how long?"*

"Well, if we can't find her yet, then Hector Foley won't," he pointed out, making me grit my teeth.

"Hector Foley." I snarled his name.

After discovering that it was as I suspected, Foley was

behind this, I had made it my mission, aside from finding my Lost Siren, that he be hunted down. I could almost feel his skull held in the hand of my Demon before I crushed it to pulp. I would first rip it from the rest of his body, hoping it survived just long enough to see it in the mirror I would do it in front of. Or perhaps I would perform the blood eagle on this one?

A most torturous way to die as you sever your victim's ribs from their spine with a blade and pull their lungs through the opening to create a pair of 'wings'.

Either way, Hector Foley was a dead man walking.

"She can only run for so long, as that bag of hers contained very little in the way of funds," Van reminded me, drawing me out of my bloody thoughts. But knowing this fact, once again, arose an internal battle within me. I knew that the less money she had, the less time she could spend in running. But then to know that she had nothing was an even more painful thought to swallow.

Simply put, *I worried about her.*

Worried where she was sleeping, what she was eating, if anything. I worried for her safety and if she was warm enough. The thought of her sleeping out in the cold on a fucking park bench somewhere was another reason most of my office had not survived.

Van had to continue to tell the office staff that I was planning on remodeling. This before sending them all home on paid leave fearing what they would see from one day to the next. My rages were sometimes out of control and to the point that damage control had to be undertaken, as I would forget to mask what the human minds saw in me. I had sent quite a few people off running in fear of their lives making the sign of Christ over their chests. Which meant that Van then had to then chase them down and wipe their memories.

In fact, I knew that if it continued to get worse, I would be forced to take a trip to my home just so as I could be locked away in my vault for a few days. This would be the only thing to calm the Prince of Greed enough to fucking function. But I did now wonder if, even then, it would do me any good, for my cravings for treasure had evaporated quickly. Now being replaced by something far more priceless to me.

The ultimate treasure.

A Demon's Siren.

It also made me wonder if any of the other Enforcers had found their Siren yet or was I the first? I would have reached out to some of those I considered friends. Comrades at arms, but my jealousy and fear of desperate Enforcers wishing to claim her for their own, kept me from doing so. It was too much of a risk in my mind and I was possessive by nature. It was why not a single living soul of this world, or my own, knew the whereabouts of my horde.

Just like I didn't know where my father's horde was kept. Which was the way of the King of Greed, the 4th President of Hell and, well, like that age old saying went, *like father, like son*. But that did make me wonder how my father would be should he ever find his own Fated one. Would he then question the treasure he valued? Would he be willing to burn his golden city, reducing it to a flowing river of shimmering lava all so as he could claim the one true God's gift?

Would he do as I would?

"Ryker?" my second questioned as I picked up the now painted mask she had worn, and one of the only things that had survived my rage. Gods, but the rage I had felt when discovering her door was no longer locked, it had been a good job she had escaped. For I had burst into my room as my Demon and roared loud enough it destroyed most of the fucking room.

Especially when I saw all that was left of her was that golden dress laid out like she had simply disappeared while sleeping. In fact, I would have believed sorcery involved had I not taken in the rest of the evidence. The chaos left in my closet, telling me she had stolen my clothes. The bitter scent of bile clinging to parts of the toilet basin telling me how she had managed to rid herself of the drugs in her system so quickly.

Gods, I would have been fucking impressed had I not been so fucking furious at her! I even found the pot of shoe polish and balls of blackened wash cloths that she had obviously used to paint her golden mask. She had thought of fucking everything!

Thankfully, I had been only minutes behind her. Which meant that by the time I followed her scent out the back door leading to the alleyway, I found two things, one was her mask and the other...

A car waiting for me.

Van, as cocky as the fucker was, he was also a damn good second in command, taking no time at all to issue orders at everyone around us. Which then allowed me to try and chase after her incase she had only just made it to the street.

Thankfully, we had known where she was heading and wasted no time in getting there.

She was going to make a run for it.

After all, it was what she did. Her natural fight or flight response kicked in each time. A habit of a lifetime was hard to break but by the Gods, it was one that I intended to shatter the first chance I got. Well, that was if I actually managed to tie her down for long enough!

In fact, right now, the thought of tying her down was the only thing that saved my desk, something I actually needed, along with my computer. Because the truth was, one of the only things that kept me from losing myself completely, was not only knowing that she was out there, but it was also the hours upon hours of recordings I had of her.

Because watching her had been the only thing that had kept me sane. Just like it had kept me from being too hasty and stealing her away the first time. But I was not making that same mistake a second time, as once I found her, then there was no stopping me.

I would claim her.

Or at the very least, she would be my prisoner until she agreed to it. A prisoner I would very much enjoy chaining to my bed.

"I am not sure I like that look on your face," Van commented with a raise brow.

"No? And what look is that?" I enquired, lifting my gaze from the mask in my hand.

"The look of a man determined to make a girl scout pay for the crime of running from you."

"Then it is a look I suggest you get used to, as that is precisely what I intend to do." At this Van's phone beeped, prompting him to get it out of his leather jacket and read the text that just came in.

"Then I won't have to wait long before another expression takes your face."

"And what is that?" I asked, feeling hopeful the moment I saw him grin.

"Satisfaction."

I tensed when hearing this before demanding, *"Tell me."*

He granted me a smirk before holding up the phone for me to see a picture of my girl wearing an apron in some shitty diner taking orders.

After this, there was only one thing left to say…

"Your little bird has been found."

CHAPTER 30
TOO GOOD TO BE TRUE
EVIE

A week later and I still couldn't get my mind off him. Oh, I had tried. Boy, had I tried. Going so far as to shout at myself consistently whenever I did think about him. In fact, to the point, I was starting to think that whoever slept in the motel rooms either side of me, most likely believed I had Tourettes. Well, if the funny looks I received off them were anything to go by. Strange looks I usually received while I was feeding dollars into the vending machine near the reception desk.

Of course, there wasn't much left to do on my time off working at the diner. Nothing but eating crap and watching even crapper TV in what felt like the crappiest room for rent. But then, at the very least, it was a roof over my head, it was cheap, and now that I had a job, I knew I wouldn't starve in it. If anything, I was lucky, because I had pretty much got off in Vancouver WA, after being forced to jump on the first train I could. Which wasn't the ticket I bought but luckily, no one seemed to notice. I then got on a bus and went as far as I could without using all of my funds, which brought me to a place called Woodland.

It was only about thirty minutes to Portland, Oregon, so suited me because I found it easier to get lost in a city. The problem with this though was the cost of living was much higher. Which meant that I was forced to settle just outside the city where I found myself a cheap motel. And opposite to this was where I found myself in a crumby diner with a handwritten sign in the window saying waitress needed.

And thank the Lord they had been desperate. Nearly as desperate as I had been. Because by the time I got to Woodland I had spent a lot more than I had wanted to. But if it meant that I couldn't be traced, then it was worth it.

As for the future, well I had no real destination in mind, only that it would be safer to try and settle in a city. But for that to happen I needed a better job to pay for it, which meant saving everything dollar I earned so that I could make that next move. Basically, it was a vicious circle and if I'd had more time in Seattle, then I might have had the chance to start off that way.

But I hadn't.

So, this was my new plan. To wait it out here in Woodland, work every hour they had available at the diner and save until it was time to move on. Basically, I was playing the long game. Of course, the only problem with that was I was constantly questioning my decision to run. Especially now I knew bad men were after me, and it stupidly felt as if I had run from the one man capable of keeping me safe.

Then of course I would chastise myself for my continued stupidity, telling myself he was also one of the bad guys and had fucking drugged and kidnapped me. Oh, and let's not forget the obvious surveillance he's had on me, and the fact that he seemed to be so superhuman that he could kill people with his bare hands!

I mean, I had tried to put everything else down to more believable explanations. Like the cloud I saw could have just been a smoke bomb being used, and the Demonic face he seemed to have was just another mask to combat against the effects of it. The speed of his men could have been adrenaline driven. Or the most likely reason could have been that I was not in my right mind at the time. And therefore, it wasn't beyond the realms of possibility for me to be seeing things.

But that didn't take anything away from the fact that the guy was a psycho, clear and simple. Albeit a totally droolworthy, handsome one that could kiss with enough power it was like a secret weapon he was firing straight at me.

Christ, I didn't think I would ever get over that kiss! I mean, I didn't think it was possible for anything to beat the first but holy hell, had I been wrong! That second kiss was disarming enough that I had been ready to throw myself at him and beg him to take me with him. Potential undercover cop be damned!

But then after seeing him taking those guys out the way he did, I think it was safe to say that he most definitely wasn't a cop. No, if anything, I think I was going with brutal mob boss over all else. Plus, I couldn't forget his reaction when I accused him of being a cop. No one was that good an actor.

Either way, I think it was still safe to say that I had

something he wanted and, clearly, he wouldn't stop hunting me until he got it. Now what that was exactly, I didn't know. Because it made no sense to me that the answer to that could simply be... *me*.

He was gorgeous, rich, and obviously powerful, meaning he could get any woman he wanted. Especially without needing to chase them around the West Coast of America. Because despite what he said, *I wasn't that good a kisser!*

No, he was just using my attraction toward him as a way to manipulate me. That was the only explanation. But like I said, what he wanted was what baffled me the most. I honestly didn't know and the more I thought about it, the crazier I became.

Damn that kiss!

And damn my mind for trying to make me believe that none of it felt forced or faked in any way. Damn him for messing with my head this way. For making me question every single second we had spent together. For acting like he genuinely seemed to want me. Like he needed me and with such intensity, it had made my head spin and, admittedly, it hadn't stopped since.

But then there were the scarier facts that kept breaking through. Like how none of his men seemed to be hurt at all, despite the number of bullets flying. And the fact that they had somehow managed to take them down without the aid of any weapons themselves. How on earth can you win a gun fight without any guns?

By breaking their bones, that's how.

None of it had made any sense. But then, hey, wasn't that my life now? Where one day I was a coffee shop girl and the next I was working in some worn, tired old diner where no one gave a shit about how sticky the menus were. Or the fact that there wasn't a single coffee cup or plate that wasn't chipped. That every single booth or stool was cracked and faded. Even most of the food that was served looked like it was ready to say fuck it and walk out of there half cooked.

But then I kept having to remind myself that it was just a job and, pretty soon, another one would come along. So, I continued to work, serving soggy pies and scrambled slop off chipped plates… oh, and not forgetting burnt coffee in thirty-year-old mugs.

Oh, and because my brain didn't think I had enough to deal with, I also continued to dream of him. Dream of him while shamefully sleeping in his shirt and wishing it still held the scent of him. Just like how I wished my lips still remembered the feel of him there. But mainly, I wished I didn't want to remember at all.

It was too painful.

"Order up on six!" The sound I had quickly come to loath bellowed from the kitchen. It seemed I hadn't lucked out with my new boss. Not like the last one. Not like Denise. Fuck, how I missed her. *Missed my friend.* And because of this, I had broken my one rule and contacted her, needing to let Denise know that I was alright before the guilt ate away at me. In fact, I was surprised to find that no one had been around, asking her questions. But then I was also thankful for this. Because I had never wanted to bring trouble to her door. Even if that was precisely what I had been from the start.

Speaking of trouble, I walked over to the hatch to grab

my order, trying to resist the urge to turn my nose up at the sight, wondering which was worse, the food or the man who cooked it. Well, if you could even call it cooking, that was. I mean, seriously, why did people still even come here? Had they just become immune to the taste of old grease and burnt food? Or had it once upon a time been good enough that they had just forgotten and therefore not even realized when exactly that had stopped?

I had seen two people fishing egg shell out of their scrambled eggs this morning, and another man scraping the burnt parts off his toast. How bad does your food have to be at home to think coming here was a good idea and parting with hard earned money to pay for this shit? Jesus, Oliver Twist ate better than this.

"What you waitin' for, a fucking garnish?" Buck snapped, making me grit my teeth and stop myself from saying,

"Something edible would be nice."

Naturally, I didn't eat the food here, hence my new unhealthy obsession with junk food. Cheetos and snickers bars were my current favorites but I had to admit, there was only so much junk food I could eat before feeling like crap.

I grabbed the plates and made my way over to the table, already feeling like delivering it with an apology and a pep-talk about making good life choices. One being not to ever come here again. To be honest, I think the only reason I made any tips at all was that people felt sorry for me. It was that or they appreciated the look of pity I gave them when handing them their food.

I walked over to my table and placed down the order, overhearing a conversation the woman in the next booth was having on her cell phone. She was a beautiful black lady in her early thirties with long lengths of thin black plaits that she twisted all off to one side.

She also looked to have curves in all the right places, because let's just say that there was more than one man in the diner that obviously appreciated the view. And boy, did she have style. She was currently wearing a teal-colored business suit that was both flared at the cuffs and at the bottom of her trousers. Even the lapels of the jacket were cool, as they were a shiny satin material that matched the black satin shirt she wore underneath.

Of course, I had noticed her when she first walked her killer, spiked silver heels in here, just as everyone else had. Now just what a woman like that was doing in a place like this was anyone's guess, because it most definitely wasn't for the food or coffee. For starters, she had wrinkled her nose up at the place just like most people did, but they were also the people who usually just walked straight back out again.

But then, she must have had no other choice, because unbelievably she had taken a seat and stayed for far longer than I would have guessed she would. Perhaps she liked shitty coffee and the persistent, zombie-like stares off locals.

"No, I told you, there is nothing wrong with the job offer, it's just the late hours that is making it hard to fill. They aren't even asking for references, or past experience. All they want is for you to take a few basic tests… oh, you know, if you can type so many words per minute and basic filing… that type of thing." She paused a second for whoever was speaking on the other end before answering,

"If you can use the operating system with confidence and

put dates in a calendar, then I'm telling you, its child's play. Office junior shit with a more than decent salary."

She paused again and looked up at me as I approached. She had a beaming smile that transformed her from beautiful to knockout in seconds. She also had rounded cheeks that made her look a lot younger than she most likely was, and big, pale green eyes that sparkled with mirth. She nodded her head to me when I made the silent, universal motion to ask if she wanted anymore coffee.

I then turned to grab the coffee pot that still kept me within hearing distance of her conversation.

"I told you, it's the hours. My boss works mainly at night, so her assistant would need to do the same." I started filling up her cup when she said,

"Well, I don't know where I am going to find this person, I only know that I have been asked to find people to interview but so far, no one is interested."

I swear I felt as if all my Christmas's had come at once! So, holding my breath and hoping this woman on the other end wasn't about to shout, 'sign me up', I waited, lingering close by until she hung up. Something she did with a dramatic sigh.

Then I practically pounced.

"Erm, so sorry, but I couldn't help overhearing about the job you were talking about."

"Ha, don't tell me, you have past office experience or actually know how to turn on a computer, because that would be all it would take at this rate," she replied with a roll of her eyes that I knew wasn't aimed at me, but more like the obvious frustration at not yet being able to find someone. At this I grinned, slipped into the seat opposite her and said,

GREED'S SIREN

"I also know how to make great coffee."

At this she grinned big and said the words I knew might be too good to be true...

"Well in that case..."

"...When can you start?"

CHAPTER 31
DANGEROUSLY CONTINUED

That night was the first time I actually managed to sleep and, perhaps, it was thanks to the prospect of a new job. But then, it wasn't just a new job, but actually one I could see myself staying in and working my way up the ladder. I knew at this point it might have been a foolish dream, because it would only take one little thing and I would be on the run again. A single sighting of someone I thought was watching me. Or hell, if a cop let his gaze linger for too long in my direction I would have been spooked enough to get the hell out of dodge.

But I had to at least try.

Because, in reality, just how long could I keep this up for? Just how long did I intend to run? Ted Bundy had once escaped by jumping out of the window of a courthouse library and fleeing to the mountains, only to give up after seven days. This was because he couldn't hack living on the lamb out in the Aspen wilderness. Of course, he had also lost about 25lbs and when he was found, he was barefoot, starving, and on the verge of hypothermia.

Of course, my circumstances weren't quite that dire yet, with the emphasis on the word *yet*. In all honesty, I didn't know how long it would be until I admitted I wasn't cut out for this way of life, despite my past. Despite all that Arthur had taught me. In truth, I was just surprised I had lasted this long without being either caught by the cops or wore. Like wound-up dead in a dumpster, down some back alley, in some city I didn't know and had only been in for less than a week.

Although, there was also the possibility that the reason for my good night's sleep was that I finally allowed myself to dream of him again. A dream so vivid, had I not woken in the morning to find myself alone in my depressing motel room and with only myself on this lumpy bed, then I would have believed it to be real.

My dream had started a lot like all the others I'd had of him. Waking up within my dream, only to feel someone watching me. A sight that startled me enough to gasp, making me wonder if I had done so in my sleep with no one around to hear it. Because there he was, now sitting in the corner of the room. His eyes glowing in the darkness like I had thought I had seen them do a few times before.

"Don't be frightened." The deep timber of his voice only added to the reasons why I should be afraid. Almost as if there had been a growl there, waiting to escape, a deep rumble sound in the back of his throat that would only have displayed anger, not pleasure. I made a move like I was about to bolt from the bed, prompting him to stand and silently telling me I was a fool if I thought he would let me run again.

It was like being in the room with a lion and watching as

it prowled slowly toward you. In your mind you told yourself, no sudden movements, while simultaneously you heard the screaming echo of survival mode kicking in, telling you to run for your life!

Of course, I didn't have a chance at this because he stalked closer to the bed, his large body looking even bigger as it towered over me. A sight that made me shrink back, as if this would help me.

"Do not fear me," he said again and just as forcefully as the first time.

"Is that a joke? You're terrifying, even in my dreams," I told him and surprisingly, this made him smirk a little.

"And what is it you would prefer to dream of, I wonder?" he asked, and the sexual intent in his voice was easy to detect. So, I told him honestly,

"I don't know, maybe you topless coming out of a waterfall with a smile on your face, and not one where you look like you're about to eat me." At this he fully grinned, and it was bad to the unbreakable bone.

"See, that look right there! That's the one that makes you look like you're about to eat me!" I said, knowing I was only being this brave because it was a dream, and therefore I knew I had no chance at dying. But then, it wasn't lacking in its power over me, as he leaned in closer, using a hand to skim along my jaw before capturing my chin so he could hold my head up.

"Oh, sweetheart, when I eat you, it is not something you will ever fear but instead... *beg me for.*"

I swallowed heavily and replied, the only way I knew how.

"I didn't know my mind was capable of creating such

vivid sex dreams, but if this is the start of one, then I am all for it." At this he threw his head back and laughed, as if I had surprised him, before he shook my chin in a playful way, and told me,

"You are a delight, Little Dove."

"I am?" I questioned.

"Yes, but only when you do not continue to try and fly away from me that is… which means it will soon be time to clip those wings of yours."

I shivered at that.

"Then I better keeping flying, so you won't catch me," I told him. Something that, again, made him smirk, before leaning further into me. Then with his lips at my ear, he informed me,

"What makes you think I haven't already caught you in my net?" I gasped at that, but it was one he quickly captured with his kiss, invading my mouth with his tongue and making my shock turn to the sound of bliss. Then I felt the sheet being yanked from between us and he pulled back long enough to stroke me with his gaze. One hot enough that I felt it like a heated caress along my skin.

"You sleep in my shirt?" I blushed at this.

"Tell me, my little runaway… does it smell of me?" My answer was to bite my lip and it was one that he didn't miss. But then his hand was in my hair and with the demanding hold over me, he pulled my head back.

"Answer me," he ordered, making my mouth open in surprise.

"No," I forced out.

His eyes hardened, and I didn't know why but the sight only added to my arousal.

"Then let's change that, should we?" he said firmly, before wrapping me in his arms and lowered himself down over me, kissing me once more. And this time, it only ended when I was gasping for breath. The feel of his strength above me felt so real, I knew I would mourn its loss when the morning came. Because I wanted him to be real despite how hazardous that wish really was. But then I guess that was the safety of dreams, we could dare to wish for the dangerous without true fear of it ever hurting us. We could dip our toes in the flames without concern of ever getting truly burned.

And he was most definitely the untouchable flame.

The fire that was just waiting to ignite me and burn me whole. And God, I badly wanted him to! I found myself gripping onto his biceps and marveling at the size and strength of them. They were like unyielding rocks beneath my palms, just like his hands that felt as if they would never let me go. The way they held me to him, like shackles around my body. In fact, I swear, any minute, he was going to tear the shirt from my body. The sound of seams pulling apart would have echoed in the room, had my pounding heart not added to the should-be silence.

But then my dream started to unravel slightly, as he pulled back not allowing me the full experience of this sexual encounter. As if he was actually real, and therefore, he knew that this was not how he wanted our first time to be. In this cheap, shitty motel room with him invading it like some phantom that had seeped into my room and stolen these few moments with me.

So, he pulled back and instead of disappearing from my mind completely, he buried his face in my neck and breathed me in deep.

"Oh, little Evie..." He sighed, pausing long enough to lift his head, pushing my hair back with both hands and framing my face while he told me,

"Soon... *soon I will have you."* This sounded nothing short of a vow, and one I would have taken seriously had it not been all in my mind. Which was why I told him on a saddened whisper,

"Only in my dreams."

"Well, that's the things with dreams, sweetheart... *sometimes they come true,"* he told me and before I could argue, he kissed me once more. Only this time, it was soft and gentle, and it finished on an insistent whisper,

"Sleep, Little Dove, and this time... dream of me for real."

The next time I opened my eyes, it was to the sound of a buzzing alarm. One set to remind me that I had something important to do today. So, I turned off the old digital clock that, in my dreams, had cast a red glow against his face. Along with the motel outside lights that I remembered had streamed through the thin flimsy curtains.

My dream phantom.

I swear, even my body wanted me to believe it had been real as I reached up through the sheet, to then run my fingers over my lips. Lips that felt as if they had experienced real kissing. I swear I nearly cried knowing that they hadn't. Christ, how could I miss his touch like I did when, in reality, I barely knew it at all? Like the scent of him and the way my mind had started to conjure it up, as if he had been really here.

"Wait... how is this...?" My question trailed off as I lifted up the shirt I wore, now convinced even more that I was going crazy because I could actually smell him on me.

"...possible?" I finished my own broken question after letting the material fall through my fingers. This before looking around the room, scanning it and half expecting to find evidence of him being there. But other than his scent left on the shirt, there was nothing.

In the end, I forced myself out of bed, shaking away the pieces of the dream clearly trying to cling to my mind and torture me. Then I made my way over to the bathroom because it was time to get ready for my interview, starting with replacing what I knew was a phantom scent.

However, it was only when I had finished ringing out my hair with the towel, that I noticed another thing I couldn't explain. Which was why I let the towel fall to the floor and instead picked up the shirt I had taken off before slipping into the shower.

"Impossible," I uttered, as I saw the ripped seams of the shirt at the back. Tears in a shirt that told a story that never should have been there, because it hadn't been real. The story of passion and what happened when wrapped in the arms of the man who wanted you, as much as you wanted him.

A story that clearly was left...

To be dangerously continued.

CHAPTER 32
THE FEAST OF FATE

I forced myself to let go of the shirt, along with the crazy idea that last night had been real. Because that was exactly what it was... *crazy*.

Just a way for my mind to linger and cling onto what I knew would never be. A fantasy pure and simple. Because that was all he was... *all he could ever be.*

So, I told myself that I had just been tossing and turning in my sleep and torn the shirt myself. That the scent of him clinging to the shirt had always been there, I just hadn't allowed it to register properly in my mind before then.

For starters, the door was still locked from the inside and with the chain across. The windows were also shut tight and with no other way inside, it was impossible for him to have actually been there.

So, I pushed the thought from my mind. Knowing that if he had actually found me, the last thing to have happened, would have been him turning up to kiss me, only to leave again. No, I wouldn't have been allowed to simply stay in my bed, blissfully unaware of the dangers that seemed to persistently want to follow me around West Coast America.

Which also meant that I felt safe enough to get ready for my interview, hoping that it wasn't too good to be true. Especially considering I had been forced to spend some of my tip money in a secondhand store, buying anything that would be considered appropriate enough for office work.

Which left me wearing a pencil skirt that I would have considered to be way too tight. But it had been that or a pair of black pants that were way too big, so I took my chance with the skirt and skipped breakfast so it would do up at the back. It was a woolen, plaid print, in creams and light browns, with lines of burgundy that matched the dark red V-neck sweater I bought. I wore a plain white shirt under it and, once again, it wasn't the best fit but thankfully its tightness was hidden under the sweater.

To this, I added the pair of skin color tights and a pair of brown boots that were worn at the heel and therefore had been reduced in price. But these were exactly my size and thank God too, because being in mismatched sizes for most of my outfit was bad enough. Did I really want to add blisters to insult...? Nope, I could definitely do without that.

So, after pulling my hair up into a neat ponytail, I grabbed my jacket. One that definitely didn't go with my outfit but it was on the practical side. Meaning that I felt warm as I walked to the nearest bus stop with my fleece-lined blue parker, which had fake fur around the hood.

I had two different buses to catch and was prewarned by another waitress at the diner that traffic could be a nightmare. So, I was leaving with plenty of time to spare because the office was in Portland, Oregon. I also realized that if I did manage to get the job, that it would be a pain in the ass getting to work each day, but I could worry about that further down the line. Because I didn't intend to just live in the motel for the rest of my days, but just until I received a few paychecks so I could put up first month's rent on a place.

I also knew the first thing I would need to do would be to buy some more office outfits, and things that I could mix and match so it didn't look like I was wearing the same stuff all the time. So basically, I was going to have to fake it until I made it, and by making it, I meant basic surviving.

So, with this new plan in place, I made my way into the city feeling optimistic for the first time in weeks. Because I had come far enough, that hopefully no one would hope to look for me here. I had a new ID, going by the name of Matilda (my favorite book) and Cameron, (after my favorite director). And this time, I was hoping it was one I would have long enough to at least get used to, before it had to change again.

But before I let that niggle of doubt worm its way into my good mood, I pushed it back. Because this time it felt different. It was more than just feeling positive. For some reason, I felt as if this could be the new start I was looking for. As if the coffee shop version of me had been nothing but a prequal to my story. A trial run to ensure I didn't make the same mistakes twice.

So, I would be friendly and nice but without forming attachments. I would be on my guard and not allow myself to get complacent. I wouldn't trust those around me and would not give in to the temptation to form friendships or, the more dangerous... *relationships.*

It was like that movie, Point of No Return with Bridget Fonda and Gabriel Byrne. She had committed a crime and was given the chance of a new life instead of being executed. But this was only if she agreed to live it as an assassin, doing jobs for the government. It had been one of the VHS's Arthur had in his small collection and I remember him telling me, the mistake she made was falling in love. She had formed a relationship with a guy but couldn't trust him enough with the truth of her past.

But as for me, a young girl running from her own past, and one that would unfortunately dictate the rest of my life had I been found out… then I too felt like I would be forced never to be honest with anyone. Because not even Arthur knew the reasons I ran away from my home.

The horror I left behind.

So, watching that movie felt more like an important life lesson, rather than just a fleeting moment of entertainment. It was also why I went to bed that night as a young girl and cried myself to sleep. Because I knew that forming relationships would only be dangerous, just like it had been for that government made assassin.

Now obviously, I didn't grow up with the skills to become some top-secret spy, but I knew how to fire a gun and hit the target. I knew how to run and what it took to stay hidden.

I was a survivor.

A forever lonely survivor.

Because that's what the movies didn't tell you. That, in fact, the hardest thing about running was the loneliness. It was a nagging need to feel wanted by someone. To feel needed. To be loved and treasured but, above all, it was to feel safe enough to open yourself up and bare all to the person you loved.

To have the bravery to allow yourself to be vulnerable.

That was the hardest part to surviving alone.

I released a sigh, feeling my optimistic mood burst like a cartoon bubble floating down to a giant pin. It popped and left me doubting my decisions. But then, as my bus stop came into view, I knew this was one opportunity I couldn't afford to run from. Because I knew that life at the diner was only going to get worse. That despite the lonely future I had ahead of me, I still needed to focus on the important things. I needed a home, I needed food and warmth. I needed water, clothes, and basic comforts. All of which wouldn't be achievable without money and with that came a job that wouldn't make me want to commit murder… *again.*

Okay, so that wasn't funny but still, I needed to work for a boss I didn't want to slap with a spatula at the very least. So, with this in mind, I walked the few blocks and soon found myself looking up at the large skyscraper. Then I told myself that I could do this.

However, then I caught sight of something behind me and turned quickly, expecting to be faced with the impossible. And this time, it wasn't one that came with smoldering good looks, a sinful smile, and eyes that stripped me bare.

No, it had been a ghost from my past.

But as quickly as it came, it was gone again because the man I thought to be watching me from across the street had disappeared with a truck driving past. One that cut the haunting figure from view, leaving an empty sidewalk in its wake.

I shook my head and forced that brutal, sneering, bloody face from my memories, pushing it down as far as it would possibly go. Back to the abyss where there lived a snarling monster full of nightmares that had tried once before to steal my voice. It was a chilling memory that was usually coiled tight and sleeping, which is exactly what I had forced it to do in the back of my mind.

The snarling monster, I had named fear.

It was a cruel creature, only tamed by the sound of my mother's voice, telling me with her last dying breath…

To run.

To run fast and to run far.

So, I did so now, turning quickly and rushing into the office building, despite knowing the danger was most definitely all in my head this time. Because it was impossible. Ghosts couldn't hurt you. No, it was the living I feared.

"Miss Cameron?" I jerked back a little at the sound of someone speaking to me because I was not yet used to my new name.

"Miss Cameron?"

"Oh, yes," I replied the second I realized they were trying to confirm this.

"Are you alright?" The cute man asked, who looked like a cross between a geeky gamer and a high school heartthrob. In fact, he couldn't have been that long out of college, unless he just had an eternally young face. But he was dressed for the office, so he was obviously old enough to work here.

Although even that may have been a stretch, because he still wore a pair of blue jeans, white converse high tops, and a light blue shirt. A shirt he wore under a light-gray blazer jacket that he had pushed up at his forearms. He had a young, friendly face but the body of a guy who looked like he knew the inside of a gym, despite how slight of frame he was.

He was tall, slim, and fit, with the body of a long-distance runner rather than the obvious bulk of my Thief. Oh, and he was also now looking over my head toward the wall of windows, where I had been transfixed.

"Oh yeah, sorry… just… erm worried I was late," I said making the excuse, despite the guy not looking entirely convinced.

"No, in fact, you are right on time… should I escort you up to the right floor?" he asked, making me wave his offer off, telling him,

"Oh, that's alright, if you tell me which floor it is and…"

"Nonsense, it's no trouble," he said, holding out his arm in a gesture that meant I should go ahead of him as he now pointed the way toward the bank of elevators.

It was also the first chance I allowed my mind to take in the entrance, one filled with little else but a security desk to one side and a curved desk at the center, that I gathered was where people signed in. Prompting me to ask,

"Should I sign in first?" Strangely, the question seemed to take the guy off guard, because he blinked twice before looking back to the receptionist.

"Oh, of course… I swear I would forget my head if it weren't attached," he said, and I couldn't help but shudder at this as a memory flashed back to me, one of the man lying bloody on my apartment floor, a broken TV being where his head should be.

"Miss?"

"Oh, me too..." I added, so he didn't think I was a simple fool who was prone to blanking out. I also took the opportunity to try to get my nerves to calm the fuck down while signing in. I then offered the receptionist a small smile as I slid the clipboard back her way. After this I turned back to the man who was waiting for me, clearly intent in escorting me to my floor.

"Katra should be waiting for you," he told me, making me frown in question before voicing it.

"Who?"

"The woman who told you about the job... you are the girl from the diner, right?" he asked, making me shake my head a little.

"Ah, yeah... sorry, I guess I forgot her name... not exactly a good first impression, huh?" At this he smirked and said,

"Oh, I don't think you have that to worry about."

The way he said this put me instantly on edge. Although thankfully, it didn't stay that way for long as he must have seen my look of confusion and thought it best to elaborate.

"Well, she did practically offer you the job, despite going through the motions of an interview, so I would say you've got this one in the bag," the young guy said before winking.

"I'm Faron by the way," he said, holding his hand out to me, making me shake it and tell him,

"Well, you know my name."

To which he smirked again, telling me, "I do indeed."

Christ, if I didn't know any better, then I would have said he knew my actual name. But then perhaps that was just his way. He seemed like the cheeky, teasing type. The type whereas life was one big playground that was his to enjoy. I always envied those types of people, as for me, it was one big assault course. A precarious gauntlet to run and navigate my way through without getting knocked down.

The doors opened and Faron led me out onto an office floor that was so fancy, it instantly put me on edge and made me wish that I had forked out the little money I had left for a better jacket.

"Don't let the fancy black marble intimidate you, we are all quite laid back here," he said after he must have noticed the way I tugged down on my jacket nervously. I also had to say that his easy-going boyish smile certainly helped. It was friendly enough that I hoped he worked on this floor too, prompting me to ask,

"Erm thanks. So do you work for Katra's boss too?"

"That I do," he replied in a happy tone. Holding his arm out, he made sure the next set of doors didn't try to close on me as he let me go first. I had to say, the more time I spent with him, the more familiar he started to sound. However, I just couldn't place where I would have heard it before.

"Well, it will be nice knowing at least one person here," I said making him grin again.

"Oh, but I think you will know more than one," he replied cryptically, chuckling while he said this. And the way he spoke, was like some hidden information I wasn't yet partial to. My look must have said it all as he replied,

"Katra."

"Oh yeah," I said, feeling like a fool and therefore forcing myself to calm down and stop being so damn paranoid.

"Here, let me show you around."

"Pretty sure I have to get the job first," I reminded him, making him nudge into me playfully.

"Oh I wouldn't worry about that, I bet it's a done deal." I grinned at that because it was obvious he was trying to put me at ease.

"Man, you guys must really be desperate," I joked, making him smirk this time.

"Nah, it's mainly just the unsociable hours that puts most people off, don't worry, no scary skeletons in closets around here... although the boss might be considered to be a monster from time to time," he joked, making me wince.

Fuck, I needed to relax!

"Anyway, here we are," he said after leading me into a kind of boardroom that was set up with a large oval table in the middle and was big enough to sit at least sixteen people. Off to the side was a long table that, for some strange reason, was set out with plates full of finger food and hot coffee that made me nearly start salivating.

"Please help yourself." My eyes widened at the offer.

"Oh, I couldn't."

"Of course, you can, after all, it will only go to waste and the rest of the office has already had their fill."

I frowned at this. "What do you mean?"

"All the food was ordered in for a board meeting that didn't happen in the end, something came up last minute and it was something the boss declared as being far more important... nothing more important, were his words in fact... anyway, it will all go to waste if no one eats it." My face must have said it all, because he chuckled before saying,

"Let me guess, you skipped breakfast?"

"And lunch," I admitted, making him gesture toward the large spread of food and say,

"Then have at it."

I laughed the once before pointing out,

"I'm not sure that's gonna look good, Katra coming in here to interview me and there I am stuffing my face."

"Ah don't worry about it… besides, you've got a while yet before Katra gets here."

"I thought you said she was waiting for me?" I asked suspiciously.

"Oh yeah, sorry, I should have said, but I got a text from her saying she will be about an hour late."

I frowned, wondering when I had seen him looking at his phone, but then again, I had walked in front of him most of the way here. He might have been young, but he had clearly been brought up as an old school gentleman… which also meant that he could have checked his phone real quick and I could have missed it.

"Ah okay, well then I guess it can't hurt," I said timidly, now staring at all the food and as if right on cue, my stomach growled.

"Not at all… here, allow me," he said, pulling out a chair and making me sit down before I knew what I was doing. Then as if he was totally used to waiting on hungry girls, he started piling up the plate with what looked like two of everything.

"Really, you don't need to…" I tried to protest but, again, he wouldn't hear of it.

"Nonsense," he said, before placing the towering plate down in front of me, along with a bottle of water, a bottle of juice and a can of soda for me to choose from.

"Now eat up and I will come back and check on you later if Katra hasn't shown up by then."

"Are you sure?" I asked, nodding down at the food and making him laugh.

"Of course! Whose idea do you think it was? Katra hates the waste. So, relax, enjoy the food and help yourself to coffee. I will see you in a little while, Matilda."

"Thanks, Faron." At this he bowed a little and told me,

"It has been my pleasure."

Then he left, after granting me a little wink and leaving me to question if the guy had been flirting with me?

If so, he would soon be left disappointed because the idea of having an office romance was about as far away from any reality I could get. As in, *it would never happen.* Even if I had been willing to allow myself foolish enough to have one, I'm not sure I would ever get over the man that I welcomed to haunt my dreams.

My thief.

In the end, I was once again forced to push him from my mind because now was not the time to continue my obsessing over him again. So instead, I focused on the mountain of food in front of me, knowing the zipper on my skirt would not have survived had I eaten all of it. In fact, I was just disappointed I couldn't take it all home with me because this spread could have fed me for a whole week!

There was everything from sandwiches, fried chicken, bowls of pasta and potato salad, slices of gourmet pizza, pastries, cakes, cheese and crackers. Oh, and the healthy stuff I knew my body was most likely crying out for, like sliced fruit and vegetable sticks, with dips.

In fact, I had just finished my coffee when Faron walked back in and told me,

"Katra is running later than she thought so asked someone else to interview you, if that's alright?" At this my heart sank and he chuckled because it must have been obvious.

"Relax, it's nothing to worry about. Like I said, you pretty much got the job, this is nothing but a formality, that's all."

I tried to look convinced but knew I was obviously failing when he patted me on the shoulder. So, I let his easy grin win me over and I forced myself to move, wishing I hadn't eaten so much. But then knowing that my belly hadn't felt this full in ages, admittedly it had been hard to stop. Which meant that, at the very least, I had gotten a free meal out this, even if this interview went horribly wrong.

An interview that was about to begin as Faron led me across the open space, one filled with desks, before rounding a corner and making our way down a hallway with offices either side. However, it was the large double doors at the very end that made my insides start to knot up.

Because whoever was behind those doors, I knew had to be important around here. Especially, to have an office the size that required not one door but two.

"Is this person high up in the company?" I asked, and Faron granted me a curious sideways glance down over his shoulder at this, but only replied when we reached the door.

"As high up as you can get seeing as he owns the company."

I gulped at this and suddenly felt like bolting back down the hallway. But the doors were opening, and it was too late to back out now. No, I would just have to try my best and hope for better.

Like a job.

So, I took the first few steps inside, seeing a huge office richly furnished and perfectly decorated. The large desk dominated the center of the room with a glass wall behind showing the entire city beyond. A high back, leather desk chair was currently facing it, keeping whoever was sitting in it a mystery. But the sight also made me stall, and it was only when I felt a little encouraging push from behind, did I take the last step to officially put me in the room.

"Go on in and don't be shy… *Girl Scout,*" Faron whispered from behind me, but the second I whipped my head back to face him, it was no use, because my whispered question ended up aimed at a pair of closing doors.

"What did you just call me?"

"He called you Girl Scout," a masculine voice said, one so full of authority and strength I almost whimpered.

"But of course, to me, you will always be known as so much more."

I swallowed hard and forced myself to turn back and face him.

To face my Thief.

Doing so with my heart feeling as though it would beat its way out of my chest or crawl its way up my throat.

Something that felt strong enough to choke me, as he started to turn in his seat, until he too was now facing me. A masterful figure that only last night had been standing over me, dominating my dreams and making himself the ruler over them.

"Hello, Evie… *my little runaway,*" he purred, and his

voice alone should have told me how much danger I was in. But if it hadn't, then one other sound would have, and that was the distinct click of locks as they slotted into place.

Sealing me in and, with it, my fate.

For he didn't know it yet, but he hadn't just captured a girl that murdered the once.

But someone who had killed...

Twice already.

To be continued in...

Evelyn's Enforcer.

ACKNOWLEDGEMENTS

Well first and foremost my love goes out to all the people who deserve the most thanks which is you the FANS!

Without you wonderful people in my life, I would most likely still be serving burgers and writing in my spare time like some dirty little secret, with no chance to share my stories with the world.

You enable me to continue living out my dreams every day and for that I will be eternally grateful to each and every one of you!

Your support is never ending. Your trust in me and the story is never failing. But more than that, your love for me and all who you consider your 'Afterlife family' is to be commended, treasured and admired. Thank you just doesn't seem enough, so one day I hope to meet you all and buy you all a drink! ;)

To my family…

To my crazy mother, who had believed in me since the beginning and doesn't think that something great should be hidden from the world. I would like to thank you for all the hard work you put into my books and the endless hours spent caring about my words and making sure it is the best it can be for everyone to enjoy. You, along with the Hudson Indie Ink team make Afterlife shine.

To my crazy father who is and always has been my hero in life.Your strength astonishes me, even to this day! The love and care you hold for your family is a gift you give to the Hudson name.

To my lovely sister,
If Peter Pan had a female version, it would be you and Wendy combined. You have always been my big, little sister and another person in my life that has always believed me capable of doing great things. You were the one who gave Afterlife its first identity and I am honored to say that you continue to do so even today. We always dreamed of being able to work together and I am thrilled that we made it happened when you agreed to work as a designer at Hudson Indie Ink.

And last but not least, to the man that I consider my soul mate. The man who taught me about real love and makes me not only want to be a better person but makes me feel I am too. The amount of support you have given me since we met has been incredible and the greatest feeling was finding out you wanted to spend the rest of your life with me when you asked me to marry you.
All my love to my dear husband and my own personal Draven… Mr Blake Hudson.

To My Team…
I am so fortunate enough to rightly state the claim that I have the best team in the world!
It is a rare thing indeed to say that not a single person

that works for Hudson Indie Ink doesn't feel like family, but there you have it. We Are a Family.

Sarah your editing is a stroke of genius and you, like others in my team, work incredibly hard to make the Afterlife world what it was always meant to be. But your personality is an utter joy to experience and getting to be a part of your crazy feels like a gift.

Sloane, it is an honor to call you friend and have you not only working for Hudson Indie Ink but also to have such a talented Author represented by us. Your formatting is flawless and makes my books look more polished than ever before.

Xen, your artwork is always a masterpiece that blows me away and again, I am lucky to have you not only a valued member of my team but also as another talented Author represented by Hudson Indie Ink.

Lisa, my social media butterfly and count down Queen! I was so happy when you accepted to work with us, as I knew you would fit in perfectly with our family! Please know you are a dear friend to me and are a such an asset to the team. Plus, your backward dancing is the stuff of legends!

Libby, as our newest member of the team but someone I consider one of my oldest and dearest friends, you came in like a whirlwind of ideas and totally blew me away with your level of energy! You fit in instantly and I honestly don't know what Hudson Indie Ink would do without you. What you have achieved in such a short time is utterly incredible and want you to know you are such an asset to the team!

And last but by certainly not least is the wonderful Claire, my right-hand woman! I honestly have nightmares about waking one day and finding you not working for

Hudson Indie Ink. You are the backbone of the company and without you and all your dedicated, hard work, there would honestly be no Hudson Indie Ink!

You have stuck by me for years, starting as a fan and quickly becoming one of my best friends. You have supported me for years and without fail have had my back through thick and thin, the ups and the downs. I could quite honestly write a book on how much you do and how lost I would be without you in my life!

I love you honey x

Thanks to all of my team for the hard work and devotion to the saga and myself. And always going that extra mile, pushing Afterlife into the spotlight you think it deserves. Basically helping me achieve my secret goal of world domination one day…evil laugh time… Mwahaha! Joking of course ;)

Another personal thank you goes to my dear friend Caroline Fairbairn and her wonderful family that have embraced my brand of crazy into their lives and given it a hug when most needed.

For their friendship I will forever be eternally grateful.

As before, a big shout has to go to all my wonderful fans who make it their mission to spread the Afterlife word and always go the extra mile. Those that have remained my fans all these years and supported me, my Afterlife family, you also meant the world to me.

All my eternal love and gratitude,
Stephanie x

About The Author

Stephanie Hudson has dreamed of being a writer ever since her obsession with reading books at an early age. What first became a quest to overcome the boundaries set against her in the form of dyslexia has turned into a life's dream. She first started writing in the form of poetry and soon found a taste for horror and romance. Afterlife is her first book in the series of twelve, with the story of Keira and Draven becoming ever more complicated in a world that sets them miles apart.

When not writing, Stephanie enjoys spending time with her loving family and friends, chatting for hours with her biggest fan, her sister Cathy who is utterly obsessed with one gorgeous Dominic Draven. And of course, spending as much time with her supportive partner and personal muse, Blake who is there for her no matter what.

Author's words.

My love and devotion is to all my wonderful fans that keep me going into the wee hours of the night but foremost to my wonderful daughter Ava...who yes, is named after a cool, kick-ass, Demonic bird and my sons, Jack, who is a little hero and Baby Halen, who yes, keeps me up at night but it's okay because he is named after a Guitar legend!

Keep updated with all new release news & more on my website

www.afterlifesaga.com
Never miss out, sign up to the
mailing list at the website.

Also, please feel free to join myself and other Dravenites on
my Facebook group
Afterlife Saga Official Fan
Interact with me and other fans. Can't wait to see you there!

        facebook.com/AfterlifeSaga
        x.com/afterlifesaga
        instagram.com/theafterlifesaga

Also by Stephanie Hudson

Afterlife Saga

Afterlife

The Two Kings

The Triple Goddess

The Quarter Moon

The Pentagram Child - Part 1

The Pentagram Child - Part 2

The Cult of the Hexad

Sacrifice of the Septimus - Part 1

Sacrifice of the Septimus - Part 2

Blood of the Infinity War

Happy Ever Afterlife - Part 1

Happy Ever Afterlife - Part 2

The Forbidden Chapters

*

Transfusion Saga

Transfusion

Venom of God

Blood of Kings

Rise of Ashes

Map of Sorrows

Tree of Souls

Kingdoms of Hell

Eyes of Crimson

Roots of Rage

Heart of Darkness

Wraith of Fire

Queen of Sins

Knights of Past

Quest of Stone

*

King of Kings

Dravens Afterlife

Dravens Electus

*

Kings of Afterlife

Vincent's Immortal Curse

The Hellbeast King

The Hellbeast's Fight

The Hellbeast's Mistake

The HellBeast's Claim

The HellBeast's Prisoner

The HellBeast's Sacrifice

The HellBeat's Hate

The HellBeast's Past

*

The Shadow Imp Series

Imp and the Beast

Beast and the Imp

*

The Lost Siren Series

Ward's Siren

Eden's Enforcer

Wrath's Siren

Emme's Enforcer

Greed's Siren

*

Afterlife Academy: (Young Adult Series)

The Glass Dagger

The Hells Ring

The Reapers

*

Stephanie Hudson and Blake Hudson

The Devil in Me

Milton Keynes UK
Ingram Content Group UK Ltd.
UKHW030949140324
439440UK00001B/26

9 781916 562677